Montana Rose

by

Sherry Derr-Wille

S

Published by
Satin Romance
An Imprint of Melange Books, LLC
White Bear Lake, MN 55110

Montana Rose ~ Copyright © 2014 by Sherry Derr-Wille

ISBN: 978-1-61235-938-0

Cover Art by Caroline Andrus

Prologue

St Louis, Missouri—1857

Darius McKinney walked the streets of St. Louis. It had been four months since Josie Sullivan's parents sent her away in shame. She'd disappeared completely and now Darius was on a quest to find her and make an honest woman of her. Josie was the younger sister of his best friend, and he always thought they would marry someday. It didn't matter she had an unwanted child on the way. His only thought was it would be much easier for her to raise her child if she had a husband to care for her.

Considering no one knew where she went, he had only the word of a man who came to the farm looking for work of where she was. He had been a hired man on several farms around the area, and he told Darius and his father he'd seen Josie in one of the cathouses in St. Louis.

Darius' father muttered it served her right for being in a family way without a husband to provide for her before he stormed off without offering the man any hope of employment. For Darius, his father's departure had been the opportunity to ask the man more questions about Josie. Although the man couldn't remember the cathouse where he'd seen her, he was certain the redheaded woman with the big belly had been Josie.

For the last two days, Darius had asked questions and gotten few answers. Last night he had talked to a man who told him about a woman who could easily be Josie. He said he'd seen her at a cathouse called the Purple Moon. A woman by the name of Madam Devereaux ran it. She

1

was known for taking in fallen ladies, helping them through their unwanted confinement, and then accepting them into her house as companions for the men who came to her establishment.

A doorman looking as if he was ready to throw out anyone who bothered the girls, answered his knock at the ornate door.

"Can I see Madam Devereaux?" Darius requested.

The man scowled at him. "What business do you have with her? You don't look old enough to be here. Why don't you come back when you know what to do with a woman?"

Darius fingered the gun in his holster before answering. He knew the man didn't miss the gesture. "I know what to do with a woman, and I'm old enough to be here. As for my business with Madam Devereaux, it's no concern to anyone but me and the lady in question."

The man continued to eye the gun strapped to Darius' hip. He then nodded and stepped aside to allow Darius entry into the house. "Wait here. I'll talk to the madam and see if she has time to see you."

Darius took a seat in the exquisite parlor. The chairs were covered in velvet and heavy draperies covered the widows so that prying eyes from the street couldn't see what happened inside.

"You look mighty young to be callin' on the likes of us," said a young woman dressed in a scandalous nightgown.

"I...I—"

His response was cut short by the entry of a very large woman who showed more bosom than Darius had ever seen before.

"Are you looking for me, young man?" the woman said.

"Ah yes, ma'am. I'd like to talk to you."

"How old are you, young man?"

"I'm seventeen."

"Are you looking to bed one of my girls?"

"No ma'am, but I am here about one of the young women living here with you."

"And just who are you looking for?"

Darius looked around the room. He certainly didn't want Madam Devereaux's whores knowing he'd come for Josie. "Is there a place where we can talk in private?"

The older woman nodded and indicated he should follow her. The office to which she led him was furnished with plush chairs as well as a large oak desk.

"I assure you we're completely alone," she said. "Won't you have a seat?"

Darius sat down in one of the chairs the woman indicated. He'd never been so uncomfortable in his entire life. How could Josie have come here of all places? She was barely fifteen years old, and if anyone asked him, he would have sworn she knew nothing about relations between a man and a woman. Of course, the fact she was in a family way meant she knew more about such things than anyone thought.

"I'll ask you again, young man. Who are you looking for?"

He took a deep breath. "Her name is Josie Sullivan. Someone said she's here."

"Just what is Josie to you?"

"I've been told Josie is in a family way. I want to marry her and give her child my name."

"Are you the father of her child?"

The fact she posed that question gave him hope he'd found the right place. "No Ma'am, I'm not, but that doesn't matter. I've always loved Josie. If this hadn't happened, I would have asked her pa for permission to marry her."

"You're mighty young. Do you have a job?"

Darius hung his head. "No, ma'am, I don't, but I'm headed west. I've been told there are ranches that could use a good man to work for them. I plan to get my own ranch and—"

"And nothing. I've heard enough. It seems like there are a lot of people telling you things. Now you're going to listen to the things I have to tell you and you will listen. Josie gave birth to a baby girl this morning. I've hired a woman to raise the child and be a wet nurse for her. You see, you're too late. Josie died in childbirth. Since you were willing to marry her, do you want to give this child a name?"

He swallowed hard. "She can't be dead. I love her."

"Love is a strong word for someone so young. If you're thinking of taking the child, you can forget it. You're a very young man. There is no way you can care for a newborn. I will care for her and raise her."

"Can I see her?"

"Only if you agree to give her your name."

Had he married Josie, he would have gladly given the child his name and raised her. "I will give her my name, but I want to name her as well. I want her to be called Rose, for Josie's mother."

"That's fair enough."

"I also plan to send money for her care. As far as I'm concerned, she's my daughter"

"Even though she isn't?"

"Even though she isn't. If Josie had lived we would have been a family, and the fact she wasn't mine wouldn't have been a question."

The older woman got to her feet and led him from the room. After going through several hallways, they came to a room with a small crib. The newborn lying in the bed was a tiny replica of Josie. He thanked God the child bore no resemblance to the man who fathered the baby.

The woman who cared for the child picked her up and held her out to Darius. He took her in his arms as he'd taken his brothers and sister in his arms when he cared for them to help his mother.

As though the child thought he was someone special, she opened her eyes and made contented cooing sounds. When she wrapped her tiny hand around his finger, he knew she'd stolen his heart. No matter what, this child would be cared for and he would send money for that care in the hopes that someday she would come to him and call him Pa.

After returning the child to her crib, he left the house. He knew Madam Devereaux never expected to hear from him again, but she was mistaken. He'd made the promise to Josie's daughter, and he never went back on his word.

Instead of heading south to the farm where his parents were expecting him to return, he rode to the west. There had to be ranches that needed a hand. With luck, he could work his way to Montana territory where he planned to buy land. Over the past several years, he'd been saving the money he received for working for the neighbors. His father insisted he give him the money he made. He'd lied about how much money he made, giving his father only a small portion and keeping the rest for himself. It would give him a stake, and if he was as frugal with his wages as he had been in the past, he could afford a ranch within five years.

"Good-bye, Rose McKinney. I promise I won't ever let you down."

Chapter One

The incessant knocking on her bedroom door brought Rose McKinney from a sound sleep. It had been late when her last customer left the night before and in no way did she want to get out of bed. She pulled on her wrapper to cover her nakedness and hurried to answer the door.

"What do you want?" she said before she recognized her boss, Madam Celeste Devereaux.

"Get dressed, Rose. There's a lawyer here to see you."

"Tell him to come back tonight. I don't do anyone in the mornings, you ought to know that Celeste."

The older woman smiled. "This one isn't a customer. He's here on behalf of your father."

Rose felt like the floor had been pulled out from beneath her feet. All her life she'd heard the story of how Darius McKinney came looking for her mother on the night she was born, but he'd been too late. Josie Sullivan was already dead when he arrived. Since then he'd sent money several times a year to leave her with a substantial bank account. Letters had come with the money always asking her to come to his ranch in Montana. She certainly didn't want to go west. Life wasn't perfect here, but she couldn't fathom fighting Indians, and living on a cattle ranch didn't sound much better.

"Now get your tail dressed and downstairs," Celeste ordered when Rose made no reply.

Rose didn't take time to do more than wash up, put on some

6

makeup, and don a day dress before going to the parlor. The lawyer sitting there was one who graced her bed more than once over the years.

"It's good to see you again, Rose," Thaddeus Waldman said when she entered the room. He got to his feet and kissed her hand in greeting. "I'm sorry to bring you bad news, but your father has been murdered, leaving you his ranch, the Rocking M. The will says you must go to Montana to claim your inheritance."

"Can't you just sell the damn thing and bring me the money?" she said. With the sale of the ranch, she could easily meet the price Celeste was asking for the Purple Moon.

"I'm sorry, but that isn't an option. The will is very specific about the fact you must live on the ranch for at least a year before you can sell it."

Rose looked around the parlor. This was the only home she'd ever known. Celeste had raised her since birth. She had also handled the money Darius McKinney sent with great regularity. How could she leave here to go to the wilds of Montana?

"This is a good opportunity for you, my dear," Celeste said. "You need to find out if this is something you might like."

"How could I like living anywhere but here?" she protested.

"You won't ever know unless you try. I can't say I won't miss you. I feel as though I'm your mother, but as such I think this is an opportunity you need to take."

Rose knew Celeste was right, but it was hard for her to accept she would be leaving St. Louis behind.

* * * *

Cameron Blake looked out across the ranch he called home. So much had happened in the past few weeks, he wondered if he'd still be welcome here by the end of the year.

He'd left Nebraska ten years ago after his wife died in childbirth leaving him with a three-year-old son to raise on his own. In the blink of an eye, he'd lost his beloved Martha as well as the daughter who would have been their second child.

Cameron worked for Martha's father and against his wishes, married his daughter. On the day after the funeral, Martha's father, Cornelius

Slade, started legal proceedings to take Cameron's son, Joshua, away from him. As soon as he heard the news, he took Joshua and left Nebraska. The first thing he did was to change their names and disappear.

After three years of drifting, he'd finally found a place to put down roots when he arrived at the Rocking M ranch located close to the Canadian border. From his friends and family back home he heard his former father-in-law hadn't given up his search for Joshua, but Cam felt he was safe here.

His boss, Darius McKinney, took the two of them in and treated them like family. He'd taken a liking to Joshua, treating him more like a favored nephew than the child of one of his hands.

Just weeks ago Cam found Darius on the north range. They'd been losing a lot of cattle and each man on the ranch took turns riding nighthawk. It had been early morning when Cameron went to relieve his boss and found the lifeless body, along with at least twenty head of cattle missing.

Within hours of Darius' funeral, a lawyer came out from town to tell the hands the ranch had been left to Darius' daughter, Rose, and she would be arriving to take over the running of the ranch within weeks.

The announcement sent a shock wave through the hands causing several of them to quit rather than work for a pesky woman. Being short-handed Cameron put Josh in the saddle with the men. He had no idea what would happen when school started again in the fall. He refused to cheat his son out of an education just because the Rocking M was short handed. With any luck, the new owner would insist on a new foreman and he could find a more suitable job to support Josh.

"Pa, Pa, you gotta come quick," Josh shouted as he reined his horse to a halt in front of his father.

"Slow down, son, what's wrong?"

"Ned and I were on our way to help Dave when we found him shot. Ned stayed with him and sent me back to get you and the wagon so we can get him back here. He ain't dead, but he's bad off."

Before Cam could answer his son, a cloud of dust indicated a wagon was on the way into the dooryard. "This has to be the new owner. You go and hitch up the wagon, and I'll stick around here long enough to meet her then come down to the corral and ride out with you."

Josh nodded and rode toward the barn where the wagon would be hitched and waiting for Cam to join him.

* * * *

Rose expected someone to meet her at the railhead with a carriage, but when no one was there, she inquired about getting to the Rocking M. To her dismay, the only transportation she could arrange was a buckboard. After the two and a half hour ride, she concluded, these people had never heard about springs on wagons. If she didn't know better, she would have accused the driver of hitting every hole and rock along the road on purpose.

"I'm sure this ain't what you're used to, ma'am," the man said as he leaned over the side of the wagon to spit a stream of tobacco juice to the ground.

"No, it's not, and it's Miss and not ma'am."

"I didn't know. I figured no one your age would be unmarried. Guess girls do things earlier out here than they do in the big city."

Inwardly, Rose groaned. The last thing she wanted was to be married. She enjoyed the attentions of the men who came to the Purple Moon. As soon as she could dump this ranch she'd inherited on some unsuspecting slob, she would return to St. Louis and buy Celeste out.

The road leading to the ranch was long and dusty. All the way, she fretted about what the dust was doing to the dress she'd chosen to wear today. She'd hoped to make a good enough impression on the men who worked for her that by nightfall she'd have one of them in her bed. With luck, she could charm one of them enough to talk him into buying this ranch so she could get back to the only life she knew.

She didn't know what she expected, but it certainly wasn't the sprawling ranch house that seemed to appear out of nowhere once they crested a hill. It looked well kept and in the dooryard was a man waiting for her. As they pulled up to where he stood, she studied his face. He couldn't be much over thirty and was ruggedly handsome. His brown hair was neatly trimmed, and he was clean-shaven. She liked that in a man.

"You must be Miss McKinney," he said, extending his hand to help

9

her down from the wagon. "I'm your foreman, Cameron Blake, but most folks call me Cam. I'd like to stay and help you get your things into the house, but I need to ride out. There's a problem out on the north range. Once you're settled, you'll realize the ranch comes first. The house has been cleaned out for you."

He turned his attention to the driver of the wagon. "Can you help Miss McKinney get her things inside, Pete?'

"Sure thing, Cam. You mentioned the north range, you ain't having more trouble with rustlers are you?"

"I'm afraid we are. I'm on my way there now to bring Dave in. Can you send the doc out here when you get back to town? I just sent Josh down to hitch up the buckboard to bring Dave here. He was with Ned when they found Dave shot."

"You got Josh riding with the men? What are you thinking? He's hardly more than a kid?"

"I don't have much choice in the matter. We've lost more hands than I like to think of in the past few weeks. Guess everyone's edgy since Darius got himself shot. After this, they'll probably be leaving in droves."

Rose watched as Cam turned from them to make his way to the barn. "What in the hell have I got myself into?" she muttered, more to herself than anyone else.

"There's been a pack of trouble out here ever since Darius was killed. Your pa was one of the best, but folks are worried. More and more ranchers are losing cattle, and the ones riding nighthawk are getting shot and even killed for their efforts."

"Then how can I get rid of this place?" she demanded. "I don't intend to get myself killed."

The man spit tobacco juice onto the ground. "Ain't likely to happen anytime soon. Until these rustlers are caught, you won't be able to give this place away. No one in his right mind wants to take on something like this. It just ain't right what's going on, but no one seems to be able to do anything about it."

She looked one last time at the man who was climbing onto the wagon, along with the young man who must be Josh. This was going to be an interesting place to live, at least until the rustlers could be caught and she could sell out.

"According to the will, you have to stay one year," Thaddeus had said.

A year seemed like a lifetime, but she needed the money the sale of this ranch would bring her. Somehow, she'd make it. It would give her plenty of time to get to know the men in this area and find out which one would be willing to buy the ranch.

Turning back to the house, she noticed Pete staring at her cleavage like a hungry kid looking at the jars of candy in the store. "I get five dollars for two hours," she said in her sweetest voice.

Pete turned six shades of red. "Oh no, Miss McKinney. I ain't interested in anything like that. My wife would have my hide. She don't even like me going down to the saloon for a drink 'cause of the women there."

Never in her life had she been as ashamed of her actions as she was now. She'd lived in a house where men were part of her livelihood. She hadn't ever considered what she did was wrong. Just the look on this man's face told her he considered her dirty, and it wasn't just because of the dust on her clothes.

Tears stung her eyes as she made her way into the house behind Pete. Inside, she was pleasantly surprised. The big living room was clean and dominated by heavy leather furniture that screamed the man who lived here had not had a woman in his life. Could it be he really loved her mother? If so, why weren't they together? Celeste only said he appeared out of nowhere on the day she was born and left within hours of her mother's death.

All her life, she viewed men as playthings, people who came to her to get away from the stress of their lives and not to be depended on. Were things different here? She doubted it, but Pete's reaction to her earlier suggestion told her perhaps men lived by different standards in this backwoods wilderness than those she knew in St. Louis.

She thought of the man Cam going to the north range to bring back a man. If he were injured badly, the doctor would need hot water to clean the wound. After starting the stove, she brought in water from the well and put it on to heat. It would certainly be hot by the time any of them got here.

11

* * * *

"Was that the new owner, Pa?" Josh said as Cam climbed onto the seat of the wagon.

"Yes, it was. I don't have a good feeling about this."

"We ain't gonna leave here, are we?"

"The word is 'aren't,' Josh. You know better than that. To answer your question, I don't know. I don't want you going up to the house like you did when Darius was here. This woman isn't the kind of person I want you around."

Josh's expression was one of puzzlement, but Cam didn't expand on his opinion of his new boss. How could he tell his thirteen-year-old son that Darius' daughter was little more than a whore? He'd never seen a more outrageous dress on a woman before. If she sneezed, her breasts would pop out of the low cut bodice of her dress. Just seeing her, told him it was time to move on, but at what cost to Josh?

"But why, Pa? Iffn she's the owner, ain't we supposed to be talkin' to her about things on the ranch?"

Cam didn't even try to correct his son's choice of words. There'd be time for that later. Now they had to get out to the north range.

"I have to deal with her, but you have no business with a woman like her. It won't be long before she decides she doesn't want us working here anymore. When that happens, we'll move on."

"But I like it here, Pa."

"I do too, but I don't know if we'll be able to stay. It just depends on how much she'll be sticking her nose in our affairs. Right now, we have to worry about getting Dave back to the ranch. I told Pete to send the doc out here when he gets back to town."

Cam was relieved when Josh didn't ask a million questions that all started with why. His son was growing up and uprooting him now wasn't something he relished doing, but he certainly didn't want him around Miss Rose McKinney.

In the distance, he could see Ned's horse. Scanning farther across the expanse of grass, he saw Ned kneeling next to a prone form that could only be Dave. He whipped the horses to a gallop and drove toward the two hands that remained loyal to the Rocking M.

"How's he doing?" Cam said once he jumped down from the seat of the wagon.

"He'll make it, but he won't be much help for quite a while. I thought you'd be sending Josh in for the doc."

"I didn't have to. Pete brought out the new owner. I asked him to take her belongings into the house and then send out the doc."

"The new owner is here? What's she like?"

Cam shot Ned a look that said Rose McKinney was someone he didn't want to discuss in front of his son. "She's a woman, that's for sure. I'll let you draw your own conclusions. Now, help me get Dave into the wagon. You get in first, Josh, and you can hold his head, keep him from moving around too much on the ride back to the ranch."

Josh nodded and hurried to get into the wagon so he'd be ready when his father and Ned lifted Dave's lifeless looking body into the bed of the wagon.

Cam smiled at his son for remembering to put in blankets. He'd seen other gunshot victims and knew once they started coming out of the shock, they usually got the shakes. It would be best if they were able to keep him warm as well as secure.

As carefully as he could, Cam lifted Dave by his shoulders, while Ned took his feet. Once they had him in the wagon, Josh pillowed Dave's head in his lap while Cam tucked the blankets around his friend's body.

"It's best if you ride back here with the boy, boss. I'll tie my horse on behind the wagon so I can drive. I'll try to give you as smooth a ride as possible."

Cam appreciated Ned's offer. He was worried about the wound Dave sustained. He'd seen men shot before and knew Ned's words of encouragement were more for Josh's sake than for his. If they got him back to the ranch alive, it would be a miracle. He could only pray the doc would be there when they arrived so he could tend to Dave's injuries and give him a fighting chance of making it.

* * * *

As soon as Rose finished in the kitchen, she searched through the trunk Pete took into the bedroom just off the living room. She needed to find a less revealing dress than the one she wore. She hated the expression of disgust on Cam's face when he looked at her. He saw her as a soiled dove as others referred to women like her.

When Celeste first learned Rose was going to the ranch, she'd tried to tell her the clothing she'd packed wasn't suitable. Instead, Celeste had taken out half the clothes Rose had packed and added things she deemed proper for her new life as the owner of the Rocking M. Now, all Rose had to do was find them and see how well they fit.

In the trunk, she found a dress with a high neckline that made her look as pure as driven snow. She also found other dresses along with britches and shirts she could wear when she went riding.

As a child, Celeste insisted Rose learn to ride both sidesaddle like a proper lady and astride. Her riding instructor told her the astride part made her look more like a wild Indian than a proper lady.

Rose laughed at the memory. If the man who taught her to ride knew the life she'd lived for so long, he wouldn't call her a proper lady. While she had the education her father financed over the years, she also received an education living and working at the Purple Moon.

She'd often heard the other girls talking about getting out of the business and leading respectable lives, but they were never able to do it. Things were different for her. She now had the chance, but did she really want it? She longed for the life she'd led in St. Louis, not the one she would be living on a ranch in the middle of nowhere. Unfortunately, the terms of her father's will required she stay at least a year before she could consider selling the ranch. If that were to be the case, she would have to learn to be the respectable lady for which her father bought and paid.

She just finished changing her clothes when she heard a commotion outside the house. When she went to investigate, she saw the buckboard Cam took to the north range earlier pull into the yard outside the front door of the house.

Earlier he said the men who killed her father weeks before had wounded a man. She needed to see if there was anything she could do.

"How bad is it?" she said, as soon as she stepped out onto the porch.

"Bad enough that the doc better get here soon or we're going to lose him," Cam replied.

"Bring him in the house. There's a second bedroom. You can put him there. I'll see what I can do until the doctor gets here."

Cam looked at her as though she was a poisonous snake waiting to bite the wounded man. "Just what the hell would someone like you know about taking care of a wounded man?"

"Probably more than you do. Just bring him in here and let me see what I can do. What do you have to lose? The doctor will be here soon, but at least I can make him comfortable and check the severity of the wound."

She knew Cam was still skeptical, but the boy with him as well as the man who drove the wagon finally convinced him to do as she said. While they got the man out of the back of the wagon, she went into the house and pulled down the covers on the bed in the second bedroom.

* * * *

"Damn woman," Cam muttered, half under his breath.

"She don't look so bad to me, Pa," Josh said as he trailed along behind his father and Ned.

"Don't let her fool you. I know what kind of a woman she is, and I don't want you anywhere near her. She's not as respectable as her pa thought she was. Skunks don't change, and they can't wash the stink off themselves no matter how hard they try."

As soon as they entered the downstairs bedroom, he realized Rose wasn't there. Just like a woman to make claims she couldn't complete. She probably got one look at all that blood and bolted like a scared calf.

"Can the two of you take off his shirt so I can see to his wound?"

Cam turned to see Rose enter the room, an apron tied around her waist and a pan of steaming water in her hands. Without saying anything, he helped Ned peel off Dave's shirt. With that done, he stepped back.

To his surprise, Rose sat down on the bed and started checking the wound. "It went in here," she said, as she laid a cloth soaked in the hot water on his chest. "Thank goodness it wasn't a few inches to the left or it might have gotten his heart. I could see from his shirt it didn't exit. That means it's still in him. I'll clean the wound as best I can. Then it's up to the doctor to get it out of him. I've taken care of wounded men, but I've never done any cutting on them. I leave that to the professionals."

Cam was shocked as Rose took charge of the situation. From the way she carefully cleansed the wound in Dave's chest, it was evident she done this kind of thing before. She probably had to tend to some man who got out of line with one of the whores with whom she worked and got himself shot for his efforts. There was no other explanation.

Seeing the ugliness of the wound on Dave's chest made Cam sick to his stomach. What she said about it being where it was made sense. At least it didn't hit his heart. There was a chance he could make it if the doc got here soon. Otherwise, it was anyone's guess.

* * * *

Rose wanted to cry at the sight of the injury to Dave's chest. It was bad. She hoped the doctor would be able to extract the bullet without doing further damage.

Before she could do anything other than clean the wound, Doctor Myers arrived and took over the care of the man.

"You must be Rose McKinney," Dr. Myers said, acknowledging her for the first time. "I've known about you for as long as I've known Darius. It's a pleasure to get to meet you. I saw you sitting next to the bed and assumed you were caring for Dave before I got here. Do you have any experience with things like this?"

Rose nodded. "As part of my education, I learned a bit about medicine. I can assist you if you need me."

"I would appreciate any help you could give me. You can start by bringing me more hot water."

Rose turned to leave the room. The look on Cam's face was one of disbelief. She knew he doubted her abilities anywhere but the bedroom. However, the next year would prove him wrong. If she had to stay in this god-forsaken country, she would make the best of it and use the education her father's money bought.

Thankfully, she had a kettle of water heating on the stove when she went to the bedroom to care for Dave. As she ladled more water into another pan, her mind went back to the number of people she'd helped like this in the past.

When Rose was fifteen, Celeste had asked Dr. Wilson to train Rose to nurse the women in the house when they were sick or injured. If Rose were truthful, she'd enjoyed this portion of her education. Dr. Wilson took care of all the girls at the house and sometimes brought patients there to nursed. It was never talked about, but Rose was certain these men were outlaws. As she recalled, one of the men had been gut shot. Although she didn't have enough education to help in taking out the bullet, she'd cared for him as he recuperated. Dr. Wilson told her that without her expert care, the man might have died.

Returning her thoughts to the man who now lay in her downstairs bedroom, she prayed she would be able to do the same for him. It would not bode well if he died while in her care.

Shaking the memories from her mind, she picked up the basin of hot water and left the kitchen. She needed all her senses about her for the task. It didn't matter that Cam looked at her as though she was lower than dirt. The education she'd received while she lived at the Purple Moon would serve her well in her new life in Montana.

Both Cam and the man he'd identified as Ned looked pale when she returned to the room. It was understandable, considering the amount of blood Dave lost combined with the severity of the wound. She had no doubts the men who did this didn't expect Dave to survive.

"Here's the water. What else can I get for you?"

Dr. Meyer looked up at her question. "I'll need someone to help me with the surgery. Are you up to the task, young lady?"

Rose nodded. "I've helped with gunshot wounds before. I would have helped him while we waited for you to get here, but I don't have the expertise. I'm a decent nurse not an accomplished doctor and that's what this man needs."

"You should know what a man needs." Cam muttered.

"I know more than you think I do," she retorted.

Cam turned on his heel and left the room with Ned following in his wake. As Rose watched them, she knew by suppertime every hand on the ranch would know the new boss was a woman and one with a past none of them could forget. She'd been right when she told him she knew more than he thought she did. She was well versed in literature, medicine and knew enough about accounting that she had been keeping the books for Celeste for the past several years in addition to gracing the beds of some of the highest paying clients at the Purple Moon.

No matter what, she refused to allow Cam's behavior to hinder her duties as nurse to Dr. Myers. Focusing her attention to the task at hand, she worked side by side with the doctor in order to be of assistance in the removal of the bullet.

"I don't give him a snowball's chance in hell," Dr. Myers said when he finished stitching up the wound. "If he's to have any chance at survival, he'll require around the clock care. Since that's impossible with only one of you, I'll send Mrs. Johnson and Miss Cranston out from town to assist you."

Rose started to protest, but Dr. Myers silenced her with a wave of his hand. "Don't argue with me, young lady. I know more about you than you think. If you're going to be accepted by these hands of yours, it's best if you have help in caring for Dave. As I said, I don't think he'll make it, but if he doesn't, it won't be me who takes the blame. I saw the look on Cam's face, and I realize he knows of your background as well as I do. Accept any help you can get and don't question it. Neither of the women who will be coming out to help you will know of your past, unless you tell them everything you did in St. Louis. I'll send them out as soon as I get to town, and I'll be back again tomorrow to see how things are going here."

Rose nodded. He was right, she had no right to expect the people who knew about her to accept someone who had grown up in a house like the Purple Moon and who had aspirations of purchasing it for herself. If she'd been smart enough to dress more demurely when she arrived, she wouldn't have made such a bad impression on her new foreman. Her problems with the men were of her own making, and she would have to work her tail off to prove she was worthy to be the owner of this ranch.

Chapter Two

"What do you have against the new boss, Cam?" Ned asked once they were outside.

"You heard what I told Josh. She's not the kind of woman Darius thought she was. If you had seen her when she first got here, you'd think the same way as I do. She looked more like one of those floozies down at the saloon than the owner of this ranch."

Ned shook his head. "You can't prove it by me. She looked like she belonged when we got back here with Dave. I give her a lot of credit for the way she pitched right in there and took care of him. I couldn't stomach all that blood to say nothing of the way the wound looked. She acted like it wasn't anything she hadn't seen before."

"Well," Cam continued, "we'll see, but for now I'm making sure Josh doesn't get anywhere near her. He'll find out about that kind of woman soon enough. He doesn't need to contend with anything like this when he's just a kid."

"You'd better take another look at him. He's been doing a man's job ever since Darius was killed and we started losing hands grand right and left. The boy, as you call him, is better help than most of the men we've had working for us."

"That may be, but he's still only thirteen. This will be his last year in school and I want him learning the things he needs to live a good life. What I don't want is for him to learn the things that woman can teach."

Without waiting for a response from Ned, Cam turned toward the corral. He needed to get back up to the area where Dave had been shot and see how many head of cattle they'd lost in this raid on the herd.

* * * *

Rose watched as the doctor left. She knew there would be little for her to do for Dave until he woke up and yet she didn't want to leave his side. If he should awaken, someone needed to be there to reassure him everything was going to be all right.

Before going back to the bedroom, she searched through the kitchen to find something to use for making broth. When she found nothing, she realized her father probably took his meals with the men. She didn't dare go out to the cookhouse to tell whoever was doing the cooking that she would need something for herself to eat as well as broth for the injured man in her care. Her only hope of getting anything to eat lay with the women who were coming out from town. If she was lucky, she could leave Dave in their care and go in search of the cook. It would be even better if they would bring food with them.

Giving the situation no further thought, she went back into the bedroom. She'd been sitting beside the bed only a short while when Dave began to moan in his sleep. It was evident he was regaining consciousness and experiencing pain.

As she opened one of the packets of pain relievers Dr. Myers left, and after mixing it with water, she prepared to help Dave drink the liquid.

Dave's screams of pain filled the room, tearing at Rose's heart. "What the hell is going on?" Dave shouted as soon as he was fully conscious.

"You were shot. I don't have any broth for you, but I do have something to take away the pain."

Dave looked at her, his eyes belying the pain he was in. "Who the hell are you?"

She marveled at his language. It seemed the word hell must be a permanent part of his vocabulary. "I'm Rose McKinney, the owner of this place and your boss. Of course, none of that matters now. For the time being, I'm your nurse, and I don't intend to lose my patient. This medicine will allow you to sleep and that's what you need to heal."

"Am I going to die?"

"Not if I can help it. I haven't ever lost anyone I cared for before. Now if you do as I say, I will see to it that the next time you wake I'll have been out to the cookhouse to get you something to eat."

Dave said no more, but allowed her to hold him in an upright position so he could drink the liquid in the glass. He made a face attesting to the terrible taste of the stuff. She certainly didn't need him to tell her that. She'd administered this medication enough times in the past to know the taste of it was downright nasty.

"Did you patch me up?" he asked, his voice sounding weaker as the medication began to take effect.

"No, I helped Dr. Myers. I've been trained to be a nurse, but not a doctor. You were very lucky. If the man who shot you had been a better shot, you'd be dead. Now I have to be certain you remain alive. It wouldn't do me any good if you were to die while I was caring for you. It's going to be hard enough for the men to get used to having a woman boss without knowing I didn't do my best for you."

The silence from the bed told her Dave had fallen asleep and probably hadn't heard a word she'd said. She knew it was foolish for her to have put voice to her frustrations, especially when the man she was talking to couldn't hear her, but she didn't care. It had done her good to say the things that were on her mind.

An hour later, a knock at the door startled her. Getting up she went to the living room to see who it was. As soon as she saw the two women standing on the front porch, she realized they were Mrs. Johnson and Miss Cranston.

"Thank you so much for coming on such short notice," she said as she held open the door. "I'm Rose McKinney."

"We know, dear," the older of the two women said. "Dr. Meyer told us you needed help. We knew your father and he was such a dear man, we're pleased to be able to be of assistance. I'm Verna Johnson and this is Minnie Cranston. We'd appreciate it if you would call us by our first names."

Rose nodded. She'd never been close to women in the past. The girls at the Purple Moon had been more like mothers to her than friends. Even when she became an adult, they treated her differently because of the money her father sent for her education and care. She wasn't there because the only thing she had open to her was to be a whore, but she'd been raised in the house and knew no other lifestyle. She prayed on this ranch she could learn how to be a decent woman who had friends and lived a normal life.

"You look beat, dear," Verna said. "Doc said you just got in this morning and then this had to happen. He also told us he was certain you didn't have a thing to eat in this house. We brought out some canned beef. While I'm taking care of Dave, Verna is going to make up some stew for you and some broth for Dave."

Rose had never eaten canned beef before. She was used to some of the best beefsteaks and seafood St. Louis had to offer. She could never remember eating stew, not with the gourmet cook who prepared all the meals at the Purple Moon.

"Can I help you?" Rose asked as she followed Verna into the kitchen.

"I can handle the work, but I'd enjoy your company."

Rose pulled out a chair from the table and sat down. It amazed her at how exhausted she felt. It didn't seem like she'd done much since she got off the train, but she must have. Celeste would have said her fatigue was from tension, but she'd never put much stock in the theory.

"Doc says you have been living in St. Louis. Do you have family there?"

The word family brought back memories of Celeste and all the girls at the Purple Moon. They were her family, not blood family, but they were the only kin she knew.

"Not really. My mother died when I was born and Miss Celeste took me in. When my father came, she told him there was no way he could support a baby. She told me he wasn't much more than sixteen, and she was certain he didn't have a job. He sent money regularly, and Miss Celeste used it to buy me the best education possible."

Verna turned and looked at her intently. "Just what kind of an education did Darius's money buy you? Do you know how to cook and how to run a ranch?"

Rose hung her head. "No, but I learned how to ride a horse, act as a nurse and how to keep the books for any kind of business. I'm anxious to look at my father's books and see what kind of shape this ranch is in. I hope he didn't send so much money for my education he neglected either his property or his hired hands."

Verna laughed. "You're a strange girl. I would think being raised in the city you would be selfish and not worry about such things. Darius was a generous man. He built this ranch out of nothing, pays top wages, and gives money to the church. As for your education, he always said it was his top priority, but we also knew you were learning other things. Those of us, who were his friends, knew all about the Purple Moon and why he left you there. I prayed night and day someday you'd come out here and make your father proud."

Tears welled up in Rose's eyes. She'd come here with one idea in mind, but when she saw the reaction of her foreman to the way she was dressed, she saw the Purple Moon in an entirely different light. Celeste tried to tell her, her formal education was more important than her dreams of owning the Purple Moon, but Rose hadn't listened. The Purple Moon was exciting and the men who came there paid her well for the attentions she gave to them. She wasn't a common whore like the women on the streets. She was one of Miss Celeste's girls and had the respect of many important men.

"I guess I wasn't the daughter my father wanted. Before I came here, the only life I knew was at the Purple Moon. I never thought of myself as anything but respectable until I saw the look on Cam's face when I first got here. He made me feel down right dirty. Can you teach me what I need to know?"

Verna smiled. "I can teach you how to cook and how to sew, but I can't teach you how to run this ranch or gain the respect of your men. That's something you'll have to gain for yourself."

"Do the men know where I've been all these years?"

"Darius was very careful never to tell them too much. He was only upfront about where you were with only a few of us, you know, the ones who came to this country at the same time. We were like family back then. Still are today."

"Was he ashamed of me?"

Verna left the stew simmering on the stove and came over to embrace Rose. "He would never be ashamed of you. He loved you unconditionally. The story he told me was your mother got in trouble, and her parents sent her away in shame. He tracked her down at the Purple Moon hours after you were born. He was the one to name you, but when he wanted to take you with him, Miss Devereaux realized he couldn't care for a newborn. He knew where he left you, but she promised him you would get the best education possible. In turn, he made a promise as well. It was that he would send money for your care regularly. He had no fancy ideas about the kind of life you would be living. The one thing he always told us was that no matter what, he loved you and that was all that mattered."

"If he hadn't left me this ranch, I would have bought the Purple Moon. I came out here with the idea I wanted to sell this ranch and go back to the life I wanted. Then I found out I had to stay here for a year. I want to fit in. I want to be a good boss for my men."

"I figured as much. Now, let's take this broth into Dave. I'm sure he'll want something to get his strength back as soon as he wakes up."

Rose picked up the tray Verna prepared being careful not to allow the broth to slosh over the sides of the bowl.

They'd just stepped into the living room when Minnie came running out of the bedroom where Dave lay. "Something is terribly wrong. Dave is breathing really funny and thrashing around."

Rose handed the tray to Verna and rushed into the bedroom. Dave thrashed in the bed and sweat beaded on his forehead as he moaned. "I need a basin of cool water and a cloth. He's running a fever. It's possible he has an infection. I also need some rope. If he continues to thrash around like this, he could easily tear open the wound. I need to keep him as quiet as possible. I realize he's in a lot of pain, but I refuse to allow him to do himself more harm."

Both women stared at her as though she'd suddenly grown two heads. "Go now, please. I'm afraid if I don't do what I can I'll lose him. Oh yes, bring me a bottle of whiskey if my father kept such a thing in the house."

Minnie was the first to leave. After Verna set down the tray, she followed. With them gone, Rose did what she could to quiet the man who was obviously in pain although he was unconscious.

"What in the hell do you think you're doing?"

Without turning toward the door, Rose recognized Ned's voice. She also realized what her position on top of Dave might look like to someone who just walked in.

"Dave ain't one of those men who come to you for relief. Are you trying to kill him?"

"I'm trying to save his life. I sent Minnie and Verna to bring me cool water for his head, ropes to restrain him, and whiskey to deal with the infection that may have settled into his wound. Now you can either stand there condemning me or you can help. If I don't get him restrained, he'll keep thrashing around and break open the stitches from where Doc dug out that bullet. If that happens, we won't have to worry about the infection, because if he loses any more blood, he'll bleed to death."

"I...I—"

"I really don't give a damn about what you're trying to say. Either help me or get out. The choice is yours. I meant it when I said I wasn't about to let one of my hands die. I've been trained as a nurse and that means I try to save lives not take them."

"I got a rope for you, but I couldn't find any whiskey," Minnie said. "I knew your pa for a long time and I never saw him take a drink."

"I'll just have to make do without it. Help me tie his hands to the sides of the bed. That should keep him still for a while at least."

By the time, she finished securing Dave's hands and feet, Verna returned with the basin of cool water and a cloth. While she bathed the sweat from Dave's brow, Rose removed the bandage. She'd seen infections after surgery before, but never one that started so quickly. The only thing she could do was to wash it out with hot water as quickly as she could and pray her efforts would be enough.

"Minnie, get me some hot water. I know there's a kettle on the stove with some in it. When you bring it, I also need a clean cloth. It won't be the same as washing the wound with whiskey, but it will have to do. Hopefully, Doc will stop back here tonight. I don't have time to go into town and get him, so the only thing I can do is my best."

Minnie hurried to do as Rose asked. While she waited, she unwound the bandage and assessed the ugly red of the wound.

"Is this what you need?"

She turned to see Ned holding out a bottle of whiskey. "Yes, but where did you find it?"

"Let's just say when Dave is done with work, he likes to take a drink. I never said anything to either Darius or Cam about it because they

25

were both so set against drinking. I figured what a man did on his time off was his own affair. Dave kept his drinking to himself. In the past, others decided they should drink while they were working and that really set Darius off. He fired them on the spot."

Rose merely nodded as she took the bottle Cam offered her. She knew all about people who drank while they were on the job. More than one girl at The Purple Moon had lost her job because they thought drinking with the customers was acceptable. While the men drank whiskey, the policy was the girls should drink only tea with the same color as the whiskey and brandy the men usually wanted.

"Hold him down. This is the only thing I can do until the doctor comes. This wound is infected."

She swallowed down the gall that rose in her throat as she looked at the ugly red skin around the wound and the puss oozing from it. It wasn't as if she'd never seen such things before, it was that she'd never seen it so soon after surgery. It was entirely possible the doctor's instruments weren't as sterile as the ones used by the surgeons in St. Louis.

Ned went around to the other side of the bed and held Dave while Rose poured the whiskey over the wound. The pain cut through the unconsciousness bringing a scream from his lips. Rose was glad Ned held Dave down, because otherwise he would have moved violently in the bed.

After the initial outburst, Dave slipped back into unconsciousness lying still on the bed.

"Thank you," Rose said. "I couldn't have done that alone. Let's hope the whiskey will help to counteract the infection until the doctor can get back here."

When she looked up, she saw the color had drained from Ned's face. "I can handle things from here," she said, dismissing him. She knew if she didn't, he might pass out, and she'd have two patients rather than just one.

"He's so still," Verna observed. "Are you sure you didn't kill him."

"I'm not sure about anything. I've seen men with infections after surgery before, but never so soon. I have neither the knowledge nor the medications the doctor does. The only thing I can do is disinfect the wound and hope for the best."

By the time the room darkened with the evening shadows, Rose could see Verna and Minnie were getting tired. "If the two of you want to go up to bed, I can take the evening shift."

"Are you certain?" Verna said. "You had a long trip to get here and now this happening within hours of your arrival has to be tiring."

"It is, but I know I can do it. I trained in one of the best hospitals in St. Louis and the hours were long."

"This training you had," Minnie commented, "it sounds as though you had formal training in many areas. Why was that?"

"My guardian wasn't certain what would be needed if my father ever sent for me, so she made certain I had training in many different things. I understood the training in accounting, since I might have to keep the books for the ranch. Of course, the riding lessons were necessary, but I questioned the training in nursing. I couldn't see any reason for it, but I'm so glad she insisted I learn from the best. I'm not a doctor, but at least I know what to do for an infection. I also know the two of you look dog-tired. I'll be fine. I'll see you in the morning and am looking forward to a good breakfast. As I told you earlier, the one thing I was never trained to do was to cook. Without a good cook around, it's entirely possible I could starve."

Minnie laughed at the comment, but it was evident Verna could easily see through the brave front Rose was trying to portray. It came as a relief when both women went off to bed without making any further comment.

The minutes ticked by but the passage of time didn't ease her mind. The fever still raged and she wished the doctor would arrive and take the burden of Dave's care out of her hands. Over and over she went for fresh cool water and continued to bathe his forehead with the cloths she dipped in water in the hopes of reducing the fever.

She sensed someone entering the house before she heard the sound of a man's boots against the wood floor of the sitting room. Turning in anticipation of seeing Dr. Myers, she was surprised when Cam entered the room.

"Ned told me Dave took a turn for the worse. Are you sure you did the right thing for him?"

The tone of Cam's voice showed his distrust of her. Rose couldn't help but wonder if her choice of outfits poisoned his mind against her.

"Yes, he did," she replied, getting to her feet. For some reason she felt more at ease standing face to face with Cam rather than looking up at him. "An infection set in. I'm certain the conditions for surgery were less than sterile. This isn't a hospital setting, and an infection was inevitable. I was hoping you were Dr. Meyer coming to check on him. I was foolish to think he would be coming back tonight. I'm doing the best I can. Thank goodness, Ned was able to find a bottle of whiskey among Dave's things. I think it kept the infection from spreading farther. Now I just need to keep bathing his brow to keep the fever down. I'm certain Dr. Myers will be back in the morning."

"Will Dave make it through the night?"

"I'm not a doctor, but I think so. It will be a long recovery, but nothing I've never been through before."

"I didn't realize you were educated in nursing. Darius never said anything about that."

"I doubt he ever knew exactly what kind of an education the money he sent to St. Louis actually bought. Celeste made certain I was well versed in many things. Not only did she insist I learn nursing, but she also made certain I could read, write, do accounting, and ride a horse. It seems at this ranch I'll need all those skills and more."

"I don't understand. Why would she teach you all that? I thought all girls like you worked best on their backs."

"I find your description of me to be rude. Yes, I worked at the Purple Moon, but I assure you I was paid ten times better than most of the girls. A lot of men wanted me for more than my body. I had a mind that matched theirs, and often we talked about literature and other things before getting down to business. Had I stayed there, I was going to buy the place.

"If I was lucky, maybe I could have repaid Celeste for everything she did for me. A lot of working girls find themselves in trouble. Most times, some back street butcher makes certain they don't carry the child to term. I was lucky my mother ended up at Celeste's house, and my father found me. He knew he couldn't care for me, but Celeste promised I'd have a good education bought with the money he sent. She kept her word, and I have my education. Now, I will thank you not to continue to

28

poison the minds of the men who will be my employees."

Cam didn't say anything. Instead, he pulled out his pouch and rolled himself a cigarette.

"I'll thank you to take that out of my house," she said before he could strike a match to ignite not only the paper but also the tobacco.

"Have you lost your mind, woman? I've always smoked in the house when I was talking to Darius."

"In case you haven't noticed, I'm not Darius. He's dead and I'm here in his place. I don't object to you smoking, even in the house, but not when Dave is battling this fever. Any other time, I would enjoy the aroma of a good cigarette. I've even been known to smoke one myself, but I don't enjoy it as much as the men I've known do."

She watched as Cam took the cigarette from between his lips and tucked it behind his ear before returning the match to his pocket. It pleased her to think he honored her wishes without her having to ask him twice. He may not like her, but at least he respected what she said where Dave was concerned. The fever was bad enough without taking any chances of making things worse.

"I saw Verna and Minnie come out earlier. Why aren't they taking care of Dave?"

"Because when it comes to nursing, I know what I'm doing and they don't. It's the same with cooking, they know how to do things like that, and if it were up to me, I'd probably starve to death. Do you have any more questions or are you just curious as to what my answer would be?"

"Just concerned about Dave. He's a top hand. I'd sure as hell hate to lose him."

"My feelings exactly. Now, if you've satisfied your curiosity, I suggest you get some rest. It's been a long day. Tomorrow I suggest you go into town and talk to the sheriff. I don't like having my herd raided and my men shot any more than you do."

"You sure do have a way with words. It's true, you wouldn't be my choice as a boss, but you're the one Darius left this spread to. I'm way ahead of you about the sheriff. I sent word into him earlier. He said he'd be out first thing in the morning to talk to you. He's probably more interested in you than he is in the rustlers, though. I've sent him word about the cattle we've been missing for the past month but this is the first time he's seen fit to even say he'd come out and investigate."

"Well, that means I must be good for something. I have a long night in store for me, and it sounds like you have plenty to do in the morning. So Mr. Blake, I think it's best if you get a good night's sleep and allow me to take care of my patient."

Cam nodded and touched his fingers to the brim of his hat. His gesture was one of respect. If that was all she was going to get out of him, so be it. It was better than out and out hatred.

Chapter Three

Cam spent a restless night. Rose bothered him. He thought he knew exactly what kind of a woman she was, and he didn't approve of her. Why was it then that she dominated his thoughts? The way she took care of Dave reminded him of one of the nurses he'd seen at the hospital in Omaha where he'd taken his wife when her pregnancy went terribly wrong. It had been what his father-in-law wanted, but it had been too late for them to do anything to save her. By the time they arrived, the doctor said she'd lost far too much blood for either her or the child to survive. Even though the memory broke his heart, he knew the women who worked in the hospital as nurses did all they could to save his wife and daughter. It had been just too little too late. If only he'd gotten her to the hospital earlier, he might still have both of them in his life. Instead, he and Josh were forced to live like fugitives running from his former father-in-law.

Rather than dwell on the past or on Rose McKinney, he got up and pulled on his britches. There was work to do, and once breakfast was finished, he would have to deal with Sheriff Pollard. It would be easy for him to ride out for the day and leave Rose to talk to the old bastard, but that wouldn't be right. All Rose knew was one of the hands had been shot. She couldn't take Pollard out to the range where Dave had been shot and the steers taken.

Before leaving the bunkhouse, Cam checked Josh's bunk. The boy was still sleeping. If he'd been any of the other hands Cam would have rousted him from his bed, but this was his son. He wasn't even old enough to shave, and yet he was doing the work of a man. It wasn't fair.

He hoped, once all this trouble calmed down, he'd be able to hire some hands to take the responsibilities off his son's shoulders.

"What do you want us to do today?" Ned asked.

"The sheriff is due out today. He'll want to talk to all of us. Once he's gone, we'll round up the rest of the herd and pasture them up closer to the house. It ain't exactly what I want to do, but I can't afford to have more of our cattle disappear or anyone else to get shot. I know we brought up the remainder of the herd from the north pasture yesterday, but we have more steers out there. If we don't round them up, this ranch ain't gonna be worth the powder and shot to blow it to hell."

"What about Dave?"

"I checked on him last night. He didn't look too good to me, but the new boss was taking care of him. He'll be mad as a wet hen when he finds out he was too sick to enjoy it."

Ned got to his feet. "You're too hard on her, Cam. It ain't like she's gonna turn this place into a whorehouse. From what I saw yesterday, she seems like a real lady."

Cam wanted to protest, but from the corner of his eye, he saw Josh enter the cookhouse. He hoped his warning glance would silence the men before his son overheard the conversation that could easily turn into an argument.

"The sun's been up for almost an hour, Pa, why didn't you wake me?"

"There wasn't any need. We're not heading out until after the sheriff is done with his investigation."

Josh nodded and made his way up to the cook to get his breakfast. Cam hated having his son live in the addition Darius had built onto the bunkhouse for them and work like the rest of the men, but he had no choice. It wasn't like Josh knew any other life. He'd been too young to remember what it was like to have a mother to fuss over him and cook his meals.

* * * *

In the morning, Verna came with a breakfast tray. Rose felt drained, but it wasn't the first time she'd stayed awake all night. While she ate, Minnie took over bathing Dave's forehead with the cool water. Both women looked well rested. That was good, since she needed all the help she could get.

Once she finished eating, she'd go up to her bedroom. She'd take a sponge bath and change her clothes. That would refresh her so she could continue monitoring Dave's care. She was certain the doctor would return today, and she wanted to be able to give him a detailed report of everything she'd done overnight.

She'd just stripped off her soiled dress and started her sponge bath when she heard a commotion downstairs.

"Are you up there, Miss McKinney?"

The voice of the man asking the question was strange to her. It had to be the sheriff. To her horror, she heard him coming up the stairs. It was entirely possible he'd heard about her life in St. Louis and was hoping to sample what he'd heard about. If that was what he had on his mind, he had another think coming. She might be a whore, but she was a well-paid one and not free for any common man who wanted her.

As quickly as possible, Rose finished her sponge bath and put on a clean shift. She grabbed her blouse and was just buttoning it when the bedroom door burst open.

"I was hoping to find you here," Sheriff Pollard said as he strode into the room. "From what I've heard, this is the perfect place for you."

"If you're referring to anything other than the fact this ranch is losing cattle, and I've had a man critically wounded, I'll be very upset."

"Then you'll have to be upset. I know all about your past, and I figure if I play my cards right, I'll be the first one in the area to taste your honey."

He reached for her and pulled her close. In the past, she'd contended with other men who were intent on the same thing as the sheriff. The difference was they were drunk and this man was stone cold sober.

With survival the only thing on her mind, she brought up her knee between his legs. As in the past, it worked like a charm. He howled in pain and doubled over giving her a chance to escape.

"My former life is just that, Sheriff Pollard. Today is what matters, and today I'm the owner of this ranch. From what I can see, we're in big trouble here, and you haven't done a thing about it. Cattle are the lifeblood of any ranch, and if mine are disappearing, then we're looking at the death of this property. Now, what do you plan to do about it?"

Pollard was still doubled over in pain and gasping for breath. At this moment, she was certain he hated her, but that didn't matter. She was here to run this ranch not fulfill the sexual fantasies of every man within a hundred mile radius. At least for the next year, she was to be the owner of the ranch left to her by her father, and she planned to make it a profitable venture.

The sound of more people coming up the stairs drew her attention from the sheriff to the men who were now crowding into the room. She hadn't met most of her crew, but she immediately recognized Cam and Ned.

"What's going on up here?" Cam asked as he looked around the bedroom.

"Sheriff Pollard and I had a misunderstanding. I think we both understand each other much better now. Isn't that right, Sheriff?"

Pollard nodded as he struggled to straighten up. "We had a bit of a difference of opinion. I agree with Miss McKinney we understand each other much better now."

Everyone turned to leave the room, leaving Cam and Rose alone. "Just what were you and the sheriff discussing in your bedroom?"

Rose looked into his eyes. All her life she'd been trained to know what a man was thinking by the look in his eyes. Cam hated her for what she'd been all her life. She couldn't change the past, but she could do something about the future.

"It wasn't my idea. I made a big mistake when I first came here. I should have thought more about what I was wearing when I got off the train yesterday. As for being in the bedroom, I have been riding a train for the past week to get here. Once I did, I find one of my men has been shot and in need of medical attention. I've been up all night and I needed to wash up as well as change my clothes. That said it was only natural for me to come to my bedroom in order to make the change. I certainly didn't expect to be accosted by the sheriff. I know what you're thinking, but I didn't come here to start a whorehouse."

Without waiting for a response to what she said, Rose pushed past Cam and went downstairs. It was one thing for people to judge her, but for her own men to think the only thing she had on her mind was getting them into bed was another. Yesterday morning when she first arrived, the idea had crossed her mind, but after her first twenty-four hours on the ranch, she was having second thoughts. Her father made certain this ranch paid for her education. She couldn't stand to lose it. Even if she had questioned Celeste's reasoning when it came to the things she had studied, she now knew each of them would come in handy in the new world she was now experiencing.

* * * *

Cam stared at Rose's back as she disappeared down the stairs. He knew, as well as the next person Sheriff Pollard was the one who initiated the confrontation with Rose. He had absolutely no business being in her bedroom. It didn't take a genius to realize what was on the man's mind when he burst in on Rose.

He smiled at the memory of seeing Pollard doubled over in pain. Rose had most likely kneed the man. It was better than he deserved. If Cam thought his father had been a rutting old goat, he couldn't hold a candle to Pollard.

Cam waited a moment longer before following Rose down the stairs. He'd come to the house to check on Dave, but he'd seen Pollard's pinto out front at the same moment he heard the man yell. That brought every hand in hearing distance running to the house.

His mind jumped to all the wrong conclusions when he'd seen Rose with her blouse half buttoned giving Pollard hell. He was grateful to think Josh hadn't witnessed that.

Pollard stood in the parlor talking to Rose when Cam finally joined them.

"I can't tell you much, Sheriff," Rose said. "As you know, I only just arrived yesterday morning. The person you should be talking to is my foreman as well as the other men in my employ. They're the ones who have been dealing with this problem."

"But, my dear Miss McKinney, you are the owner of the Rocking M. It's you I should be talking to," Sheriff Pollard protested.

Cam wasn't content to listen to anymore of Pollard's lame comments. "Rose is right. We've been coming into town ever since Darius was killed trying to get you to come out here. Other than the day we found Darius dead, you haven't gotten off your fat ass long enough to come out here and investigate our losses. It's been over twenty-four hours since we found Dave and you've just decided to come out. I sent someone into town to get you and the doctor at the same time. Doc came out right away but you waited until you thought you would be able to catch Rose alone."

"I don't have to talk to you, Blake. You're nothing but a hired hand."

"In case you haven't noticed, I'm the foreman of this ranch and I've been responsible for it ever since Darius's death. You can and you will talk to me. As far as I can see, the rustlers have been driving the cattle north. For all we know, they could be in Canada by now, but something tells me they're somewhere in the area. There are just too many canyons where they could hide a herd. Is there anyone else who is losing cattle?"

The look on Pollard's face was one of confusion. "Not that I've heard, but you know the people around here. They don't come running to me every time one of their steers wanders away."

"Look, Sheriff," Rose began, "I haven't had a chance to look at the books yet, but believe me I will be looking at them very carefully. Right now, I'm more interested in the cattle disappearing from my herd. Now either you do something about this, or I'll get in touch with the U. S. Marshal in Denver. I'm certain they would be more than happy to do the job you don't seem able to handle."

Cam smiled as Sheriff Pollard started to squirm. It was one thing for a woman to knee him and yet another for the same woman to threaten his authority with the possibility of calling in a U. S. Marshal to solve something Pollard didn't want to look into himself.

"You don't need to do that, Miss McKinney. I'll ride out there with Cam right away and see what we can come up with. I just wouldn't expect miracles. If we believe your foreman here, this has been going on ever since Darius was killed. We did a lot of investigating then and didn't come up with anything. It's possible your steers are in Canada by now."

Cam could tell by the look in Rose's eyes she didn't believe Pollard any more than he did. He had his own theories about this, but it was best if he kept his mouth shut until he came back and could talk to Rose

36

alone. It was possible Darius had given her a clue in one of the letters he'd written her prior to his death.

* * * *

The excitement of the morning ended when Cam and the sheriff left to investigate the rustling. With them gone, Rose went back to the room where Dave was still sleeping. Minnie seemed to be happy to have her return.

"I don't see any change, Rose," she said. "Are you sure he's going to be all right?"

"At this point, I'm not sure about anything."

"One thing I know is that you gave Sheriff Pollard something to think about. Ned told us that you kneed him. I don't think there's a woman in town with the guts to do that to him."

"Do you mean he's assaulted other women?"

Minnie nodded her head. "No one likes to talk about it, but let's just say single women try to stay out of his way."

Minnie's words bothered Rose. If she were still in St. Louis, she'd make a visit to the chief of police and complain. Here there was no one to whom she could go. The only way that man could be put out of office was by an election, and she knew the men wouldn't vote him out. It was the way things were. She only wished the women were allowed to vote. If that were the case, Amos Pollard would be looking for a new line of work in the fall when the elections were held.

Rather than dwelling on what she couldn't change, Rose turned her attention to her patient. Dave slept fitfully. It was evident his fever hadn't lessened overnight. She knew no amount of cold cloths on his forehead would bring it down.

She'd expected the doctor to come last night, but she hadn't seen him. It was getting late in the morning and she still was on her own. She had to do something, but without modern medicine, she was at a loss.

"I've made some willow bark tea," Verna said, as she came into the downstairs bedroom. "It's a good fever reducer. I went into town right after I got up this morning to get it. I also stopped by the doctor's office. He's still over at the Alton ranch delivering a baby. I doubt we'll see him until late this afternoon. Tillie always has long labors when she delivers."

Rose took the cup of tea from Verna along with the spoon. While Minnie lifted Dave into a sitting position, Rose spooned the tea into his mouth. She was pleased to see him automatically swallow the medication.

"I hope this works," she said, more to herself than to her companions.

"We haven't always had a doctor in town," Verna said. "When I first came here, we had to do our own doctoring. My mother always used willow bark tea for fevers. I try keep some in my kitchen since I never know when I'll be called on to help the doctor. All the neighbors call me the medicine lady."

Rose wished she knew more about the natural remedies. If they had been good for the pioneers, it was a wonder the doctors didn't recognize them.

* * * *

Cam saddled his horse and rode out of the dooryard with Sheriff Pollard and the rest of the hands. The only one he left behind was his son, Josh. He certainly didn't want his son involved in this investigation. It was better if the boy spent the time cleaning out the barns and catching up on the reading he'd neglected ever since he had to start riding with the men.

Yesterday, the men moved the cattle from the north pasture to grazing land closer to the house. At least it discouraged any further activity. After checking them this morning, he knew there hadn't been another raid.

"That boss of yours needs to be taken down a peg or two," Pollard said as he rode up to ride next to Cam.

"Why, because she wouldn't let you rape her the way you do every other female you get a chance to be alone with?"

"Rape, hell, I don't know who you're listening to. Every woman I've been with has wanted me in her bed. As for raping your boss, that's a laugh. Everyone knows you can't rape a whore. That's what she is, you know. I saw her get off the train, and I've heard stories about how she was brought up in a cathouse in St. Louis. I've been waiting for her to get here so I can get a decent roll."

"Then why did she knee you? I'm not thrilled about the life she's lived, but I also don't approve of what you've done to the women of this town. If it was up to me, I'd make certain you were run out of town. It will be interesting to see what happens when you come up for reelection this fall."

Pollard laughed. "And just who is stupid enough to run against me? I've held this job for the past ten years. There's no one who wants to do this shit work."

"What does that say about you? If it's shit work for someone else, why do you keep doing it?"

"Why not? I make good money, and the work is usually easy, unless I get called out on some wild goose chase. If you ask me, those steers are long gone. I told you as much when we were at the house. The only reason I'm out here is to show you I'm right."

Chapter Four

Rose soon learned neither Verna nor Minnie wanted to be in the sickroom. She found it strange because Verna bragged she'd worked with the sick before they got a doctor in town. Perhaps Verna realized working with the sick was not something she enjoyed. In St. Louis, she would have been called an herbalist and would have helped the doctors in a way that wouldn't involve being with the patients.

Even though Verna and Minnie had been cordial to her the previous day, Rose sensed they wanted to keep distance between them and her. For the first time in her life, the way she grew up and the life she'd lived was embarrassing her. These good women looked at her as the scum of the earth.

She wasn't a terrible person. She'd gone to the best schools and been educated in fields she never thought she would use. Now, she was in a position where that education was useful. Couldn't they see she was a decent person? She'd only ever known one life, and it was the same as what they knew.

"I've fixed plenty of food for you," Verna said, as she entered the bedroom and ended Rose's mental ramblings. "There's also a supply of willow bark for tea. It's in a jar I labeled for you. I can't imagine you'd know what it was just by looking at it."

Even though it was true, the comment hurt. Rose knew she was ignorant in the ways of natural medicines, but she was a damn good nurse, and she hated having this woman think otherwise.

"I appreciate all you've done. When I'm settled here, I'll find a way to repay you. I'm certain you and Minnie have people in town who depend on you."

Verna looked relieved. Although she had, more than likely, come into the room to tell Rose she was ready to go back to town she was having a hard time saying the words.

"I hope you'll be all right here alone, but you're right, Minnie and I do have other obligations. I'm certain the cook for your men will keep you supplied with food, but at least you have something here so you don't have to depend on someone you don't know."

"I'll enjoy the food you've left. I'm certain I'll see you when I'm able to get to town."

Verna nodded as she turned to leave the room. For years, Rose had been trained to read the body language of the people with whom she dealt. With such knowledge, she knew Verna was secretly praying their paths would never cross again. Rose wasn't respectable enough for this woman who probably never ate a meal in a fancy restaurant or bought a ready-made dress.

Verna came to say good-bye, but the fact that Minnie didn't, hurt. She liked both of these women and knew they had much they could teach her. Unfortunately, their preconceived notions about Rose stood in the way of any friendship might have formed.

Beside her Dave moaned, taking her mind from the women who, by now, were driving their wagon back to town.

"Get out!" Dave shouted. "Get off this land. These cattle ain't yours."

He thrashed around in the bed, causing Rose to get to her feet. As gently as possible, she pushed him back down against the pillows and whispered soothing words to him.

It took a few minutes for Dave to calm down and slip back into a peaceful sleep. When she was convinced he was again sleeping, she placed her hand on his forehead. To her relief, the fever that raged hours earlier was now back to normal. She made a mental note to contact the hospital she'd worked at in St. Louis to let them know of the wonders of willow bark tea. Even with the modern medicine she used, it usually took longer to work than this home remedy that the doctors would probably not acknowledge.

It was mid afternoon when Rose finally left the chair next to Dave's bed. She knew she should be there in case he woke, but her stomach growled in protest because she'd eaten neither breakfast nor the noon meal.

She was surprised to see a young man mounting the steps of the porch. Considering none of the hands had been up to the house today, she was fearful of who could be coming up to the house as though he belonged there.

"Miss McKinney," the young man who stood outside the closed screen door said. "I came to see if you're all right. I saw the other women leave and the cook said you haven't been down to the cookhouse for anything to eat."

Rose tentatively opened the door. The person standing on the porch was far from a man. Seeing him without the screen separating them allowed her to see he was little more than a boy. Even though he wore cowboy boots, a chambray shirt, denim britches, and a hat like the ones she'd seen on the other men, she could tell he was far too young to be employed as a ranch hand.

"I'm fine, thank you," she replied. "The ladies who were here left me some food, but I haven't taken the time to eat any of it. I appreciate you coming to check on me, but I'm afraid you have me at a bit of a disadvantage. You know who I am, but I don't know your name."

The boy held out his hand to shake hers. "I'm Joshua Blake, but my friends call me Josh. My pa is your foreman."

It was difficult to comprehend Cam having a son who looked so young and acted so mature. "I'm pleased to meet you, Josh. My friends call me Rose. I'm hoping I can call you my friend."

"I'd like that, ma'am. Pa wouldn't let me ride out with the men and Sheriff Pollard this morning. He gave me some chores to do here, but I have them all done. I was glad when the cook asked me to find out if you needed anything to eat. It gave me a chance to see how Dave is doing."

"Why don't you come in? I don't like to leave him alone for too long. You can sit with him while I fix myself something to eat. There hasn't been much change except his fever has gone down."

Josh smiled at the invitation and followed her into the house. She pointed him toward the bedroom while she went to the kitchen to see what the women left. A kettle of broth simmered along with a kettle of stew on the back of the stove. After ladling out a bowl of stew for herself, she returned to the room where Josh sat with Dave.

"I didn't think," she said as she entered the room. "Have you had your noon meal?"

Josh looked up at her. "Yes ma'am, I mean Rose, I ate at the cookhouse earlier."

Dave continued to sleep while Rose ate and watched Josh hold the older man's hand compassionately. "Do you know Dave well?" she said, once she finished her stew.

"As well as I do most of the hands. Pa wouldn't let me ride with the men until this summer after your pa died. That's when our men started quitting, and I had to ride with my pa."

"What does your mother think of you doing a man's job this summer?"

"My ma died ten years ago. Pa says she was having my baby sister and they both died. Pa doesn't like me working with the men, but he says he doesn't have any choice. He's more interested in me getting educated. I'd rather be out riding like he does."

"Your father is a wise man. Everyone should have an education, and you have a father who is willing to see you get it."

"But it ain't the same as riding with the men. Who cares about what you read in books?"

Rose smiled at the question. "There's more to life than riding the range, Josh. I agree with your father. An education is worth more than anything else in this world. Of course, when I was your age, I used to grouse about having to study."

"I don't mind studying, but I can't see the sense in it when we're shorthanded. I need to be out there helping Pa and the others. With the rustlers takin' our steers, he needs every hand he can get in the saddle. There are still a lot of strays in the canyons that have to be rounded up."

"I would imagine there are, but the men can handle it. Now the sheriff is involved and things are more settled here, we'll hire more hands and things can get back to normal. In the mean time, I noticed a shelf with lots of books in the parlor. Anytime you want to read one of them, feel free to come up here and take any of them."

A heartwarming smile spread across Josh's face. He was a good boy but he was also one on the verge of manhood. His father was right about education, but by the same token, Josh was right about wanting to ride with the men. From what she'd heard in town, plus what she'd seen for herself, there were problems at the Rocking M. The sooner she could ride with the men and see the problems first hand, the better she'd like it.

Josh turned his attention from her to Dave, giving Rose time to think about the situation she was in. This was her ranch, or at least it would be once she stayed here for a year. She owed it to the man who religiously sent the checks for her care to find out what was happening and avenge his murder.

She yawned broadly, and prayed she would be able to stay awake for the night to come. The trip out had been draining to say the least. All she thought about during the last days on the train was a hot bath and a soft bed. Since arriving here, she had only taken enough time for a sponge bath in tepid water. As for the soft bed, she had eyed it as though it was a hot meal and she was starving. It would have to wait, but how long would her body allow her to go without the rest it craved?

* * * *

The sun was slipping down past the mountains to the west when Cam and the others returned to the ranch. Sheriff Pollard had been less than diligent about his investigation. Rose was right, it was time to call in a U. S. Marshal and get to the bottom of things. Cam certainly didn't want to wait for another of his hands to be murdered like Darius had been.

The men filed into the cookhouse for the supper waiting for them. There had been a lot of hard riding between now and the breakfast they'd eaten hours earlier. Even though they'd eaten a noon meal of cold beans, it hadn't been enough to ward off the hunger that clawed at each of their stomachs.

Rather than join the men, Cam went to his quarters beside the bunkhouse. He was certain he'd find Josh there resting, considering the barns looked as though they had been cleaned meaning the chores he'd left for his son had been completed.

To his surprise, the bunkhouse was deserted. He went back to the cookhouse, thinking Josh might already be there to eat. Unfortunately, he wasn't there either.

"Have you seen Josh?" he asked the cook.

The man looked up from the food he was putting on the plates of the hands. "I saw him around lunch time. I sent him up to the house to check on Miss McKinney. She hasn't been down here for anything to eat and I saw those all old biddies from town leave just before lunchtime."

"You sent him up there? What were you thinking about? I don't want him around that woman. She's not the kind of woman who..."

"Settle down, Cam," Ned advised. "The horse is out of the barn. Josh went up to the house, and there's nothing we can do about it. Just go up there and bring him down here for supper. She's here to stay, and you'd better get used to it. It doesn't matter what she did before she arrived here. Since she's arrived I haven't seen any behavior that would bother me. I'll go up to the house and get him."

"Like hell you will. I'll go up and let him know I don't want him associating with that woman."

Ned shook his head. Cam knew his friend didn't approve, but Josh wasn't his son. Cam would raise the boy in the way he saw fit.

Crossing the dooryard, Cam headed toward the main house. As soon as he stepped onto the porch, he could hear his son speaking in an even tone from within the house.

Without knocking, he opened the door and crossed the parlor to get to the downstairs bedroom. Once he entered the room, he saw Josh sitting next to Dave's bed, reading from one of the books Cam recognized from those in Darius' bookcase.

Across the room Rose sat in an overstuffed chair and looked up at him as he entered, interrupting Josh's reading.

"What in the hell are you doing up here, boy?" Cam demanded.

"I came up to check on Rose and..."

"And nothing. I told you not to come up here, and you know better than to call her by her first name."

To his surprise, Rose sat in the overstuffed chair on the other side of the room. "Your son was courteous enough to come up to see if I had enough to eat," she said. "As for calling me by my first name, I gave him permission. He was very formal and it certainly didn't seem right. We were talking about his education and I suggested he select some of the books from my father's library and take his time reading them. I also thought hearing Josh's voice might be enough to bring Dave back to consciousness.

"Whether you realize it or not, you have an extraordinary son. He's so worried about this ranch being short-handed he feels he has to take on a man's job. I don't agree, but after talking to him, I understand why he's taken to the saddle, at least for the summer. As soon as Dave can be left alone, I plan to start riding with you in Josh's place. When fall comes, he can continue his education."

"You? Riding with us? How do you expect to do such a thing? What do you know about ranching? Do you even know how to ride a horse?"

Sparks flew from Rose's eyes. "To answer your questions, yes, I do intend to ride with the men. My father would have ridden and done the work, and I plan to do the same. As for what I know about ranching, it isn't much, but I've been learning things all my life, and I can learn this as well. That brings us to what I know about riding a horse. I've been taking riding lessons since I was five years old. I can ride as well, if not better than any of the men on this ranch."

"This isn't one of those fancy bridle paths I've heard they have in St. Louis. Out here, it's range riding, and the range is full of gopher and snake holes. A man has to be an experienced rider to miss them."

"Because I'm a woman you don't think I could do the same. You aren't giving the horse much credit. Another thing, although I did ride on the bridle paths, I have ridden out in the country on more than one occasion. I haven't done any riding in Montana, but I doubt it's much different from riding in Missouri."

"It still isn't right. Women out here don't ride with the men just because they think it will be fun. They're smart enough to know they belong at home doing the things women do best."

His comment seemed to agitate Rose. She got to her feet and took a step forward. He wondered if she had gotten up too quickly when her face drained of color and she began to shake. Before he could caution her to sit back down, she pitched forward in a faint.

Josh was immediately on his feet and at her side before Cam could react. His son caught Rose before she reached the floor.

Knowing his son wasn't strong enough to lift Rose's dead weight,

Cam scooped her into his arms and carried her into the parlor to put her on the sofa.

"There should be water in the kitchen," Cam ordered. "Bring me a wet cloth for her forehead."

It had been over ten years since Cam held a woman in his arms. No matter how much he resented her coming to the ranch to take over, the feelings generated by this woman he now held were ones he thought died with his wife.

Before he could examine his emotions further, Josh returned with the damp cloth.

"What do you think is wrong, Pa?" Josh showed concern for this woman.

"It could be she's just exhausted."

"Miss McKinney, I've come to check on our patient."

Cam turned toward the door to see Dr. Myers enter the parlor. Relief flooded Cam. He had no idea why Rose collapsed to say nothing of what to do for her.

"Am I glad to see you, Doc. Rose just collapsed, and Dave is still unconscious."

By the time Dr. Myers came over to the couch, Josh was caressing Rose's forehead with the damp cloth.

"How long has she been unconscious?"

"Just a few minutes," Cam replied. "We were having a discussion, and she got up from the chair where she was sitting, and then she collapsed."

"You were fighting, Pa, and you know it," Josh corrected.

"We were disagreeing," Cam corrected.

"It doesn't matter. Has this young lady had any sleep?"

"No sir," Josh said without allowing Cam to speak. "I thought she looked tired when I first came up to the house. That was why I stayed and read to Dave while she relaxed. She was just about asleep when Pa came."

"I heard her say this morning she hadn't slept well on the train, and she'd been up all night with Dave," Cam added.

"What about the women I sent out to help her?"

"She said they had things they had to do in town, so she sent them

47

back this afternoon," Josh replied.

Cam thought about the cook telling him the 'old biddies' from town left shortly after noon. At the time, he'd been thinking only about his son being with Rose when he'd told Josh he couldn't go up to the house. Since Dave was still unconscious, why did those women even consider leaving Rose here alone?

Dr. Myers was holding Rose's wrist to check her pulse when she began to stir. "Dave, I have to get back and check on Dave," she said as she tried to get into a sitting position.

"I don't think so," Dr. Myers said. He forced her back down against the pillow Josh placed on the sofa before Cam laid her down.

"There's nothing wrong with me. My patient needs me."

"Dave needs you to be healthy, not completely exhausted. It seems to me healthy young women don't pass out without a good reason. I'm going to check you over and then see how things are going with Dave. Is there a reason you haven't rested, considering Verna and Minnie were here to help you?" Cam was interested in hearing her reasoning as well.

"Dave's incision was infected and I was trying to get the fever down. I didn't think I should be sleeping when he might need me. I treated him throughout the night. I think I cleaned out the infection, but he was still running a fever. That was when Verna went into town and brought out some willow bark tea. It did help, but I still didn't want to leave him alone."

"That's all fine and good, but I'm certain when you were training to be a nurse, one of the first things you learned was the nurse needed her rest as much as the patient."

Rose lowered her eyes. "I did, but then I had people who could take over. I could tell Verna and Minnie were not comfortable taking care of Dave. It's one thing for Verna to care for sick children, but gunshot victims are an entirely different matter. They meant well, but my instincts told me they also didn't approve of me. Rather than all of us feeling uncomfortable, I suggested they go back to town. Thankfully, they left me some broth for Dave and some stew for me."

Cam saw the questions in his son's eyes at Rose's statement. He didn't want to have to explain about Rose's past to someone so young, but now that she mentioned it, Cam had little choice in the matter.

"What's she talking about?" Josh whispered.

"It's best if we talk about it later," Cam replied.

Josh's expression told Cam his son wanted answers. "It's because she came from St. Louis and was brought up in a cat house isn't it?"

"How do you know that?"

"The men are all talking about it. I don't see what difference it makes. She's very nice, and from what I can tell, she knows about a lot more things than what goes on in a place like that. We were talking about me riding with the men, and she said the same thing you have been telling me all summer. She wants me to continue with my education and told me I could read any of the books in her Pa's library. She even said if there was anything I didn't understand, she'd be happy to help me."

"She sounds like a wise woman. I just hope the things she's talking about aren't things you shouldn't be learning."

"Pa, it ain't… ah, I mean isn't like that. She's been well educated, and she wants to share her knowledge with me. Rose told me she's planning to find more hands to work for us so when school starts in the fall, I can finish the rest of my education."

Cam looked from his son to Rose. He shouldn't have judged her without knowing her, but the way she looked when she first arrived indicated she was a whore.

Over the years, he'd heard Darius telling about the fine education she was receiving in St. Louis. He'd believed every word of what his boss said, but seeing the way Rose was dressed when she arrived brought doubts to his mind. Then this morning, Verna told him the story was Rose had been brought up in a cathouse in St. Louis called the Purple Moon. He didn't know where Verna got her information, but it made sense.

Looking over, he saw Dr. Myers tending to the new owner. Cam was overwhelmed by a flood of emotions. Suddenly he wasn't on the Rocking M. Instead, he was sitting in the hospital room in Nebraska. For a fleeting moment, the woman being ministered to wasn't Rose, but was his wife.

He blinked his eyes several times to rid himself of the unwanted memory. It had been over a year since such memories found their way to his mind. Over a year since the horror of losing his wife and daughter within hours of each other had completely engulfed his being.

"Are you all right, Pa?" Josh said, successfully dissolving the memory Cam couldn't rid himself of on his own.

Cam nodded. "Doc don't need us in here. It's best we go in and sit with Dave."

* * * *

Rose resigned herself to the role of patient. It was true, she hadn't taken the time to care for herself since arriving at the Rocking M, but there hadn't been time. Verna and Minnie meant well, but they knew nothing at all about nursing. That, added to the severity of Dave's wounds, left them virtually useless. It would have been easier to doze off if the infection hadn't set in so quickly.

"Now, young lady," Dr. Myers continued, "where are Verna and Minnie?"

"I… I thought I told you. I… I sent them home."

Dr. Myers looked at her disapprovingly. "I told them to stay as long as you needed them."

"It was evident they weren't comfortable here. Besides, they had duties at home just as I have duties in the sick room. Rather than bothering with me, shouldn't you be checking on Dave? He ran a temperature all night after the wound became infected. I did the best I could. It was Verna who brought out the willow bark tea and reduced the fever."

"That damnable woman and her folk remedies. How many times do I have to tell her they have no place in modern medicine?"

Rose felt her blood boil in anger. "No place? If it hadn't been for those herbs, Dave's temperature would still be raging. Instead, he's sleeping peacefully."

"What you don't understand, young lady, is a doctor's orders cannot be overridden by—"

"By what? Someone who knows how to remedy the problem? I couldn't reach you, and the fever was consuming him. I've already made note of its healing properties and plan to forward them on to my friends at the hospital where I trained in St. Louis."

"They will dismiss it as poppycock. It is said a little knowledge is a dangerous thing, and it seems they were referring to you when they said it. You have the knowledge of a nurse, but not of a doctor. You are interfering in things best left for men who are trained to be doctors. As a nurse, I am certain there are none better than you, but remember, you are only a nurse, not a doctor."

Rose made no further comment. In her training, she'd encountered doctors who considered nurses as little more than hand holders and someone to administer medicine. One man called them medical whores. At the time, her fellow students laughed at the term, even though when she had no homework, Rose often worked at the Purple Moon as the whore he'd called her. She could see no comparison between what the whores at the Purple Moon did and what the nurses at the hospitals did.

As a whore, she gave men the pleasure they needed to relieve the ache in their bodies. As a nurse, she tended to sick men, women, and children, with the compassion they needed in order to get well. The difference was as vast as the Mississippi River and could not be, in any way, compared one to the other.

"I can tell you are healthy, but you are also exhausted. My orders are to rest. I'll be instructing Cam and Josh on what to do for Dave to keep him comfortable. Of course, I don't trust you to do as I say, so I want you to drink this."

Rose looked at the beaker of medication he held out to her. "What is it?"

"Just a mild sedative. You're so worked up over Dave I know you can't begin to rest. This will take the edge off and make you sleep for several hours."

She made a face she hoped would tell him she didn't need his sedative, but he forced her to take it. Once she swallowed, the bitter liquid burned its way down her throat. She knew, from experience with patients, it would begin to take effect within minutes of her swallowing it. Rather than fight it, she closed her eyes and allowed the medication to work.

* * * *

Dave looked up when Dr. Myers returned to the downstairs bedroom. The older man was shaking his head in dismay. "Is she all right?" Cam said.

"She's one of the most bull-headed women I've ever met. As a trained nurse, she should know the one thing she needed to do was get her rest. Instead, she sat up all night after being on a train for the better part of two weeks. Then she was stupid enough to allow Verna to give her some folk remedy. For all she knew, that willow bark tea could have killed Dave."

"But it didn't," Josh protested. "The fever is down, and he's been sleeping peacefully all afternoon. I've been here and watched her."

"She was very lucky," Dr. Myers conceded. "Let me do an examination."

Cam shot his son a look he hoped would tell him to back off. Over the years, he'd heard about the fever reducing benefits of willow bark tea. He'd even used it himself when Josh had been little and there wasn't a doctor within a hundred miles of this ranch. Then it hadn't been Verna who brought it out to him, but he had gotten it from Darius.

He watched as Dr. Myers finished his examination. "Miss McKinney was right," Dr. Myers said, once he finished his examination. "If there was an infection, it's been cleared up and the fever is down. Right now, he's sleeping, and that's the best medicine I can think of at this point. Did I hear her say something about some broth on the stove?"

"Yes sir," Josh replied. "The ladies left that and some stew for Rose simmering on the stove. Do you want me to get some of it?"

"No, I just want to check it for myself. If they made that up last night, I doubt it's any good. In this heat, food has a tendency to spoil. If I'm right, I want you to go out and talk to the cook and have him make up some fresh broth and bring up fresh food for Miss McKinney when she wakes."

"Her name is Rose," Josh said. "She told me friends don't call each other Miss or Mister. She also said she was uncomfortable with such formality."

Dr. Myers put his hand on Josh's shoulder. "I think you're just what this young lady needs right now."

"What do you mean by that?" Cam questioned.

"I have a feeling she could use a friend. It's evident just about everyone in town knows who and what she was, and they've decided to judge her on that information alone. This young man is judging her as a person who is just like everyone else. I think the two of them will be good for each other. From what Darius told me, she's well educated and won't take any lip from this scamp about not doing the best he can in school."

Cam looked at his son and saw the boy who was becoming a man all too quickly. With the trust of someone his age, he'd made friends with the woman who was going to be their boss and found her to be worthy of his friendship.

"I'll check the stew and the broth, Doc. You just take care of your patients, and I'll take care of the rest."

Chapter Five

By the end of Rose's first week on the Rocking M, Dave was well enough to be up and around. At his insistence, he moved back to the bunkhouse, leaving Rose alone in the house. At first, she had been too busy with Dave and then getting settled to become bored, but soon those responsibilities ended.

Considering the cook was delivering her meals, Rose realized it was just one more reason for the men to keep their distance from her. The house was extremely lonely and she craved the companionship she couldn't find within its walls.

Pushing her dresses to the back of the closet, she pulled out a pair of denim britches along with a shirt like the ones her hands wore, a pair of boots, and a Stetson hat. The hat had been a gift from Celeste before Rose left to claim her inheritance.

She finished dressing just as the cook brought her breakfast. "There's no need for that this morning," she declared when she opened the door.

"But you gotta eat," the man protested.

Rose smiled at his words. "I don't plan to go hungry, just as I don't plan to eat alone this morning. I'll be coming out to the cookhouse with you and sharing breakfast with the men."

"But—but you can't, I mean…"

"I know very well what you mean, but I own this ranch and it's high time I find out exactly what it is when I ride out with the men this morning."

"Cam ain't gonna like this," the man muttered as he led the way to the cookhouse.

"It doesn't matter what Cam does or doesn't like. I'm his boss in the same way that I'm yours, and I think I need to start acting like it. I doubt my father spent his days sitting in the house watching the dust accumulate on the furniture."

The man turned his back on her and stormed off in the direction of the building she could only conclude had to be the cookhouse. After closing the front door of the house, she followed him.

She stepped into a room filled with long tables, right behind the cook. As she did, every man in the place turned to look at her. In the past, such attention would have meant money in her pocket, but here it was different. She wasn't a whore out to make as much money in an evening as she could. Here she was the owner of the Rocking M and these men were in her employ.

Dave was immediately on his feet to greet her. "Boys this is the new boss, Rose McKinney," he said as he introduced her. "I don't know what she knows about ranching, but I can tell you she's one hell of a nurse. From what I hear, if it hadn't been for her, I might have died from the infection that set into my shoulder while the doc was out tendin' to someone else when I needed him."

"Thanks Dave," Rose said.

"So just what is it that brought you out here this morning?" Cam demanded before she could say anything more.

"I plan to start acting like the owner of this spread and not a guest staying up at the house. It seems to me that I told you I planned to start riding with the men, and today is as good a day as any for me to start. After breakfast, I'm certain you'll be able to find a horse for me to ride. I know I don't have my own tack here, but my father must have those things, and I don't see any reason why I shouldn't put them to good use."

"As long as you plan on using his tack, you might was well ride his horse," Cam replied. "I'll be more than happy to saddle Renegade for you."

"You can't do that, Pa," Josh protested. "Everyone knows Renegade is the most unpredictable horse on the ranch. As far as I know, no one other than Darius ever rode him."

"Don't worry about me," Rose said, winking broadly at Josh. "I'm a good horsewoman. I have no doubts that I can handle him, but not until I get something to eat."

Josh and the others sitting on the long bench beside him slid down, making room for her across the table from Cam. Once she seated herself the cook brought a plate of food and set it in front of her.

"I threw out the stuff I brought up to the house. It was gettin' cold. I thought you'd like somethin' hot."

"Thank you, Red. I do enjoy hot biscuits and gravy and hot ham much more than I do eating it cold."

"Didn't think the like of you would be content with the kind of food we eat on a daily basis," Cam commented. "'Course if you're planning to ride with the men this morning, you need to get your stomach filled with good food. Don't suppose you ate things like this in St. Louis."

She smiled thinking that she never ate breakfast in St. Louis because her day never started much before noon. "I can't say I did. Of course, I wasn't doing manual labor there that would need the heavier meal to sustain me. My usual morning meal was more like toast points and jam along with assorted fruit. There, I preferred to eat light to keep my girlish figure. Here things are different. I need all the strength I can get to keep up with the duties of a ranch owner."

Cam scowled at her and continued eating his breakfast. She knew the others were casting sideways glances at her to see exactly who and what she was. It was evident they had all heard about her past, but it wasn't the past that concerned her now. She was more interested in the present and future. For now, she had to find out who was stealing cattle from the ranch and how they played a role in her father's murder as well as the wounding of Dave.

As she ate, she thought of the books her father kept. They were far from the perfect ones she'd studied in St. Louis, but they showed the ranch was a money-making proposition until late last winter when the first cattle started disappearing from Rocking M land. His journal told the story more than his books.

It started out in March with the loss of ten head. At the time, he'd chalked it up to Indians looking for meat to supplement the supplies sent from the government. When it kept up week after week, Darius went up to the reservation and spoke with the elders. When they were surprised about the rustling, he realized he was being targeted for some reason he couldn't put his finger on.

Through April and May, his losses continued to mount until they cost his life. Throughout the journal were references to the number of times Darius called on Sheriff Pollard and been told there was nothing he or anyone else could do. Either the rustlers were too crafty to be caught, or Pollard was in on it up to his eyeballs. Whichever scenario, Rose was more than ready to find out what was going on and stop the loss of cattle and lives from her ranch.

* * * *

Cam wondered what wheels were turning in Rose's pretty little head. She'd grown strangely silent as she dug into the biscuits and gravy the hands were enjoying for breakfast.

As far as he was concerned, she was as out of place on the Rocking M as he would be in St. Louis. The last thing he expected was to see her sashaying in here this morning in a pair of denims that hugged every curve of her body and a shirt that accented the breasts he knew were hidden beneath the plaid. It didn't seem possible, but this outfit made her even more appealing than the revealing dress she'd worn on the day she arrived.

He finished the last of his breakfast and got up without making any further conversation with Rose. The thought of watching her try to ride that hellion Renegade brought a smile to his face.

She'd told Josh she was a good horsewoman, but good or not, he'd never seen anyone other than Darius try to ride the stallion. It should be one hell of a show for the boys to watch.

As he saddled Renegade, Cam thought about the letter he'd received from his friend in Texas yesterday. Cornelius Slade hired a private investigator to find his grandson. From what the letter said, Cam and Josh were still safe. The detectives were following leads in California as well as Oregon. Until they got closer to Montana, he didn't have anything to worry about.

It helped that his friend was sending the letters to him in California and Oregon through acquaintances out there. They'd been doing it for years. He was lucky to have friends in both areas of the country who were willing to help him hide Josh from the man who wanted to take him away from his father.

Once Josh was eighteen, Cam promised himself he would tell his son about the man who held his father responsible for Martha's death. Then it would be up to Josh as to whether or not he sought out his grandfather. Until then, it was up to Cam to keep his son close safely out of Cornelius' reach.

"Are you ready to start the day?" he heard Rose say as she swung her leg over the top rail of the corral fence.

Impure thoughts drifted through his mind, but he beat them back. "Ready if you are," he replied all the time watching her walk across the corral.

She reached up to caress Renegade's nose and speak softly to him. The horse twitched his ears as though he was as enchanted by her beauty as Cam had been moments earlier.

"You are I are going to be great friends," he heard her say to the horse.

"You'll rethink your position once you've tried to ride Renegade. I was going to have a lot of fun watching you get yourself tossed on your tail, but on second thought, I think I'd better find you one of the quiet little mares."

Rose smiled as she came around to mount Renegade. "I'd hate to deprive you of your fun," she said with wink, as she swung into the saddle.

Renegade pranced at the unexpected weight on his back, but he didn't rear and buck like Cam expected.

"Well, I'll be damned," Dave said. "That's the last thing I expected to see Renegade do. How in the hell do you think she did that?"

Cam scratched his head. "I figured she'd get thrown on her ass and learn a woman's place isn't out riding with the men. Don't know what got into that horse. He's acting like it was Darius on his back."

Rose rode around the corral and then leaned over and patted Renegade's neck. "I think he's the perfect mount for me, Cam. He's gentle as a kitten, just like my father said he would be."

"Just how did you do that?" Josh's eyes were wide with wonder.

Rose swung from the saddle and crossed over to where Josh stood.

"It's very simple. My father wrote me letters all the time. In them, he told me about how he'd tamed Renegade. His exact words were 'I used sugar cubes and wouldn't you know that devil developed a sweet tooth. As long as I gave him his ration of sugar before I mounted him, he was as gentle as a kitten.'"

"I knew there had to be a trick to it," Cam said. It irritated him there was something about how Darius tamed one of the wildest mustangs they'd ever caught. "We don't have time to stand around here jawin'. We're already late in leaving for the day. There's a lot of ground we have to cover before tonight."

Around them, the men hurried to saddle and mount their horses. "I'd prefer you stay back at the ranch with Josh and the cook, Miss McKinney."

Sparks shot from her eyes. "I'm certain my father didn't stay at the ranch while everyone else rode out."

"Your father owned this place, and he was a man. You on the other hand won't ever own it, because you won't last out the year specified in the will. Besides, riding with us ain't nothin' a lady like you should be doing."

"Why do you want me to think you're uneducated? My father told me you value education quite highly, and he considered you an intelligent man."

"Damn Darius and those infernal letters of his. Yes I'm educated, but that shouldn't be any concern of yours."

"Everything on this ranch is of concern to me. The fact you can read and write is important. Did you ever help my father with his bookwork, or were the accounting skills his alone?"

"I helped him set them up. Why do you ask?"

"They're in terrible shape. Just how many head of cattle have we lost over the past few months?"

"About a hundred and fifty give or take a few. What do the books say?"

"Just that the losses were steady. From his journal, I gather he suspected Sheriff Pollard of being in on it. Is that what you think?"

"Pollard's a fool, but he's not smart enough to be the mastermind of what's been going on around here. It's possible he's aware of who is stealing our stock. That's probably the reason he doesn't do anything about it."

Rose nodded. "That's what I thought as well. Meeting the man one time was enough to make me realize he's not very bright. So how do we go about finding out what's going on?"

It surprised Cam to think they were actually having a civil conversation. "Before Darius died, we thought we could handle it on our own. Now I'm not so sure. I've thought about sending for a federal marshal but to do that I'd have to send a letter from town, and I don't trust anyone there not to tell Pollard we sent one."

"As I recall, we stopped at a small railhead not too far east of here. I saw they had a telegraph operator there. I could ride over there and send the wire."

"Not on your life. Do you think I'd let you ride all that way by yourself? God only knows who or what might be out there."

"I didn't exactly plan on riding over there alone. I thought Josh could go along with me. I've seen him practicing with his gun. He's not a bad shot. It would give me time to get to know him better."

"I don't want my son—"

"I don't care what you want. I'm the boss here, and it's my cattle that are disappearing at a record pace. I'm not planning to seduce him if that's what you're thinking. I left that life back in St. Louis. Sure, I thought it would be easy to pick it up again once I got here, but I gave up on that idea the minute I saw the horror on your face when I arrived. As for my staying here for a year, you'd better be prepared to put up with me, because I'm not budging. This ranch was important to my father, and it paid for my education. At the time, I wondered why I was learning the things I did, but I studied them like I was told. Now I'm glad I did. I know enough about accounting to know this ranch has been losing money on a steady basis, and my nursing kept Dave from joining my father in the graveyard. That said, do you think we can work together or should I start looking for another foreman?"

Cam knew she was right. No matter how he felt about working for a woman, she'd saved Dave's life and made herself sick in the process. "I agree about the wire, but you can take Dave with you rather than Josh. The boy needs to get ready for school to start soon, and Dave's a better hand with the gun than Josh. Besides, I don't like Dave doing anything too strenuous until he mends a bit more."

Rose's stern expression of a few minutes earlier turned into a brilliant smile. He liked the way it softened her face.

"It's a deal," she said, extending her hand to him. "I don't mind Dave's company, although I would like to get to know Josh better. He's a good kid. Did he tell you I said he could use any of the books in my father's library?"

"He did, but I told him he could get along without them."

"You're being ridiculous. The books are there, and from what I can tell, there are a lot of them that would help him in school. Why not let him use them?"

"The same reason I don't want him riding out with you today. I remember what it was like to be his age. He's just learning about girls, and he doesn't need to have temptation thrown in his path."

"Did someone throw that temptation in your way when you were a kid?"

"That's none of your business. You're the boss, and I work for you, but that doesn't mean I have to like you."

"No it doesn't, but we have a year to figure that out. I'm hoping by the end of that year we'll not only be friends, but we will have found out who is rustling my cattle and have found we can work together."

Cam turned and went to where Dave was saddling his horse. "You're riding with the boss this morning."

"Where are you sending us?" Dave inquired.

"Rose thinks the sheriff is in on this rustling the same as we do. The difference is she's prepared to do something about it. She wants to ride over to the railhead east of here and send a wire off to the U.S. Marshall in Denver. I want you to ride along with her."

"Why me? Why not Josh? It would be an easy ride, and I know he's itchin' to git off the ranch for a while."

"He'll get away, just not with her. I'm letting him ride in your place. I'm not so sure you're up to hard riding yet. Watching over the boss will be a good job for you."

"Whatever you say, Cam, but mark my words, you can't keep the boy away from women all his life. I know what she was in St. Louis. I should, you told me, and so did she. Since she's been here, I ain't seen her as anything but proper. Why can't you let go of them ideas you've got about her and try to get along?"

"I've got my reasons. A skunk don't change his stripe, and a whore can't stay away from the trade for long."

Dave shook his head and pushed past Cam to head to where Rose stood with Renegade.

She might have hoodwinked Dave and Josh, but he knew what kind of a woman Rose McKinney was. He'd seen it when she first arrived. He swore if Darius knew what kind of a woman she was, he would have never left this spread to her.

* * * *

Rose watched as Cam gave Dave his orders for the day. It would be easy for her to ride to the railhead and book passage back to St. Louis, but she knew she couldn't do it. Her father built up this ranch to give her an inheritance. It bought her the best education possible, and there was no way she intended to lose it because of the way Cam felt about her. She had the ability to do more than work on her back, and she planned to show him she was woman enough to put the past behind her.

"I hear I'm riding with you today, Miss Rose," Dave said, as he approached her.

"That's what I heard, too. Please, Dave, I wish you'd just call me Rose. That Miss business makes me feel like an old maid schoolteacher, and believe me, that's one thing I'm not. I'm glad Cam decided you should ride with me rather than with the men."

"I am too. As much as I want to get back to work, I know I have a long way to go to be strong enough to do it. He's been keepin' me as penned up as he does the boy, and I was beginning to chafe under the strain."

"What do you mean he keeps Josh penned up?"

"After your pa was killed, we didn't have much choice but to let the boy ride with us. I can tell you it made Cam as mad as a wet hen. He wants Josh to get an education and make more of himself than being a two-bit cowhand. If you ask me, Cam is a highly educated man. I just don't know what he's doing on a ranch like this one."

"I tend to agree with you. I have a feeling there's something in his background he's running away from. It's a shame. Josh is a fine young man, and I think he deserves the best education he can get. I have enough pull in St. Louis to get him into one of the best schools when he's old enough to leave."

"I don't know anything about Cam's background. What I do know is that he and the boy have been here for nigh onto seven years now. I know 'cause him and me came here at about the same time. I knew right off he was an ambitious man, and when the time came that Darius needed a new foreman, it was only right Cam got the job. Course I figured right off he was as green as new grass and didn't know a cow from a steer, but by God, he learned right fast. Ain't no one better on the whole ranch than Cam. He can cut out a calf and have it castrated into a steer and branded faster than anyone. He knows a heap about runnin' a ranch, too. He figures you're aimin' to send him packin' just as soon as you know what you're doin' here."

"Where would he get an idea like that?" Rose said.

"That's just the way things work on a ranch. A new owner takes over, and the old foreman can kiss his job good-bye. You know how it is, new owners want their own people runnin' the place."

"Well, I don't. My motto is if it's not broken, don't fix it. The only thing wrong with the Rocking M is someone's running off our cattle, and I intend to get to the bottom of who is behind it. We can't keep losing steers at the rate we have and hope to stay in business. For some reason, someone wants this ranch, and they want it badly enough to kill to get it. It's going to stop.

"Now, if we're going to get to the railhead and back to the ranch before dark, we have some hard riding ahead of us. As I recall, it took the stage over an hour to get to town after we stopped for the night. With good horses, we can make it in less time."

She dug her spurs into Renegade's side and took off at a gallop, pleased to see Dave was following her lead. It felt good to be riding rather than cooped up in the house. It made her think of being in St. Louis. After several days at the Purple Moon, she always enjoyed getting out and going for a long ride.

Just thinking about the life she left behind, made her realize she honestly didn't miss the hours she spent pleasuring the men who paid highly for her company. Everything Celeste told her about the life her father led was proving to be right. He was an honest and hardworking man, and the education he purchased for her was worth more than anything else in the world. Even the thought of one day purchasing the Purple Moon was slipping further and further into the recesses of her mind. As much as she loved and missed Celeste and the other girls, she realized they led the lives they did because they had no other options.

Her options were very clear. She would find out why someone murdered her father and was stealing his stock, and would end it. She knew she couldn't do it alone, but with the help of someone in the U S Marshall's office, she would get to the bottom of things. She remembered meeting Marshall Frank O'Brien right after they pulled out of St. Louis. They'd been traveling companions all the way to Denver, and he stayed with her until she safely changed trains to continue on to Montana. They'd become good friends, and when they parted, he told her if she ever needed him all she had to do was send him a wire. She'd kept the slip of paper he gave her and brought it along today. For some reason, she'd tucked it safely in her shirt pocket this morning.

As she rode, she composed the message she wanted to send once she made it to the railhead. She and Frank shared several delightful evenings in the confines of her compartment on the train and she knew he'd come if she sent the wire to him.

The miles melted beneath the hooves of their horses, and by noon, they arrived at the railhead.

"Why, Miss McKinney, I sure didn't expect to see you back here so soon," the stationmaster greeted her. "You're not dressed for traveling, so what can I do for you?"

"I need to send a wire."

"As I recall, you were headed for Blanchard. Why ride all the way out here just to send a wire?"

"Because I don't want anyone to know I sent it or to whom I sent it. I can trust you not to tell anyone, can't I?"

"That you can, Ma'am. Don't know why you would think any operator would tell someone what your wire said, but I wouldn't tell anyone about it."

"I knew I could trust you." She batted her eyelashes for effect. "There was a young man on the train, and I'd like to have him come here. He said he was looking for a job, and I think I can supply him with one." She took a pencil and began to write down the message she wanted to send on the pad of yellow paper the stationmaster handed her.

"Who do you want this sent to, Ma'am?"

"I want it to go to Mr. Frank O'Brien in Denver. You know how it would look to the people in town if they knew I was corresponding with a friend of the opposite sex and asking him to come here. I'm afraid my reputation is tainted enough without adding this bit of information to the gossip mill."

"I understand completely," the man replied as he read the message Rose handed him.

```
FRANK—I NEED YOUR HELP ON THE ROCKING M—
WILL EXPLAIN WHEN YOU GET HERE—WILL WAIT
AT THE RAILHEAD FOR YOUR REPLY—ROSE
MCKINNEY
```

The stationmaster read over what the message printed on the paper and began to tap out the wire. "Do you really plan to stay here until you get an answer?" he said once he finished sending it across the wire.

"Yes, I do. Dave and I had a long ride to get here. Do you think you could manage to get us a meal?"

The man looked skeptically at Dave. "'Course I can, but I was hoping…"

"You can hope all you want, but that life is behind me. I'm the owner of the Rocking M ranch and nothing more."

The man laughed. "Once a whore always a whore, mark my words, it won't take long before you're back in the business, and when you are, I hope you won't forget me."

"Are you telling me if I grace your bed, you'll keep the contents of the wire I just sent a secret?"

The man looked crestfallen. "I've never told anyone what a wire contained in my life, and I'm not about to start now. I just remember what you looked like when you first arrived here."

"When I arrived here, I was a whore, but a lot has happened since then. I've realized there is more to life than being with men for money."

The man's face turned white as she heard the click of a gun cocking behind her. Turning she saw Dave standing with his gun drawn on the man who threatened her.

"I know what Miss Rose was, but I also know she's the owner of the Rocking M ranch and a damn good nurse. She cared for me when I got shot, and she cares for the Rocking M as well. Whatever she did before she got here is in the past. The future is what matters. She's a fine woman, and if she says that life is behind her, I believe her."

"I'm sorry, Miss McKinney. You can be certain no one will know the contents of your wire or the one coming in return. I've got some steak and biscuits on the stove, you're welcome to join me for dinner."

Rose nodded her thanks. She knew she'd pay dearly for the meal as well as the man's silence, but it was worth it. Just hearing Dave defend her was worth more than any money she had to pay out.

By the time they finished eating, the telegraph began to clatter. The stationmaster, she now knew was called Mike Perry, quickly took down the message.

```
ROSE—LEAVING DENVER FOR MONTANA TONIGHT—
SHOULD ARRIVE AT THE ROCKING M BY THE END
OF WEEK—HOPE YOU'RE HIRING NEW HANDS—FRANK
```

She could almost see him wink as she read the message Mike handed her. Once Frank got here, she'd have to set him straight about the life she lead now she'd come home to claim her inheritance.

"Beside you and Cam, no one else will know who Frank really is," Rose said, as they prepared to leave the railhead.

"I appreciate you confidin' in me."

"Why shouldn't I? You have as big a stake in this as I do. I lost my father to those rustlers, and you almost lost your life. As far as anyone else on the ranch will know, I sent the wire but didn't get a reply. It's not that I don't trust the other hands at the ranch, but I've always thought it was better to keep things private."

"I know what you mean. I've worked with those men for a long time, but I've learned not to trust everyone just because I think I know them."

Rose smiled as they rode out toward the ranch. She knew she could trust Dave, she could only hope she could trust Cam in the same way.

* * * *

Cam watched the horizon for Dave and Rose to return. What would the marshal say? Would he come and interfere in what should be the problem of the local sheriff? He doubted it. It was entirely possible Rose was wasting her time in going all the way to the railhead only to be turned down.

He continued to think about Rose's trip to the railhead. He'd been a fool to send Dave with her. The trip was more than likely too much for him to attempt so soon after recovering from his wounds.

Rather than continue to ride with the men, Cam headed back toward the ranch. He was too preoccupied with Rose and Dave to concentrate on the round up of the remaining cattle to move them to pasture closer to the ranch.

It was late afternoon when he rode into the dooryard as Dave and Rose returned from the railhead.

"Well?" he prompted once they dismounted.

"Well what?" Rose countered his question with one of her own.

"Did you get an answer to your wire?"

"We did, but for now, the only ones who are going to know the real answer are the three of us," Dave replied.

Cam shook his head. "What did I just miss?"

"It's simple," Rose began. "In a couple of days a new hand by the name of Frank O'Brien will be riding in looking for a job. As foreman, you'll be the one who will be hiring him. He's the U S Marshall I mentioned. He's catching a train tonight. For him to find out exactly what's going on, it's important none of the other hands know he's here to investigate the rustling. If anyone here is in on this, I don't want to tip our hand."

Cam looked at Rose in disbelief. Over the past few months, he'd suspected everyone and anyone connected with the ranch. Hell, he'd even suspected Dave until he got shot. That ruled him out completely.

"Do you suspect the hands?" he said.

Dave nodded, and Rose merely rolled her eyes. "I don't know what to think," she finally said. "I'd hate to think one of my father's own men was involved in killing him, but I can't rule anything out. I knew too many lawmen in St. Louis not to be skeptical of everyone."

Cam laughed at her statement. "Are you telling me these so called lawmen were your clients?"

"Are you telling me you've never heard of a lawman visiting a cathouse? Look, that portion of my life is in the past. I thought it was what I wanted until I came here. When I saw the way you looked at me as well as the way people like Sheriff Pollard and the stationmaster at the railhead treated me, I realized I wanted more out of life than to be a whore. This ranch is giving it to me, and I won't stand by and let someone take it all away from me without a fight."

Chapter Six

It had been almost a week since the last time the Rocking M lost cattle to the rustlers. Rose credited Cam's decision to move the herd to winter pasture closer to the house for the stop in the raids.

After riding with the men, she had aches in muscles she didn't know existed. Back in St. Louis, she would end the day with a hot bath drawn by one of the many servants who lived at the Purple Moon. Here, she had to pump the water, heat it on the stove, and pour it into the galvanized tub she'd found on the top shelf of the pantry. Instead of enjoying her bath in the privacy of her bedroom, she now bathed in the kitchen and prayed no one came to the house with a problem until she finished. Once she was done, she had to dump the water by herself. She'd just finished bathing and was wrapped in a robe when she heard a knock at the door.

"Damn," she muttered as she tied the sash of the robe tighter and padded across the kitchen to get to find out who would be calling at this late hour.

"Sorry to bother you, Rose, but I just hired a new man I thought you should meet," Cam said as soon as she opened the door.

Rose immediately recognized Frank O'Brien. She'd found him a handsome man when she first saw him on the train and decided he was even more so as he stood on her front porch.

"Won't you come in? I just finished my bath. Give me a moment and I'll get dressed. There's hot water on the stove. I'm sorry I can't offer you any coffee, but I do have tea or if you want something a little more substantial, I discovered my father kept a bottle of whiskey in the office. At least that's where I think I saw it. I don't touch the stuff myself, but I know working men like a drink at the end of the day."

She hurried upstairs to put on something more suitable to discussing business with Cam and Frank. From the closet, she chose a dress made from calico with a high collar. She was glad she'd packed the dresses she'd worn when attending classes and working at the hospital. They were more suitable to wear in Montana than the ones she'd worn at the Purple Moon.

As she dressed, she thought about the two men waiting for her downstairs. Frank had been a good lover on the train, but she would have to make it clear to him she no longer participated in the life she'd led in St. Louis as well as on the train. She had to remember he was here to do a job as a favor for their nights on the train. That left Cam, he was a handsome man with a questionable background.

Over the past week, she'd taken the time to study Cam intently. Her first impressions were proving to be correct. The way he talked and acted said he hadn't always been a cowhand. His speech sounded too well educated and his manners, although he tried to be like everyone else, were more refined. When this was all over, she planned to get to the bottom of where one Cameron Blake and his son, Joshua, really came from.

She put the thoughts about Cam to the back of her mind and hurried back down to the business facing them.

"Sorry to keep you waiting," she said as she entered the parlor.

The expressions on the faces of the two men who were waiting for her were in direct contrast to each other. Frank smiled as though anticipating delightful evenings together, and Cam looked as though he was jealous of the man who stood beside him. The jealousy she saw in his eyes came as a shock. Nothing about the relationship they'd had since her arrival at the Rocking M gave her any reason to believe he could be jealous of the marshal who came to help find out who was rustling their cattle.

* * * *

Cam knew who Frank was even before he said his name. There was something about the way he sat his horse said he was a lawman. He hoped none of the other men guessed the identity of the man. If they did, it wouldn't be good. Cam was certain someone in his employ was in cahoots with the rustlers right along with Sheriff Pollard.

"Look, O'Brien, I know who you are and why you're here," Cam said while they waited for Rose to come back downstairs. "From what Rose tells me, you don't have any idea why she asked you to come."

"I have my suspicions. I know she wouldn't take me up on my offer to help if I could if she wasn't in trouble. On the train, she mentioned her father had been murdered and she was taking over as the owner of the Rocking M. I got into town yesterday and did some nosing around. The word is no one wants to work for a woman or is ready to sign on to work at a ranch where the owner was killed and one of the hands wounded. I figured they had to be talking about this place."

"They were. I haven't been able to hire anyone since Darius was killed. I've even had my son and now Rose riding with the men. That's how shorthanded I am. To make matters worse, I'll be even shorter once my son starts school. This is his last year and I want him to get all the schooling he can. Next year I hope to send him east to finish his education."

Frank nodded. "Do you have any idea who might be behind this?"

"I don't know for certain but I don't trust the sheriff any further than I can throw him. I also think there's someone on this ranch who is in on it as well. After Darius was killed, we moved the herd, but no matter where we pastured them, we kept losing cattle. On the last move, I sent Dave out to ride nighthawk and just about got him killed. Since we've brought what's left of the herd up to the winter pasture, the rustling has stopped. Come spring, they'll have to be sent out to the open range and the whole thing will start all over again."

"Sorry to keep you waiting."

At the sound of Rose's voice, Frank moved toward the staircase. By the look on the man's face, it was evident he was disappointed in the modest dress Rose wore. It wasn't hard to realize the good marshal and Rose hadn't been engaged in idle conversation or playing whist while they were on the train together.

"We were getting to know one another," Cam said before Frank could even open his mouth. "It seems our troubles are the talk of the saloon. Frank came into town yesterday and has a good handle on what's been going on out here."

"Well, that's good. I'm sorry to have been so secretive in my wire to you, but I didn't know if I could trust the stationmaster. I really didn't want to advertise you were with the marshals. Do you think you can help us?"

"I hope so. How many people know I was coming?"

"Only three," Cam replied. "Dave, the man who was shot in the last raid went to the railhead with Rose to send the wire knows, but he can be trusted completely. I've known him for the past seven years, and I would trust him with my life."

"That's good, because the more people who know who I am, the harder it will be to find out who is in on this and who is innocent."

"I know the wages of a ranch hand can't begin to pay you for what you're going to do for us," Rose added.

"Don't worry about that, Rose. This is what I do. I told my superiors I figured there had to be real problems here. We're not far from the Fort Belknap Reservation. I rode over there this morning and checked in with the Denver office. They agree with me and said I should stay here until this is settled. We'll get to the bottom of this, even if I have to call in extra help."

"So why come all this way for someone you only met in passing on a train?" Cam said.

"I knew Rose was special when I first met her. I also knew she wouldn't ask for help unless it was necessary."

"Let's get something straight," Rose said. "If you came only for the girl you met on the train, you can go back to Denver and send someone else."

"What do you mean?" Frank said.

"On that train, I was a whore. I don't make any bones about it, but since I've come here, I've learned there's more to life than doing what I did in St. Louis. My father built this ranch from nothing and lost his life protecting it. I won't let someone drive me away now. My life is as a rancher and not as a whore. Can you understand that?"

"That's not the reason I came, Rose. I honestly liked you. I wondered how you would fit in out here, but it seems you've decided to make a go of this. I give you credit. You made my trip from St. Louis to

Denver very enjoyable, but I'm pleased to think your life is turning in a different direction."

What Rose said didn't come as much of a shock, while Frank's reply on the other hand brought skeptical thoughts to Cam's mind.

"Cam will get you settled in the bunkhouse, and I'll see you at breakfast in the morning. I hope you're ready to work, since we're going to start deciding which steers to drive to the railhead and send to Denver for sale. With winter coming, the smaller the size of the herd we have to feed, the better."

Frank nodded and held out his hand to Rose. "I'll see you in the morning, Rose. Luckily, most of the assignments I usually get take me to ranches like this one. When I joined the marshals, I thought I was getting away from ranch work. I was certainly wrong on that count."

Cam waited until Frank left the parlor to follow him. "I'll see you in the morning," he said, looking over his shoulder at Rose. As much as he enjoyed seeing her womanly curves in the denims she wore when she was working with the men, the dress she had on tonight was even more exciting.

"Are you and the boss, well, you know?"

Cam swallowed hard at the sound of Frank's question. "Hardly. I'd like to see her pack up and go back to St. Louis, but the terms of Darius' will require her to live here for a year. I'm getting used to having her around, but I'm not at all happy over her friendship with my son. He's only thirteen, and I don't want him getting any wrong ideas about women."

"I can understand that."

"Well, understand this, the boss is off limits to any of the hands on this ranch. Your job is to find out who is behind the rustling going on here. Why you came is your business, but as far as anyone is concerned, you're only here to do what I tell you to do."

"Whatever you say, boss. I think I can find my way to the bunkhouse by myself. There's no need for you to tuck me in."

Cam watched as Frank disappeared into the bunkhouse. It wasn't like they couldn't use all the help they could get in catching the men responsible for the murder of Darius McKinney, the wounding of Dave, or the loss of their cattle, because they could. What bothered him the most was the way Frank looked at Rose. It was like he knew every inch of her personally.

"What does it matter to me?" he asked aloud.

"I don't know what you're talking about, but the way it sounds it has something to do with Rose."

Cam turned to see Dave step out of the shadows. "I see we have a new man. He introduced himself as Frank O'Brien. Couldn't be he came all the way from Denver just to be a ranch hand on a spread like this one, could it?"

"You know it could. He knows you're in on all this. Just remember no one else is to know why he's here or who he is."

"Like I'd trip our hand. I'd been giving this a lot of thought. I didn't see the bunch ambushed me, but do you think it's funny they only took twenty five head of cattle when they could have made off with the entire herd?"

"I've given it a lot of thought, too, but I don't know of anyone who was trying to send a subtle message. Whoever is behind this is out to ruin the Rocking M a little bit at a time. Darius said the same thing when he first realized we were losing a few head every few days. I've run through all the hands as well as the ones we had to fire over the years, and I can't come up with anyone I'd consider behind this."

"Maybe you're looking in the wrong place. I heard something in town tonight that might be of interest."

"In town? What were you doing there?"

"Now what do you think? I had an itch that needed to be scratched, and I went in to see Molly at the saloon. She told me there's talk the railroad is running a spur into town and is trying to decide where to run it. After riding out to the railhead with Rose the other day, running it through Rocking M property would be the perfect place to bring it in."

"I never thought about anything like that, but why not just approach Darius? Why rustle the cattle and then kill him? It doesn't make any sense."

"It's only a rumor, but everything has to be looked at."

Cam agreed. "Thanks for the information. I'll let Frank know. Just remember, he's no different from any new hand. In order for him to work here he has to prove himself, to both you and me."

Dave nodded and then disappeared back into the darkness. It had been the two of them who had been the top hands for the past five years. Darius called them both in when he made his decision about who would become the foreman.

In his mind, Cam could hear the conversation between the three of them.

"I need a new foreman," Darius had begun. "The way I see it, that is a problem. Both of you are more than qualified, but there can only be one foreman. I want to hear what you think about it?"

"I don't think there's a decision to be made," Dave replied. "I enjoy working here, and you know Cam is my best friend. The thing I wouldn't like is all the responsibility. Cam is the best man for the job and besides he has a son to support. He can use the extra money in his pocket every month. I'll be happier doing what I do best and that's working this ranch and doing it to the best way I can."

The memory of that conversation brought a lump to Cam's throat. Darius had been more than fair. Even though the main responsibility of the job of foreman fell on Cam's shoulders, there had been a raise in pay for Dave as well. Together the three of them worked closely, and now Dave was as qualified to make decisions as Cam. He trusted the man with his life, and he knew the same was true in Dave's mind.

Cam finished his cigarette and ground the butt under his boot before entering the room that adjoined the bunkhouse. He remembered when Darius insisted on building the extra room with its own private entrance. He made it clear since Cam had a young son, it was important they have private quarters. At the time, Cam thought the decision would meet with opposition, but the hands had all agreed. A room filled with rough cowboys was no place for a young child.

Josh had more surrogate uncles than any boy could even hope for. The men who could read and write were adamant about helping Josh with his schoolwork and those who couldn't, pushed the boy to do his very best. It made Cam proud to call the men of the Rocking M his friends.

"Was that a new man who rode in?" Josh said when Cam entered.

"Yes it was. Maybe he will be the end of the jinx on this ranch since the rustlings started and it was announced that Rose was going to be the new owner."

"I don't know what anyone has against Rose. I understand what she did before she came here, but that's the past. Haven't you always told me what happened in the past is over and finished? I've watched her working with the men, and she doesn't shy away from any of the jobs she's been given. She's even insisted I use the library up at the house." He held up the book he was reading.

Cam halfway expected to see one of the novels Darius had so enjoyed handing Josh to read, but instead it was a book on the history of the United States. "I don't remember ever seeing that book in Darius' library. Where did you get it?"

"Rose brought it out to me. She said she sent to St. Louis for some books she thought I should be reading. They arrived yesterday, and she gave me this one to start with."

"Rose did that?"

Josh nodded. "She told me reading novels was good for enjoyment, but she wanted me to read books that would help me get into a good school next year. I'm not so sure about going away to school, but Rose says she's in favor of it, just like you are."

Cam was shocked. He knew Darius had been in agreement about Josh's education and had even put aside money to help pay for it, but to hear Rose sent to St. Louis for books that would help his son with the requirements for higher learning was a surprise.

He picked up the book, pleased to see it was a fine edition of a history book. He remembered reading a book of the same quality when he was his son's age. Of course then things like the War Between the States and the assassination of President Lincoln were still current events and weren't included. This book was the most up to date edition he'd ever seen.

"What other books did she send for?"

"She said something about mathematics, English composition, and geography. This was the one she told me was her favorite when she went to school."

It was hard for Cam to think of Rose studying the way he had when he was a kid. Back then, his father insisted he get all the education he could. The old man would turn over in his grave if he knew Cam was working as the foreman of a ranch in Montana. He'd had so much potential it was a shame it was being wasted. It wasn't that he didn't like his job, he did, but he'd been trained for so much more.

When he first started working for Cornelius Slade at the bank, he knew he was making his father proud. He'd been in charge of the loans made to many of the biggest depositors in Omaha. Against her father's wishes, Martha became his bride, using the argument that if Cam was good enough to be a trusted employee of the bank, then he was the perfect man for her to fall in love with and marry.

It was her death that sent Cam and Josh away from Omaha. His leaving had broken his mother's heart, but he knew it had to be done. Otherwise, he would have lost his son completely. Cornelius fired him and was making plans to take Josh away. He couldn't stand to lose his son in addition to his wife and his unborn daughter.

Luckily, he'd had enough warning he was going to lose everything and took his savings from the bank and stuffed them into his bags. It was late at night when his brother took him to a small town to board a stage heading west. He was cutting ties with everyone and everything he ever knew, but it was necessary.

It took three years before he finally landed at the Rocking M. With a new name, he'd felt safe in contacting his brother and then his friends. At least he got the news from home and was able to keep in touch with what Cornelius was doing to find him.

What would he do if Cornelius found them? He couldn't let that man take Josh away from him. This time he wouldn't turn tail and run, though. Josh was old enough to understand now. What if he decided life as Cornelius Slade's grandson was more attractive than being the son of a ranch foreman?

"I told you Rose wasn't as bad as you said she was. We talked about the life she lived in St. Louis, and she says that's all behind her now. She's even going to try to get me into a good school. She knows a lot of influential people back east. I don't know if that's where I want to go to school though. It's a long way away from here. I'd rather stay and help you."

Cam smiled at how adult his son sounded tonight. "As much as I like working with you, I won't let you give up on an education. I think maybe we should talk about the past and why this is the life we're living."

He watched as his son put aside the book and looked up at him quizzically. "Are you talking about what our lives were like before we came here? I remember drifting from ranch to ranch and leaving Omaha in the middle of the night. I just never knew why."

Cam swallowed hard. He had been so certain Josh was too young to remember anything about the three years before they arrived at the Rocking M. "It's a long story, but I think it's one you should be told. I'm sorry you remember any of it."

"I don't remember much, but I do want to know what happened."

Cam hoped this conversation would never have to happen, but he'd opened the door and Josh was anxious to know the truth.

"When I was your age, my parents insisted I get a good education. The War Between the States had just ended and my father returned to work in his father's store. He'd been gone a long time, but my grandfather cared for us in his absence. The two of them decided I needed an education so I wouldn't end up running a country store like they did.

"When I finished elementary school, they sent me off to Omaha to get the kind of education Grandpa wanted for my father, but and couldn't afford at the time. My brother as well as my sister followed in my footsteps and got the education to give them a leg up in life.

"After graduation, I took a job in one of the biggest banks in Omaha. That was where I met your mother. Martha was one of the most beautiful women in town. The problem was she was my boss' daughter, and he didn't think I was worthy to be her husband. We ran away and got married against his wishes.

"Of course, your mother was very persuasive and finally got your grandfather to keep me on at the bank and give me a promotion. After you were born, Cornelius softened. He fell in love with you the first time we put you in his arms. When we told him you were going to have a little brother or sister, he was thrilled.

"Unfortunately, something went terribly wrong and your sister was born way too soon. I rushed your mother to the hospital, but they couldn't save your sister and in the process, your mother…your mother lost her life.

"Your grandfather went wild and blamed me. He wouldn't even allow me to plan your mother's funeral or to attend. I knew he was going to fire me so instead of going to the funeral, I took all of my money out of the bank and prepared to leave town with you.

"While I was at the bank, I ran into a friend of mine. He worked in the office of Cornelius' lawyer and heard rumors. He gave me his condolences and told me your grandfather was starting procedures to take you away from me. I couldn't lose you as well, and so I continued with my plans to disappear."

Cam paused to take a breath. "What happened to him, Pa?"

"He's been looking for us for the past ten years. He wants you to become his son and from what I hear he still blames me for your mother's death."

"What I can't understand is why he hasn't found us? We've been here for a long time and everyone around here knows us."

Cam knew this was going to be the hardest part of the story. "When we left Omaha, I changed our names. My real name is Addison Cameron and yours is Joshua Cameron."

Josh gave him a look that said he understood. "How did we get the name of Blake?"

"My mother's sister married a man by the name of Blake. The family decided it wouldn't raise suspicions if they continued to correspond with a member of the Blake family. Since my cousin's name was Charles, they stared sending me letters under C. Blake. "

"Maybe he's stopped looking for us?"

"From what I've heard, from my family in Nebraska, he's become obsessed with getting you back. I'm telling you this because after this year of schooling, you'll be old enough to make your own decisions. As much as I want you to go to school and get your education, you should know Cornelius wants you to be with him. You're a man now and the decision has to be yours to make. All I ask is that you stay with me long enough to finish this part of your education. Then you can do what you want with your life."

Those words were the hardest ones he knew he'd ever speak. He'd just told his son about the past and given him permission to seek out the man who wanted to see Cam either dead or in prison for the rest of his life.

When Josh made no comment, Cam knew he had to say something more. "These past ten years, I've regretted the fact you didn't know my family. I've missed them too. By next summer, this business of the rustling should be over. Dave's more than qualified to take over here as the foreman. When he does, I'll take you back to Nebraska myself. I've decided it's time I faced Cornelius Slade and make him believe the last thing I wanted in life was to lose your mother the way I did."

"I don't think that's such a good idea, Pa. I have no desire to meet a man who blames you for something beyond your control. As much as I'd like to have more family than just you and me, I know going back there could mean you could be taken from me forever, and I couldn't stand that. For now, let's not even think about anything like that. I know school is important, but going back east isn't."

Josh returned to reading the book Rose gave him, indicating their conversation had ended. Cam understood. He'd given his son a lot to think about tonight. Maybe it had been too soon to tell him about his grandfather, but Cam had a feeling he would have had this conversation sooner or later.

Everything he'd heard from home indicated Cornelius had sworn out a warrant for his arrest. If that were so, how long would it take for Frank O'Brien to figure out Cam and Joshua Blake were in reality Addison and Joshua Cameron and there was a warrant out for his arrest for the murder of his wife and unborn child? Frank would have no recourse but to arrest him and take him back to Omaha.

Chapter Seven

Rose spent an uneasy night. When she'd sent the wire to Frank, it had been in the hopes of getting help in finding the people responsible for the rustling of cattle from her ranch, as well as the murder of her father. After seeing him last night, she wondered if she made the right decision.

In the past, she'd enjoyed the look of hunger in the eyes of the men who took her to their beds. Last night the look in Frank's eyes had been one of lust. Their fire had been quenched when she told him she was no longer in the business of pleasuring men for money. She hoped she was wrong, but something told her the only reason he came to her aid was so he could grace her bed.

The first light of morning was filtering into her bedroom when she got out of bed and dressed in her denim britches and plaid shirt. After pulling on her boots, she headed out to the cookhouse for breakfast.

Men sat in their usual groups, no longer shocked to see her enter the room. Many of them acknowledged her with nods of their heads. She wondered if any of them were giving the information about where the herd was pastured to the rustlers. She doubted it. She'd worked with most of them and felt they were trustworthy.

The thing that bothered her the most about all of this was since her arrival there had been no more raids. Of course, it could be because they moved the cattle to the winter pasture, but she doubted it. The original raids were directed against her father, and once he was dead, against the ranch itself. If that were so, why would they cease when she'd arrived? Did the people involved think she could be bribed? Again, she had her doubts. She suspected Sheriff Pollard, but why didn't he retaliate when she refused his attentions?

With all the questions running rampant through her mind, she decided with no answers forthcoming, it was best if she get her breakfast and get ready to work. In the far corner, she saw Cam and Frank engaged in conversation. There was an empty space on the bench across from they were seated. After filling her plate and getting her coffee, she went to join them.

"Good morning, Rose," Cam greeted her. "I thought you might stay up at the house today considering we have more help."

"Then you thought wrong." She smiled as sweetly as she could possibly manage.

She hated the thought Cam thought she wasn't able to keep up with the men. She had been riding with the men ever since her arrival and by now, she'd proven herself to him.

"I enjoy riding with the men and learning as much as I can about this ranch and the men who run it. In case you've forgotten, it was my father who built this place and left it to me. I don't intend to be an owner without getting my hands dirty."

"Well said." Frank smiled his approval. "Cam tells me as the new hand, I have to ride with him for a while. Will you be joining us today?"

"I doubt it. I promised Dave and his crew I'd be working with them today cutting out steers to drive to the railhead. I think the sooner I get my cattle to market, the less chance I have of losing more of them to the rustlers."

Frank merely nodded that he understood what she was meant. If she wasn't mistaken, Cam planned to take him to the areas hit by the rustlers, including where her father had been killed and where Dave had been shot. She hoped seeing those areas would give Frank some insight into what had and was happening.

For the second time since rising, she was second-guessing herself about having asked Frank to come and see if he could get to the bottom of the rustlings on the Rocking M. If her instincts were wrong, she could be in more trouble than she was before he arrived. On the train, she believed he was a U.S. Marshal, but now she was having doubts. What if he told her only what she wanted to hear and come because he thought he could find his way back into her bed?

She was letting her imagination run wild. What kind of a man would say he was a U.S. Marshal if he wasn't? She had to give the man a chance to prove his worth. Once this business with the rustling was behind them, they'd settle into a normal routine, whatever normal was.

* * * *

Frank watched the woman who sat across from him. She certainly wasn't the woman who gave him so much pleasure on the trip from St. Louis to Denver.

When he told her he was a U.S. Marshal, he hadn't stretched the truth too badly. He had been with the marshals for several years, but left that life behind after a disagreement with his immediate supervisor.

Of course, he was still involved in law enforcement. He just didn't wear the badge that was once his to wear with pride.

As he studied Cam, he wondered exactly what he'd gotten himself into. His face was a familiar one, since he'd seen it on the wanted poster he'd picked up on his way to St. Louis. Last night, after getting settled into the bunkhouse, he'd gone through his saddlebags and found the wanted poster he'd picked up in Nebraska while taking a prisoner to St. Louis. The name wasn't the same, but the face certainly was. It was entirely possible Cameron Blake and Addison Cameron were one and the same.

He was glad he'd taken the time to ride over to the Fort Belknap Reservation and send the wire to his superiors in Denver. Of course, he wasn't sending it to the marshal's office, but that was one bit of information best not made public until it was necessary.

In the next few days, he'd have to make another trip to the Fort Belknap Reservation and send another wire. This time it wouldn't be to Denver. Instead, he'd be sending it to Omaha.

* * * *

Cam finished his breakfast and went out to saddle his horse. He was surprised when Frank stayed behind. The only thing Cam could equate the way Frank looked at Rose was like a drunk eying a free drink. He would have thought what Rose told him last night would have put a damper on the man's lust, but apparently, it didn't.

"Are you sure you don't want me to work with the men cutting out the steers for market from the main herd?"

Cam turned at the sound of Frank's voice. "I'm positive. You're no different from any other new hand hired on this ranch. For the first week, you ride with me. It's the way Darius ran the ranch when he first started it and nothing has changed in the past eighteen years."

"But you're not the owner. What gives you the right to check out the new men?"

"Darius gave me the right when he hired me as the foreman. When he first started this ranch, he was the only one to check out the new men, but when he hired his first foreman, he gave him the right. The man worked for Darius for several years and was trusted. It was the same with me. At the time, I took over this job it was a toss-up between Dave and me for the position. Darius was torn until Dave told him he didn't want the responsibility."

"And you did?"

"I knew I could handle it, especially with Dave as my right hand man."

"Then you don't suspect him of being in with the rustlers?"

Cam was shocked at the accusation. "Dave is the last person I'd ever suspect of any wrongdoing. I'd sooner suspect my own brother than to suspect Dave. He's the most trustworthy man on this ranch."

"Then who do you suspect, other than the sheriff?"

"I have no idea. I was thinking it was someone who works here, but I've more or less eliminated everyone. I spent a lot of time thinking about it last night. There's no one here who hasn't been on this spread for a long time. As for people who have left or been fired over the years I don't think there's anyone around here with that much hatred for Darius or the Rocking M."

Several other people were coming out of the cookhouse, ending the conversation between Cam and Frank. With a nod of his head toward the people coming into the corral, Cam swung into the saddle and watched as Frank did the same. Together they rode out in the direction of the rangeland where not only the rustling took place but also where Darius lost his life and Dave had been shot.

* * * *

Rose saddled her horse and watched Cam and Frank leave. As much as she wanted to ride out with them, she knew her promise to participate in today's work was one she had to keep. It wouldn't look good if all of a sudden she changed her mind to trail along with Cam and the new hand.

"Are you ready to ride?" Dave asked from behind her.

"Just about. I only have to check the cinch on this saddle and then…" her gaze turned to the disappearing figures of Cam and Frank as they rode over the hill that would obscure them from her sight.

"You want to check out the new hand with Cam, don't you?"

"Don't be silly. I know nothing about the things Cam looks for in a new hand. Besides, I think I'm still being studied to see if I can measure up to being a hand."

"Rose, you're so much more than a hand. I appreciate your help, and you're learning more every day, but I feel bad about having you out here working your tail off."

"Well, don't. I find I rather enjoy it. Besides, I like seeing all the new calves. I never thought animals would be so fascinating."

Dave chuckled. "I have a feeling the men are enjoying another fascinating animal. I know they all look forward to riding with you. I doubt any of them has ever seen a woman wearing britches before. At first, I was shocked, but I have to admit, I like the look of a woman's curves in them. Maybe someday it will be fashionable. You might be starting a rage or something."

"Just what would you know about rages in high fashion?"

"I wasn't born a cowhand. My folks owned a fancy plantation before the war. Even when we didn't have anything and Pa was forced to move west, Ma and my sisters were always talking about the newest fashions. They were always talking about the great balls they used to have. I was the baby in the family and don't remember much about life in the old South, but I heard all the stories."

"Where's your family now?"

"The girls are all married and living on ranches from Missouri to Texas. Pa died when I was ten, and Ma remarried. Can't say I much liked the man I was supposed to call Pa. I ran off when I was twelve and never looked back. Been on my own ever since."

"Don't you miss them?"

"Not really. After the war, all Ma and the girls did was complain about how things used to be. I took to helping Pa. He worked as a sharecropper, and the work was so hard it killed him. I swore I wouldn't be like that. I'd read about life on ranches in the west and decided that's where I should be. I don't think anyone actually missed me when I left home."

"I would think you'd want to get in touch with them."

"Oh, I have. Darius made a point about that. He insisted if I wanted to work here, I needed to contact them. I hear from my oldest sister, Carolyn, on a regular basis. Ma writes about once a year and so do my other sisters, Juliet and Amanda. They're as happy with their lives as I am with mine. I know I won't ever see any of them again, but then they aren't all that thrilled about seeing me either. I don't fit into their lives any longer."

Rose made no reply. Instead, she swung into the saddle and rode out of the corral to catch up with the other men. She certainly didn't want any of them to see the tears forming in her eyes. All her life she'd known Darius McKinney was her father. Instead of a flesh and blood man, he was a signature on the many letters he'd sent her over the years. In them, he'd described the hardships of running a ranch in northern Montana. When she read them, she knew this kind of life was nothing she wanted for herself. It was strange how things changed in so short a time.

When she first arrived, all she could think about was how soon she could sell the ranch and move back to St. Louis to purchase the Purple Moon from Celeste. Now, that was the furthest thing from her mind. Her only regret was she hadn't followed Celeste's advice to visit her father sooner.

The only problem with her coming here now was she would never meet the man who loved her unconditionally. Because of his love, he'd given her the opportunity to grow up knowing she was loved and given the best education possible.

"Are you all right, Rose?" Dave said as he rode beside her.

"I will be. I'm just sad because the only family I have was gone before I could meet him. You have family, and you're content never to see them again. I used to think his letters were enough, but now I know better. Letters are just words on paper. With those words, he told me I was loved and I would always have a home on the Rocking M. I thought knowledge was enough. I always thought I would have a lifetime time to get to know the man behind the words. My life in St. Louis was far too important to me to travel hundreds of miles to meet the man who supported me all my life. Now, I can see how selfish I was. If only I'd thought with my heart rather than my head, I would have met him before it was too late."

"I hear what you're saying. I'll give it some thought. Maybe it's not too late for me to go back and see my family, but it won't happen until after the problem here on the Rocking M is resolved."

Rose knew to some the loyalty that Dave's statement suggested wouldn't make any sense, but she knew exactly what he meant. Before she came here if it had been the Purple Moon in trouble, she wouldn't have wanted to leave until the trouble was resolved either. It made her all the more grateful for the kind of men her father employed. Even knowing a woman with a not so sterling past was going to be the owner of the ranch, they'd stayed on and were willing to do whatever it took to make things right again.

* * * *

Cam wondered about the man riding beside him. When he first arrived it seemed like Frank was all business, but now Cam wasn't so sure. If he was really here on official business, putting on a façade should have been a top priority. Instead, he acted more like a dog in heat when he was around Rose rather than a seasoned lawman.

Once they reached the range where Darius had lost his life, Cam reined his horse to a halt and dismounted. No matter how much time passed, he could still see Darius's body lying on the ground, a bullet hole in his back. The vision had the same effect on him now, over three months after the actual murder, as it had that morning. He could feel bile rising in his throat and his head beginning to spin.

"Are you all right?" Frank asked, offering a steadying hand.

"I will be. Coming up here is hard. This is where I found Darius's body. He was such a good man, and he didn't deserve to be shot in the back."

"Just how long have you worked for him?"

"I came here seven years ago. It wasn't easy for a widower with a young child to find a place that would hire him. Most people didn't want a kid under foot. Josh was only six, but since we'd been drifting for three years after my wife's death, he'd gotten to be an independent child."

"Why leave your home?"

Cam didn't like the way this conversation was going. It was true he'd opened the door with his initial comment, but he certainly didn't like talking about his past with someone he didn't know. To be truthful, the only people around here who actually knew the truth had been Darius and now Josh. Knowing Cornelius wanted Josh and was prepared to see Cam captured dead or alive to achieve his goal, made Cam overly cautious.

"That's something I don't like to talk about," he finally replied. "It was a rough time in my life and something best left unsaid."

"I can understand. We all have things in our past that are painful to discuss. Was this where most of the rustling took place?"

Cam relaxed. "The only cattle we lost from this area were the ones taken the night Darius was killed. We'd just moved them here from a place where we lost several head just a week earlier. Darius thought it was best if he ride nighthawk that night, and we all agreed to take turns doing the same thing. The next morning, I rode up here when Darius didn't show up at the cookhouse for breakfast. That's when I found his body. I don't think I'll ever forget what I saw here."

"Did you continue losing cattle after that?"

"It was funny. We didn't have any more losses until the day Rose arrived. Dave rode out to check on the herd early that morning. When my son Josh and Ned rode up to help him, they found Dave shot and more of our cattle missing. Josh came back up to the house to tell me about it and get a wagon to bring Dave back."

"That had to be tough for the kid. I saw him at breakfast this morning. He doesn't seem old enough to be riding with the men."

"He's not, but I haven't had much choice this summer. When Rose insisted on riding with us, I made him stay back with Cookie and gave him lots of tack to mend. He's not happy about it, but he understands. Thank goodness first Darius, and now Rose, gave him access to the library at the main house. That boy has a hunger for learning that matches mine at his age."

"Well, now I'm here, he'll have more time for reading and such. Maybe we can even get Rose out of the saddle and into more suitable clothing."

Cam laughed out loud. "You'll get used to those britches. I know we all have. She's a worker, there's no doubt about that."

"Then you don't mind working for a whore?"

"That's a bit harsh, isn't it?"

"It's what she called herself last night."

Cam had to agree. "I wasn't happy about her being here when she first arrived, but she's proven she can do the job. On the first day, she came in here looking every inch a whore, but since then she's changed. She's serious about getting to the bottom of this problem. I couldn't believe it when she offered to ride nighthawk, but that was where I drew the line. With the cattle in the winter pasture closer to the house, it's safer, but I still don't want her out there alone. At least the men have a chance of defending themselves. I doubt she has any idea what to do with those guns she's been wearing."

"They do make her look a lot less fetching. Have any of your men made their way into her bed?"

Frank's question came as a shock. "No they haven't and I don't expect any of them to even think about such a thing. She's their boss, nothing more."

Frank shook his head. "What a waste. That woman is damn good at what she was trained to do. I can't believe she would give it up completely."

"Look here, O'Brien, if you're thinking that's the reason she sent for you, you can leave now. We had a long talk about it, and she wants an end to this rustling. Either you get to the bottom of things, or you can pack your gear and leave now. Rose is off limits to the men on this ranch and that includes you."

"Have it your way, but you don't know what you're missing. Of course, I do know why I'm here. Take me to where your boy found Dave and then maybe I can get a better handle on what's been going on here."

Cam turned from Frank. He couldn't shake the feeling this man wasn't exactly what he made himself out to be. Rather than push Frank with questions, he decided it was best if all he did was observe for the time being.

Chapter Eight

Rain pelted against the windows when Rose woke the next morning. Last night Cam predicted the storm brewing in the mountains. He told her the rainstorms coming would be only the beginning of winter.

With luck, the rain would last only for today so tomorrow they could drive the cattle to the railhead. In anticipation of the trip, she decided to take today to write some letters so she could post them tomorrow.

After dressing in the same modest dress she'd worn the night Frank arrived, she added a log to the fireplace to take the chill off the house before going out to the cookhouse to enjoy breakfast with the men.

As she opened the door to face the pouring rain, she grabbed the umbrella she'd brought along with her from St. Louis. Holding it in front of her, she shielded herself from the onslaught of the rapidly falling raindrops.

By the time she entered the cookhouse, her shoes as well as the hem of her skirt were soaked.

"Didn't expect to see you this morning," Cookie greeted her.

"Can't starve just because it's raining. I don't have anything to prepare for breakfast at the house."

The older man nodded. "Well, don't you be comin' out here for dinner or supper. If it's still rainin,' I'll bring it up to you. There's no use in you catching pneumonia by bein' out in this weather."

"I'm stronger than you think, but I do appreciate your offer. It will be nice not to have to get soaking wet. All I can think about at this point is getting something to eat and going back to the house and taking off these wet shoes."

"What about that wet dress?"

She turned at the sound of Frank's voice. "My skirt will dry once I'm settled in front of the fire, but having wet feet is more chilling than anything else."

"And here I was imagining you in the robe you were wearing when I first arrived."

Rose didn't like Frank's comment any more than she liked the wicked laugh accompanying it. For some reason, she had a feeling the man could be very dangerous.

After getting her food, she made a point of finding a spot where there would be no room for Frank to join her. She was pleased to find an empty seat across from where Cam, Josh, and Dave were sitting.

"I was hoping we could drive those beeves to the railhead today," Dave said.

"I don't think this storm will last more than today," Cam replied. "We should be able to make the drive tomorrow. I just hope those rustlers don't decide to hit us before we can get them out of here."

"Would they hit in the rain?" Rose asked.

Cam shrugged his shoulders. "Who knows what goes through the minds of men who think nothing of taking someone's life? Just to be safe, we're going to have a couple of the men out there all day."

"You'd let them go out there in the rain?"

"This isn't a fancy office in the city," Cam assured her. "There's work to do and we're all going to be out there doing it. I'm sending out teams of two to keep an eye on the herd in two hours shifts."

"When is my shift?" she teased.

"Never. We're all used to this kind of weather. You're not. If you're planning on going on the drive with us when this weather clears, you'd better get your rest today. If you thought cutting out the steers we want to sell was hard work, wait until you get on the trail. Thank goodness the railhead isn't all that far away. In the old days I'm told people had to drive their cattle for hundreds of miles."

Cam and Dave went back to the conversation they'd shared before she seated herself at their table, giving her time to study Frank more closely. He looked disappointed there was no room at the table where she sat and took a seat at the next table. It didn't stop him from leering at her and making her feel uncomfortable.

The men were finishing their meal and getting ready to leave the cookhouse, when Rose put her hand on Cam's arm. "Would you stay for a moment?" she said, her voice so low only Cam could hear her.

"Any particular reason?"

"I'd appreciate it if you would walk me back to the house. I have a bad feeling about having Frank here. He's definitely not the man I thought he was when we were on the train. Of course, then I wasn't interested in his personality as much as I was in other things. Seeing him now and getting to know him better, has changed my mind. I wish I'd never sent for him. I just don't think he's what he claims."

"I know what you mean. He may have been a lawman sometime in the past, but I doubt that's what he's doing now. He just doesn't act like he's as interested in finding out who is behind the rustling as he is in asking questions about you."

"I'm not too proud to admit he scares me. Once I'm at the house, I'm planning to lock all the windows and doors. Thank goodness, my father put locks on everything. It was a surprise. I didn't think folks out here did stuff like that."

"They usually don't, but once the rustlers started hitting us, Darius insisted on them, not only at the main house but also in the bunkhouse as well as the addition he put on for Josh and me. I thought it was a bit much, but I'm sure he had his reason for doing it. Do you want some help locking all those windows?"

Rose smiled. "I really would. I can't believe the number of windows there are in the house. I'm also glad there are heavy drapes downstairs. I can't put my finger on why I feel this way, but I don't want anyone peeking in the windows at me."

The expression on Cam's face told her he agreed with her. Of course, he'd been with Frank all day yesterday and gotten to know the man. It convinced her she needed to get more information on one Frank O'Brien before she trusted him completely.

* * * *

Before he left the house, Cam made certain every window and door was locked and he'd stoked the fire, making her father's library toasty warm.

She'd taken the time to change out of her wet dress into a split skirt and blouse and put on a pair of dry stockings along with a different pair of shoes before settling at the desk where her father dealt with the business of the ranch. She took out a sheet of paper and began to write a letter to Celeste.

Dear Celeste,

I have so much to tell you, I hardly know where to begin. The first thing I need to do is ask for a favor. The foreman here is a man by the name of Cameron Blake. He has a son by the name of Joshua who is thirteen years old. The first thing I need is for you to look into good schools for Josh. He's brilliant and needs a good education. That brings me to Cam. I have a feeling he's more educated than he lets on. He certainly didn't begin his life as a rancher. I think there's something in his past that he's hiding. Can you see what you can find out about anyone by the name of Cameron, either first or last?

She continued the letter with all the things she had been doing since her arrival until she had at least three pages filled both front and back. Rose admitted she missed Celeste and the girls at the Purple Moon more than she did the lifestyle she'd known her entire life.

Once her letter to St. Louis was finished and sealed, she took out a clean sheet of paper.

Dear Sir:

I need information on one of your marshals. I met a man by the name of Frank O'Brien. He told me he was affiliated with your office, but now I am having doubts. Since arriving in Montana, I have found the ranch I inherited has a major problem, not only with rustling but also murder. I asked for Frank's help, but now that he is here, I question his qualifications.

Any information you could supply me would be greatly appreciated.

Rose read over the letter before slipping it into the envelope and sealing it. If the storm ended as Cam predicted it would, she would be able to take both letters to the railhead tomorrow and send them on their way. She didn't expect an answer from St. Louis any time soon, but hoped within a couple of weeks, she would hear back from the U.S. Marshal's office in Denver.

* * * *

Cam left Rose and listened for her to turn the key in the lock. It surprised him to see Frank standing at the library window. The man's intent was evident; he was definitely there to spy on Rose.

"Something I can help you with?" Cam said.

Frank jumped at the sound of his voice. "Ah... I... I was checking to make certain the house was secure."

"That won't be necessary. I've made certain Rose doesn't have to worry about unwanted visitors. All this rustling has her spooked."

"I didn't get a chance to speak to her this morning. I thought—"

"Well, you thought wrong. She told me she has some paperwork that needs to be done, and she doesn't want to be disturbed. Since we'll be going out to keep an eye on the herd later this afternoon, I suggest you spend the time in the bunkhouse getting better acquainted with the hands. I've been a hand and a foreman, and I've learned they don't confide in either me, or Dave the way they once did. Maybe you can find out if they know anything to help put an end to the losses we've had lately."

Frank nodded and turned away from Cam. Rather than following immediately, Cam watched until Frank entered the bunkhouse. Once he was certain he wouldn't be followed, Cam went to the corral and saddled his horse for a ride into town. The worst of the rain had let up so his slicker offered the protection he needed.

Once in town, he went directly to the telegraph office. His wire to the U.S. Marshal's office in Denver was short and to the point.

CHECKING CREDENTIALS FOR MARSHALL FRANK
O'BRIEN—IMMEDIATE REPLY REQUESTED.

After paying to send the wire, Cam settled down to wait for the reply. He was glad Mel Peabody was the operator on duty. Of everyone who worked the wire, he was the most trustworthy.

"Ain't seen you in town for a while, Cam. That new owner must be keepin' you busy. I hear she's a real looker."

"You heard right. 'Course she's not the one keepin' us on our toes, it's those rustlers."

"Heard 'bout Dave. That was a real shame. At least they didn't kill him the way they did Darius."

"You wouldn't be saying that if Josh and Ned hadn't found him when they did. He was bad off. Doc did what he could, but Rose's nursing skills pulled him through. There's more than looks to that lady."

"Is it true she's a whore and she wouldn't let Sheriff Pollard have his way with her?"

Before Cam could reply, the telegraph key began to click. He hoped it was his reply. He didn't want to answer any more questions about Rose and add more grist to the rumor mill.

"Got your reply, Cam," Mel said, handing him the paper with the neatly printed message.

"Thanks, Mel. I'm sure this is what I'm looking for."

After paying for the message he'd sent as well as adding a little extra money to insure Mel's silence, Cam left the office. The reply to his question was both anticipated and feared. Again, he read the words.

> O'BRIEN NO LONGER WITH THE MARSHALS—
> DISMISSED OVER TWO YEARS AGO.

"So," Cam said to no one in particular, "just who is he, and why is he letting everyone think he's a U.S. Marshal?"

* * * *

The knocking at the front door woke Rose abruptly. She couldn't believe she'd actually fallen asleep at her father's desk.

"I'm coming," she called as she hurried to open the door. As soon as her hand touched the key, she felt a moment of dread. She should have checked to see who was at the door, but it was too late now.

When she opened the door, she was pleased to see Cookie with a plate for her dinner. "Is it noon already?" she asked.

"Yes, Ma'am. I brought you a bowl of hot stew and some fresh bread. Stew always tastes good on a day like today.

"It looks like the rain is finally letting up, so I'll bring the dishes back after I finish eating."

Cookie smiled at her before turning to leave. Rose knew coming up to the main house made the man uncomfortable. He brought not only this meal but also the ones she'd eaten here days earlier. She'd make certain on payday he was compensated for his kindness.

She was just closing the door when she saw Cam ride in from the direction of town. Seeing her at the door, he turned his horse toward the house.

"What are you doing out in this weather?" she said. "I thought you'd be holed up inside until it was time to ride out to check on the herd."

Cam's expression told her he wanted to talk, but where no one could overhear. As soon as he stepped into the house, Cam pulled the door shut and turned the key in the lock. Once he knew the house was secure, he took off his slicker and followed her to the kitchen.

"Cookie brought me dinner. From the weight of this plate, there's enough for two. You're welcome to join me."

She watched as Cam pulled out a chair and seated himself at the table. "I appreciate this. I wasn't looking forward to running into O'Brien at the cook house."

After getting another bowl from the cupboard, Rose divided the stew equally. "Is something wrong between you and Frank?"

"I've had my doubts about him, but they became stronger when I saw him trying to get into the library window this morning."

"Why in the world would he do something like that?"

"I don't know, but he doesn't act like any lawman I've ever known."

Rose felt her stomach begin to churn. "I thought I was the only one with doubts. I wrote a letter to the U.S. Marshal's office in Denver and was planning to send it from the railhead."

"I'm way ahead of you. I rode into town this morning and sent a wire to Denver."

"Are you sure that was wise?"

"I trust Mel and besides, I paid him enough to keep his mouth shut."

Rose watched as Cam reached into his pocket to retrieve the paper that most certainly was a reply to his wire. She accepted it from him, unable to stop her hands from shaking. As soon as she looked at the unfolded paper, the words jumped off the page at her.

"Why would he tell me he was a marshal?"

"A man will tell a woman just about anything to get her into his bed. He was probably hoping you'd get in touch with him and he could have another chance to be with you."

"Guess he thought he could get away with it since he was with a whore. So now what do we do, send him packing?"

"That's the last thing we want to do. He's asking a lot of questions that have nothing to do with the rustling. I'd like to know what he's after. Depending on what I learn, I can send another wire from the railhead and ask for help from a real marshal."

"I hope it won't be too late by the time we're able to drive the herd there. I'm getting worried about what he's here to do." She glanced at the window, almost expecting to see Frank looking in through the curtains. Instead, she saw the rain had stopped. "Since it's no longer raining, I think it might be best if I rode out with you and Frank this afternoon."

"That might not be such a bad idea. By the way, while I was in town, I picked up the mail for the ranch." He reached into his shirt and produced several envelopes.

Rose flipped through the stack of mail, smiling at the letters from both Celeste and her lawyer. It would be good to get news from home and stop thinking about rustling, murderers, and men who pretended to be someone they weren't.

"Hope there's something good in there," Cam commented. "Darius always said the only thing he ever got was bills."

"I'm certain there are some of those in this stack, but I'll deal with them later. For now, I'm planning to read these personal letters."

Cam smiled for the first time since he arrived. "I'll leave you to your reading. If it's not raining when we ride out, I'll bring your horse up so you can join us. I'm sure that will make Mr. O'Brien happy."

Rose followed him to the door and locked it behind him. Knowing Frank O'Brien wasn't the man he claimed he was, she would keep the doors and windows locked.

* * * *

Cam again listened for the key to turn in the lock before heading toward the bunkhouse. As he expected, O'Brien stood outside smoking a cigarette and watching his movements.

"Where did you go this morning?" Frank asked.

"I had some business in town, so I picked up the mail for the ranch."

"Are you sure you didn't go in to see the sheriff and let him know where the herd is pastured?"

Cam's blood boiled at O'Brien's accusation. More than anything else, he wanted to punch the man in the nose, but in doing so, he might tip his hand and let him know what he'd learned from the wire he'd sent to Denver.

"It would be a cold day in hell when I waste my time with Pollard."

"Then what was so important that you rode to town in the rain?"

"Look, O'Brien, you know and I know Rose asked you here to investigate the rustling and the murder of her father. Lately, I haven't been able to get to town to take care of my business. If you must know, I haven't had a chance to take my pay to the bank. With everything going on out here, I don't like keeping it at the ranch. With the rain, I knew I'd be able to get away and take care of my personal business."

Cam cringed at the lie he just told. Before Martha's death, he'd never told an untruth. Now his entire life was a lie.

"Sounds believable enough, but if I find you're in cahoots with those rustlers, so help me God, I'll nail your hide to the wall."

Cam seethed. This guy was playing the part of a marshal to the hilt. He acted as though he suspected everyone.

"You can scratch me off your list of suspects as well as Dave and Rose. Did you learn anything in the bunkhouse this morning?"

"Not much. Either they aren't involved in this mess, or they're covering up for who is. So why did you go up to the house?"

Nosey Bastard. "The mail isn't my responsibility, it's Rose's, so I took it to her. Besides, I thought since the rain was letting up, she might want to ride out with us this afternoon."

O'Brien's eyes lit up like a child on Christmas morning. "Now that's a right fine idea. I certainly enjoyed the look of her in them britches yesterday. It was a disappointment to see her in a dress this morning.

Cam shook his head He couldn't understand O'Brien's obsession with Rose. She already made it clear she wanted nothing to do with him in that way. Why didn't he let it drop?

* * * *

Rose changed clothes after Cam left the house. On her return to the library, she saw the letter she'd written to the U.S. Marshal's office earlier, sitting on the desk. Rather than leaving it lying there, she threw it in the fire.

Just thinking of the telegram Cam received from Denver made her sick to her stomach. How could she have been so wrong about Frank? In her heart, she knew the answer, but she didn't want to admit it.

On the train, she'd been plying the trade she knew better than any other. What she had forgotten was that men and women alike in bed lied. Whether it was to make a good impression, or to hide their true selves, didn't matter. A lie was a lie.

As the owner of the Rocking M, she knew she had to learn to recognize the lies and look for the truth. She was certain she knew the reason Frank had answered her plea for help. It wasn't because he wanted to uphold the law. Instead, he was intent on finding his way to her bed and little else.

She watched the last of the letter fade in the flames when a knock sounded at the door. This time, she exercised more caution than when Cookie brought her the noon meal. Through the lace curtain that covered the window by the door, she saw Cam standing on the porch.

She remembered packing the lace for the curtain before leaving St. Louis. At the time, she thought Celeste was crazy to suggest it, but now she was thankful for it. The lace made a perfect covering for the window her father had preferred to leave uncovered. Through it, she could see who stood on the other side of the window, but without a light behind her, she couldn't be seen by anyone standing on the porch.

"Are you ready to ride?" Cam said when she opened the door.

Rose scanned the clouds broken by small patches of blue sky. If she were back in St. Louis, she would say the storm was over, but she didn't know what to expect in Montana.

"If you're worried about more rain," Cam said when she didn't reply to his question, "I put a slicker in your saddle bag. I like to be prepared just in case I'm wrong about the weather."

Rose nodded her thanks, still eyeing the sky skeptically. She realized she had to trust Cam on this one. She wasn't as familiar with the weather here as he was and couldn't trust her instincts alone.

* * * *

Cam held the reins of Rose's horse as she mounted and prepared to ride out. He didn't miss the fact she'd bribed the black devil with sugar to allow her on his back.

"Good afternoon, Miss Rose," Frank drawled as he touched his fingers to the brim of his hat in respect. "I didn't get a chance to talk to you at breakfast."

"Cam and I had ranch business to discuss. It was a good time for us to take care of it."

Gritting his teeth, Cam turned his horse toward the winter pasture to relieve the men who were watching the herd. It was one thing for O'Brien to pepper him with questions and another for the man to make a fool of himself over Rose. Anyone would think he was in love with her or something.

Cam shook his head to silence the inner voice of reason now becoming far too intrusive to suit him. The last person in the world he would fall in love with was Rose McKinney. She represented everything he hated in a woman. She certainly wasn't the type of person he wanted in his life as a role model for Josh.

Yet, just what kind of a role model was he? He'd forced his son to live a lie for the past ten years.

Gunfire permeated the air and reverberated through the valley. "Stay here," Cam shouted to Rose as he and Frank pulled their guns and spurred their horses to a gallop.

He knew Dave was riding herd with one of the other hands. The thought of again finding his best friend lying on the ground with a bullet in him was sickening.

"I can't believe the bastards tried a daylight raid," Frank shouted as they rode into the area under attack.

"Shut your mouth and start firing that gun you're carrying."

Cam approached the area where the rustlers had Dave and Adam Green pinned behind a rock. He was out of the saddle almost before his horse stopped running and crouched behind the rock next to Dave.

Taking careful aim, he shot at the men who were now abandoning the fight. His bullet hit home, knocking one of the rustlers from his saddle.

"The son of a bitches are getting away," Dave spat.

"Not all of them," Cam replied.

Cautiously, Cam got to his feet and headed toward where the man lay.

"I'm shot, mister, shot bad. You gotta help me," the rustler pleaded.

Cam knelt beside the man and assessed the wound. "It's not much more than a scratch. We'll take you back to the ranch, and the boss can patch you up. Then you can tell us who hired you."

Cam pulled the man to his feet and forced his hands behind his back. After tying the man's hands, Cam brought the horse the man had been riding and now stood only feet away from his wounded master.

"Get on," Cam ordered.

"I can't, I'm wounded."

"You aren't hurt that bad. What little scratch you've got is nothing compared to the man you killed and the cattle you've taken off this ranch."

The man turned to Cam, fear radiating from his eyes. "I didn't kill nobody. This is the first time I've even been on this spread."

"Who hired you?"

From behind them, a shot rang out and the man crumbled at Cam's feet, dead from a shot in the back of his head.

Gunfire erupted from the rock where Dave and the others had ducked. Cam hit the dirt in order to dodge any other bullets being fired by the people hidden somewhere beyond the tree line that bordered the south end of the pasture.

When there was no answering report, Dave came out and ran toward Cam. "Are you hit?" he asked as he helped Cam to his feet.

Cam dusted off his britches. "No, I'm fine. Someone didn't want our friend here to do any talking, though. He did tell me this was the first time he'd been on this ranch. It could be whoever is behind this is hiring different people each time. Damn, I wish I knew who."

The sound of an approaching horse caused Cam to turn to see who was riding into the area that could still be dangerous.

"I thought I told you to stay back, Rose," he shouted once she dismounted. "I don't know where those rustlers are, they could still be hiding in the woods ready to kill you."

"But—but the gunfire stopped. I thought I would be safe."

He noticed tears had formed in her blue eyes. She rode to where the shooting had taken place because she was concerned for the safety of her men. Any owner would have done the same thing. Hell, if it had been Darius, he would have been there with his guns blazing along with the rest of the crew.

She wasn't Darius. She was a woman, and he was a fool to ask her to ride out here with them today. The quicker he could get these beeves to market, the better he'd like it.

"With men like these, you can't assume you'll be safe just because you're a woman. We need to get this body back to the ranch and send someone for the sheriff."

"Did you shoot him?" Rose said, her voice shaking at the horror of what had just happened.

"I shot him," Cam replied. "I didn't kill him. My bullet is the one in his shoulder. I had just asked him who he was working for when someone shot him in the head from behind us."

"Cam's right," Dave said, coming to Cam's rescue. "Those rustlers had us pinned down. I thought I shot one, but it wasn't enough to stop them from getting away. Cam got off a lucky shot and knocked this one from his saddle before he could ride out with the others. Cam had just started questioning him when one of the ones who got away shot him in the head. Whoever is behind this doesn't want anyone talking about it to us or anyone else."

"I agree with Dave." Frank added. "In all my years as a lawman I've never seen anything like this. A rustler usually doesn't shoot one of his band from behind unless they have something to hide."

Cam caught Rose's eye. He hoped she wouldn't say anything about the wire he'd received while he was in town. It wouldn't do for O'Brien to know they were aware he was no longer with the marshal's office.

By the time they tied the body to the rustler's horse, the rain had again begun to fall.

"I think Adam and I should stay out here and keep an eye on the herd," Dave suggested. "Those rustlers will expect us to all go back to the ranch, leaving the herd unprotected. I didn't get shot protecting these beeves to lose them now. You can send someone else out here to relieve us when you get back."

"What about you, Adam, are you prepared to stay with Dave?" Cam asked.

"You bet I am. I want a piece of those bastards, pardon my language, Ma'am, but that's just what they are."

"You didn't upset me, Adam," Rose said. "I'm not naïve about the kind of language men use when they're upset. If I were any good with a gun I'd stay here and help, but I'm afraid I couldn't hit the broadside of a barn. I appreciate you and Dave staying behind to guard the herd."

Cam watched as she mounted Renegade and joined them in leading the rustler's horse to the ranch. Even though Frank kept up a non-stop conversation with Rose, Cam remained silent. He was thinking of whom he could send into town to get the sheriff. He certainly didn't want to let O'Brien out of his sight for that long. At this point, there was no way of knowing whether O'Brien was in on the rustling or if it was the sheriff alone.

Josh was just coming out of their quarters when they rode into the dooryard. Much as Cam hated sending his son out in the rain, it seemed only logical to have Josh be the one to go into town, since he would be sending the remainder of the hands back out to the herd.

"Who got shot?" Josh said as he hurried to Cam's side.

"One of the rustlers. I need you to saddle your horse and ride into town to get the sheriff. I'd send someone else, but I have to get the rest of the men out there to help Dave and Adam. The only thing I can think of, at this point, is to drive the herd up to the corrals by the house. There's no other way for us to keep them safe until we can get them to market. If I didn't know better, I'd say someone on this ranch is supplying the rustlers with information."

As soon as he spoke the words, he thought about what happened today. O'Brien had arrived only two days ago, but would that be enough time for him to ally himself with the rustlers? The herd had been moved several days before O'Brien arrived, and no one had attempted to take any of the cattle off the winter range. It seemed odd that suddenly the rustlers were there to get the remainder of the herd.

Chapter Nine

Every bone in Rose's body ached. She'd been around men all her life, but never had she seen such violence. The sight of the rustler's dead body made her sick to her stomach. Added to that, she was beginning to distrust Frank more and more.

On the train, she had accepted every word he said, even though she knew better than to believe any man who wanted to get into bed with her. If he wasn't a marshal, just who was he and why had he come to the Rocking M? She'd made it clear she wasn't opening her bed to anyone, so why didn't he just ride away? Was it possible he was working with the rustlers, and if he was, how did he know it was her ranch that was targeted?

With no answers forthcoming, she dismounted her horse and headed toward the house. To her surprise, Frank followed her.

"I think we need to discuss what happened out there this afternoon," he said, putting his hand on her arm.

"Don't you think you should be helping Cam take the body to the barn? As far as I can tell, there's not much to discuss. Those men were trying to steal the herd. Dave and Adam were holding them off when you and Cam rode in there. Cam admitted he shot the man in the shoulder, and Dave backed him up. Is there something else you think I should know about the situation?"

"No, it's just—"

"It's just want? I made it clear I wasn't allowing any man in my bed. What we did on the train has nothing to do with the life I have here. Since you have nothing different to tell me, I suggest you see if there is anything Cam needs you to do. Better yet, why don't you ride out with the men and see what you can do to help with the herd?"

"Suppose there is. I could have gone to town to get the sheriff, but Cam already sent his son."

"Josh is capable of going for the sheriff. Besides, every adult on this ranch is automatically suspect. You should know that."

"They couldn't suspect you or me. All this started before either of us even arrived."

"Maybe not, but it's best if we all stay put."

Rose opened the front door and stepped inside, locking the door behind her before Frank could follow. She was relieved to be safe behind the closed and locked door. After reading the wire Cam received earlier in the day, she began to wonder just who Frank O'Brien really was, and if she should send another wire from the railhead asking for assistance from the U.S. Marshals in Denver. If she did send for them, would they arrive in time to save not only her herd but also the lives of her men?

* * * *

Cam watched as Josh rode toward town. He hoped he hadn't made a mistake by sending his son. If Sheriff Pollard was in on this, he might disregard anything the boy had to say.

At the house, he saw O'Brien speaking with Rose. He couldn't hear what they were saying, but from the expression on Rose's face, he knew she was exasperated with the conversation they were having. Once she entered the house, he prayed she remembered to lock the door. He didn't put anything past O'Brien, since it was apparent he wanted back into Rose's bed.

He continued to study O'Brien as he made his way back to the bunkhouse where Cam stood.

"That one is certainly a cold fish, ain't she?" O'Brien asked.

"I wouldn't say that. I'm sure today was a very hard one for her. I doubt she's ever seen anyone shot in the head before."

"In her line of business, she should have been used to such things. I've been in more than one whorehouse where a gunfight has broken out."

"I doubt that's the kind of house she grew up in. The sheriff should be back here within the hour. I need to check out the areas where we're going to put the herd when the men bring it up to the house. I suggest you take the time to ride out and help the men with bringing them in."

"Suit yourself. Are you sure you want me to leave you here with no one to watch your back? I doubt Rose can handle a gun, 'course that could have been an act as well."

"I'm positive. We won't hear anything more from the rustlers today. Just ride back out there and help the other men. As far as they're concerned, you're no different from them. It would look rather funny if you stayed up here while they were getting wet doing their jobs."

O'Brien nodded and went to where he'd left his horse. Once he rode out, Cam thought about what O'Brien said. Was Rose just putting on an act when she was frightened by what she saw when she rode into the area where they gunfight had taken place? Anything was possible, but he didn't think anyone could put on such an act. The color had drained completely from her face. She was shocked by what she had seen. Besides, that whorehouse where she had grown up wasn't one in a wild western town. It was in St. Louis. If he thought Omaha was civilized, it was nothing compared to St. Louis. That city had been in existence for many more years than Omaha and had most if the amenities of bigger cities like Chicago and New York.

As O'Brien joined the other men to ride out toward the pasture where Cam left Dave, he checked the corrals closer to the house. It would be tight, but until the weather cleared and they could drive the steers to the railhead, it would be necessary for them to be in cramped quarters.

Once assured he was alone, he made his way into the room he shared with Josh. Earlier, when he'd picked up the mail, he'd stashed the letter from his brother under his pillow. For some reason, he didn't want to read the letter he'd picked up with the other mail. The minute he saw it with the rest of the mail for the ranch, he had a bad feeling about it. Somehow he knew it carried bad news. He hoped it would not be to tell him something had happened to his mother.

He held the letter in his hand for a long time before he opened it. Before he did, he sat down on his bunk and prayed what he read wouldn't be disturbing.

Dear Addison

It was good to get your letter. All is well here, but had to take pen in hand to tell you what I heard at the store today.

Do you remember Jeff Benton? I think he was still working at the bank when you were there. Anyway, he's kept in touch with me. He's the one who has been telling me what Cornelius is doing.

He said Cornelius left Omaha yesterday and was heading for Montana. He said he had a lead on where you were. All I can say is watch your back.

I told you, when Martha died, you should stay here and fight him. There's no way he can make a murder charge stick against you. There's not a judge in the world that would hold you responsible for Martha's death. I know you're going to say there was no way you could fight against all his money, but I think you're wrong.

Considering all the trouble you're having with the rustlers, I'm beginning to think Cornelius knew where you were for a lot longer than Jeff thinks. It's entirely possible he's behind what's going on out there. I wouldn't put anything past him. The man has completely lost his mind where you and Josh are concerned.

Cam didn't bother reading any further. He knew the next several pages would contain chatty news about the family. What he needed to know had been on the first page. If Cornelius was hiring men to rustle the cattle of the Rocking M, it was possible he thought he was hurting only Cam. Instead, there had been a loss of life and now even Rose was in danger. The old man had no idea what kind of men were willing to take his money to rustle the cattle.

After what he read, he knew he had to go up to the house and tell Rose everything. She was the one suffering, and it now appeared it was because of him.

* * * *

Rose changed out of her wet clothes and warmed herself in front of the fire she built up in the library. The knock at the door came as a surprise.

Carefully looking out the window, she was relieved to see Cam standing on the porch.

"Is the sheriff here already?"

"Not yet, but before he gets here, there's something you should know. I think I have an idea who's behind all of the troubles we've been having on this ranch. If I'm right, we're going to need the help of the marshals in Denver."

"Come in. Something tells me we will both need a drink before we talk."

Cam followed her into the library and accepted a glass of whiskey while she poured herself a glass of wine.

"It all started in Omaha. My pa had decided it was best if I go to school and get an education. Once I finished, Cornelius Slade hired me to work in his bank. That was when I met his daughter, Martha. When we fell in love, he was livid and even more so when we ran away and married against his wishes. I thought things were better once Josh was born. He was the apple of the old man's eye, but then Martha got pregnant again. This time something went wrong. The baby came too early and the birth took both their lives.

"Cornelius wouldn't let me even go to the funeral and threatened to fire me. As I was preparing to leave the bank, one of my friends said he'd overheard Cornelius talking to his lawyer about getting custody of Josh. I couldn't let that happen. I drew out all my money from the bank and took my son out of Omaha. I changed our names and drifted for three years before we made it to this ranch.

"Darius took us in, no questions asked. It didn't take me long to trust him enough to tell him about our past. Luckily, he didn't hold anything against us and even added on the room to the bunkhouse for Josh and me.

"I've kept in touch with my family and they tell me the old man swore out a warrant for my arrest for the murder of my wife and daughter."

"That's the most ridiculous thing I've ever heard. How could anyone believe you murdered your wife when she died in childbirth?"

"Cornelius convinced someone I did something to Martha to make her lose the baby. In doing so, she lost her life. Of course none of that makes any difference now. I just had a letter from my brother and he says he thinks Cornelius is behind the rustling."

"But why?"

"The only thing I can think of is one of his wanted posters made its way out here and someone recognized me. He figures I own this place. The man is out of his mind, but from what my brother said, he's on his way here. It should all be over soon, but no matter what, we're taking these beeves to the railhead tomorrow and sending a wire to Denver for help. I just hope they can get here in time."

"What would make him think you own the Rocking M?"

"He knew what Martha and I had in the bank. She had a substantial inheritance from her mother, and when we got married, she put everything in my name. During our marriage, we managed to save quite a bit of money along with what she had. When I heard what Cornelius was planning to do, I took out all of our money. The only money I kept for Josh and me was what I had added to our savings. The remainder of it, I put in an account in Denver for Josh's education. Since it belonged to Martha, I knew it rightfully belonged to Josh. She wanted him to have a good education."

"Did you know ranching when you came here?"

"Somewhat. I'd been drifting between farms and ranches for three years, and learned a lot. When Josh was smaller, the wives of the people I worked for were happy to keep an eye on him, but I knew it wasn't anything that was permanent. By the time we landed here, he could go into town for school and entertain himself when he got home and in the summer. Darius even gave him the job of mending tack and cleaning out the stables. He even made sure he got paid like everyone else."

Rose nodded. From his father's letters, she knew he was a man who loved children and valued education. She had often written asking why she didn't live with him. His response had been she was better off in St. Louis where she was about to get the education she deserved. Hearing Cam talk about being a man alone with a child, she realized her coming here, as a child, would have been next to impossible for her father.

"So what do we do about Cornelius Slade?" she finally asked.

"I don't know. I honestly don't think we can go to Pollard with any of this. I have a funny feeling one of those bogus wanted posters landed on Pollard's desk. Knowing how money hungry he is, I'm sure he contacted Cornelius. From what my brother tells me, the likeness on the posters leaves no doubt Addison Cameron and Cameron Blake are one in the same. The fact it says I have a son is the clincher."

Rose smiled. It was ironic that Cam was reluctant to have her anywhere near Josh while he'd been living a lie for the past ten years.

"So, if Pollard thinks he knows who you are and is intent on getting the reward, why hasn't he arrested you?"

"My brother says the poster sent out reads that anyone with knowledge about my whereabouts should contact Cornelius before apprehending me. He wants to be here so he can take custody of Josh."

"That makes sense. This all has my mind reeling. I could use another glass of wine. Would you like another whiskey?"

Cam shook his head. "One takes off the chill, two would cloud my judgment. I need to be sharp to deal with Pollard when he gets here."

He no more than spoke the words when there was a knock at the door. Before she answered the door, she checked to see who waited on the porch. If came as no surprise to see Josh and Sheriff Pollard.

"Thank you for coming so promptly," she said, extending her hand.

"The kid said one of the rustlers got himself killed," Pollard said, trying to look past Rose and into the house. "Which one of those idiots who work for you did a fool thing like that?"

Indignation built up like bitter bile. "Cam only winged him. One of his own men stopped him with a bullet in his head before he could tell us anything."

"And you'd take Cam's word on that? Seems to me you're not as bright as I gave you credit for being. The way I see it, someone on this ranch is behind the rustling and I wouldn't put anything past Blake."

"Well, Sheriff, that's where you're sadly mistaken. I was there during the raid and I know the man was shot in the back of the head just as he was getting ready to answer Cam's questions."

"Why are you sticking up for him? Is he that good in bed?"

Rage replaced indignation as Rose reached up and slapped Sheriff Pollard's face.

"I heard what you just said, Pollard," Cam said as he came from the library to stand behind Rose. "You're lucky all that happened was that Rose slapped your face. I would have knocked you flat on your ass for saying such a thing. Now, I'm sure my son told you about the dead rustler we have out in the barn. Let's go out there, and you can see him for yourself."

"I'm going too," Rose declared.

Both men turned to look at her, disbelief mirrored in their eyes. "But… but you can't," Pollard stammered.

"I don't see why you would say such a thing. This is my ranch. The cattle being rustled are mine. It's my men being shot at and risking their lives, so I have every right to know what's happening."

Cam broke into a wide grin. "The lady's right. I'm learning not to argue with her about things that concern the Rocking M."

"But she's a woman."

"I'm well aware of that. She's also able to ride Renegade and has been working on the ranch books. Anyone who can make out Darius' handwriting and figure out his bookkeeping system deserves to know what's happening."

Rose grabbed her slicker before heading out to the barn with Cam and Sheriff Pollard. The rain had diminished to a light drizzle, but she didn't want to get soaking wet for a second time today.

* * * *

Cam inwardly chuckled at how uncomfortable Pollard seemed with Rose's presence. It was evident the man's opinion of women was quite low. As far as he was concerned, they were only good for one thing, and he couldn't get past that impression with Rose.

Immediately Cam chided himself. He had thought of her in the same way when he first met her. It was amazing how quickly he'd changed his mind.

Josh waited for them in the barn. "Should you be here, Miss Rose?" he asked. "It's not a pretty sight."

Rose smiled. "Thank you for your concern, Josh, but you tend to forget I was there when the man was killed. This is nothing I haven't seen before."

"Do you know him?" Cam asked Sheriff Pollard, holding up the man's head.

"Hard to tell with his face blown away like that, but I don't recognize his horse. If he'd been in town, I would have remembered an appaloosa like this one."

It surprised Cam to see Rose take the bags from behind the man's saddle. "Maybe we can find something out about him in here," she said, holding them out to Cam.

"Well, at least we know who to contact about his death," Cam said, as he held up a letter addressed to the man. The handwriting was very feminine.

Pollard snatched the letter from Cam's hand before he handed the saddlebags back to Rose. He watched as Pollard turned the paper in several directions. "I can't seem to make out this here fancy writing. Can you make out what it says?" he demanded as he thrust the paper back toward Cam.

"My dear brother…" Cam began.

"Nothin' but drivel. It doesn't say who this fellar is."

"The envelope does," Cam replied. "It's addressed to Nathaniel Kent and sent from Omaha to General Delivery in Rapid City. It seems to me Mr. Kent is a long way from home."

Pollard snatched back the letter and envelope. "I'll take this back to town and have Mel send a wire to the sister."

"What about the body?"

"Can't send him back to his kin lookin' like this. It's best if I take him to the undertaker and get him planted in Boothill."

"Do you want to take these as well?" Rose said, holding up the saddlebags.

Cam had been so engrossed in the letter he forgot he'd handed the saddlebags to Rose. He wondered if she had taken the time to go through them. Across from him, Pollard nodded before taking the bags from Rose's hands.

Together Cam and Rose watched as Pollard led the horse carrying Kent's body out of the barn to where his own horse was tied.

"So what did you find in the saddlebags?" Cam said once Pollard rode out of the dooryard.

Rose glanced from Josh and back to Cam.

"It's all right. I told Josh everything last night. You can talk in front of him."

"But not here. Come up to the house where I know no one will walk in on us."

* * * *

Rose's hands trembled as she pulled the things she'd taken out of the saddlebags from their hiding place. She had no idea what the book she'd found as well as the other papers with him would say, but she didn't want Sheriff Pollard to get his hands on them. It was best if she let Cam see them first.

Together, they made their way up to the house. Once there, Rose wished she had something other than wine or whiskey to offer Josh.

After ushering them into the library, she laid the book and the papers on the table. "I found these, but I figured it was better if we looked at them together first."

"I wondered if you'd seen the same book in there that I had," Cam said, as he picked up the leather bound book. "I didn't dare take it out in front of Pollard, though."

"From what I saw, he couldn't have read it anyway. It wasn't the handwriting that bothered him. It was the fact he can't read. How in the world did that man get elected sheriff, being illiterate?"

"Your guess is as good as mine. Up until today I had no idea he couldn't read or write. It's good information for future reference, though. As for how he gets elected, it's all in whose good graces he's won. Darius always said there was a lot of underhanded dealings hereabouts, and Pollard knew all the secrets."

Rose smiled. She knew all about that kind of politics. It was the same in St. Louis. Crooked politicians were elected every year because they literally knew where all the bodies were buried. It was a shame the women weren't able to vote. With all the information the whores had, it was entirely possible their votes alone could have ousted the crooks and installed honest men.

As soon as the thought crossed her mind, she concentrated on not laughing out loud. In her opinion, there was no such thing as an honest man. She was even more convinced after her run in with Frank O'Brien. Believing him had been the worst mistake she'd ever made.

"Well, well, well, this is interesting," Cam said, holding up a wanted poster with a likeness of him on it.

"That's a picture of you, Pa," Josh declared. "I didn't believe it when you told me about my grandfather wanting you to pay for Ma's death. How could he believe you were responsible for something like that?"

Rose couldn't help wondering what Cam's response would be. How could anyone explain such hatred to a mere child?

"Grief does strange things to a man. Your mother was his only child. He holds me responsible because your sister was my child and her birth took your mother's life. I was wrong not to stay and reason with him, but that was my grief showing. All I knew was I'd lost one of the most important people in my life and if I stayed, he would find a way to take the other one from me. I couldn't lose you too, so I ran away."

A lump formed in her throat. Cam had done the best he could for his son, just as her father had done for her. By leaving her at the Purple Moon, she had grown up knowing she was loved by the women who cared for her. Had he taken her with him, she might not have survived to see her first birthday.

She watched as Cam thumbed through the journal. "It looks like our dead friend was telling the truth. He only joined the rustlers a week ago. From what this says, he'd seen me somewhere and contacted Slade. It also says he is not to try to apprehend me, only break me until Slade can arrange to get here. It seems Slade put him in contact with the rustlers who have been hitting this ranch. If I'm right, the cattle are close by somewhere, because if Slade thinks they're mine, he'll hold them for Josh."

"Then I say the sooner we start driving this herd to the railhead the better," Rose declared. "The men should have them moved up here by tonight and tomorrow we can start. I'll definitely be sending a wire to Denver once we get there."

"You aren't going with us," Josh said, his voice sounding with shock.

"Of course I am. We'll leave a few men here, but the rest of us are going, me included. I intend to put a stop to what's happened on this ranch."

"But it's not your problem," Josh persisted. "This is between Pa and

116

me and my grandfather."

"That's where you're wrong, Josh. What your grandfather is doing is wrong, but it involves more than you and your father. What he's doing is against the Rocking M and therefore it's my business, too. Because he mistakenly thinks your father owns this ranch, he's guilty of more than rustling. His men have murdered my father and tired to do the same to Dave. Someone has to stop it and I plan to be one of the people who does it. Of course, I would like it if you would go with us tomorrow."

Josh's eyes lit up, but he sobered when he saw Cam's reaction to her suggestion. "I don't think that's wise."

"Well, I do. If Josh stays here, it's entirely possible Slade's men will kidnap him. Once he has what he wants there will be nothing to stop him from ordering your execution. Now we know who's behind this, we have to take the proper precautions."

She saw defeat in Cam's eyes. Because of him, her father had lost his life and the Rocking M had lost several hundred head of cattle. At least that's the way he saw it. Things looked different to Rose. Cornelius Slade had to be out of his mind to blame Cam for an act of God. Women died in childbirth on a regular basis. She ought to know because her birth had caused her mother's death. For those left behind, life went on. No one was to blame. It was just the way things had been since the beginning of time.

"Guess you're right. I can't risk leaving Josh here. It's not like he can't defend himself, but I wouldn't want to put him in a situation like that."

A knock at the door interrupted them before Rose could reply to what Cam just said.

"I'll get it," Cam declared, getting to his feet.

Rose followed behind only because she was curious. In the entire time she'd been here, there had been no actual visitors to the Rocking M. She certainly couldn't count the two women who had come out to help her with Dave when she first arrived. Minnie and Verna had only come because Doc made them. Once they went back to town, she was certain they told everyone about the woman who had come to lay claim to Darius McKinney's ranch. That had to be the reason no self-respecting woman had come to call in all the time she'd been there.

When Cam opened the door, she saw a young boy standing there. "Mel said I should get this wire out to you right away, Cam. Should I wait for a reply?"

Cam scanned the contents of the wire and then nodded his head. "You bet. Give me a minute." He handed Rose the wire before taking the pencil and paper from the boy to compose a reply.

Rose unfolded the paper and read the words that were neatly printed on it.

```
IF YOU'RE DEALING WITH FRANK O'BRIEN, YOU
NEED HELP—RESPOND IF YOU NEED A MARSHALL
OUT THERE—WE HAVE A MAN IN YOUR AREA—CAN
BE AT THE ROCKING M BY MORNING.
```

She'd just finished reading it when Cam handed her his reply.

```
HAVE MARSHAL MEET US AT THE RAILHEAD—
DRIVING HERD THERE—WILL CAUSE LESS
SUSPICION—LEAVING O'BRIEN AT RANCH.
```

After checking it over, she nodded her approval. Before she could go into the library to get money to pay the boy, Cam reached into his pocket and pulled out several coins.

"This should cover it," he said. "Of course, I know Mel will keep this confidential. I trust you will as well."

The boy looked at the coins that constituted much more than the cost of the wire. "Yes, sir. We'll send this off right away."

"Well, this changes everything," Cam said once they were back in the library.

Rose agreed. With Josh there she didn't want to say too much.

"There's something you should know, son," Cam began. "Frank O'Brien is here at Rose's request, because he told her he was a U.S. Marshal. We now know he isn't. A marshal will meet us tomorrow at the railhead, so we'll be leaving O'Brien here with a couple of the other hands. You can't let him know what we've learned. He could be working for your grandfather as well."

"You can count on me, Pa. I know how to keep my mouth shut."
Rose admired Cam. It took a lot for him to confide in his son.

Chapter Ten

"What do you mean I'm not going to the railhead with you?" O'Brien shouted.

"Just what I said. I need to leave someone here I can trust. The way I see it that's you and Dave. I don't think Dave's up to driving the cattle there, and you're the least experienced man. Besides, with your background, I feel better leaving you here with Dave to keep an eye on things. If they try something, you as a U.S. Marshal can handle it."

O'Brien's earlier outrage turned to a wide grin. It galled Cam to call the man a U.S. Marshal, but he didn't want to tip his hand. He and Dave discussed it last night and devised a plan they hoped would work. Playing on O'Brien's ego had been a stroke of genius.

"Cam tells me it's just you and me stayin' here," Cam heard O'Brien say to Dave.

"There's a couple of others. I wanted to be in on the drive to take the herd to the railhead, but Cam makes sense. He needs someone here he can trust."

"I know we're okay, but what about Cam and that kid of his?"

"Look, O'Brien, Cam is the foreman here. If he was good enough for Darius, then there's no reason for you to question him. As for Josh, he's a good kid. He's worked his tail off this summer. There's no reason why he can't be in on taking the herd to the railhead. This will be his last chance for something like this."

"Last chance? Why? Is Cam pullin' out?"

"Not on your life. This is Josh's last year at the school in town. Cam is planning to send him away to continue his education. He's too smart to spend the rest of his life herding a bunch of dumb cows like the rest of us. We all know he's Cam's kid, but we love that boy like he was our own. Seeing him get an education will make all of us proud."

Cam smiled at the exchange. If Dave fed O'Brien enough information, the one-time marshal could easily hang himself. Someone like Cornelius Slade would pay dearly for the information Josh would be going away to school next fall. With the coming of a real U.S. Marshal it was safe to give out this little bit of information.

* * * *

Even with the amount of rain that fell yesterday, Rose found the cattle raised a lot of dust as they were driven from the ranch to the railhead. With the men riding drag in shifts, she and Josh stayed in position at the head of the herd. Cam said it was best, since if the rustlers were going to strike while they were on the trail, then she and Josh would be safe. It made sense. Why would they try to get animals at the front of the herd when it would be easier to take the ones at the back?

"We're almost there," Cam shouted as he rode up beside them.

Rose stretched in the saddle, surprised to see the buildings that comprised the railhead looming in the distance. "I didn't think we'd get here this soon."

"We've been on the trail since sun up. It's almost noon. I thought we'd take this long. It's a lot different from when we used to have to drive them down to Cheyenne. That was a long trip. Things are getting easier than when the first ranches were established up here."

Rose agreed. In her father's letters, he'd described the drives to Cheyenne. They hadn't always had good conditions. Today there was plenty of vegetation for grazing, and the streams were full of water. Even the threat of Indian attack had lessened since the fiasco with Custer at the Little Big Horn.

Once at the railhead, Rose watched as the cattle were driven into pens to be loaded onto the cars of the next train headed for the markets in the east.

"It's good to see you again, Miss McKinney," the stationmaster greeted her. "Good lookin' herd you got here. Your timin' is good, too. The next train east should be pullin' in about an hour from now. Oh and

Cam, there's someone here waitin' for you."

Rose dismounted and went into the building that housed the office of the stationmaster as well as the telegraph office, with Cam right behind her.

"The name's Wilson, George Wilson," the man who approached them said as he extended his hand. "The wire I got said you were having problems with rustlers. Since I was in Beaverton, my boss knew I could get here the fastest."

"After being duped once," Cam said. "Can we see some identification?"

George reached into his pocket and produced not only his badge but also papers with proof of his identity.

"Thank you. You have to understand why we're worried."

"I most certainly do. When you're dealing with people who lie about their identity, you can't be too careful.

"So, do you know a man by the name of Frank O'Brien?" Rose asked.

"Not personally, Ma'am, I only know his name from what I've heard and believe me, it's not good. After he got booted out of the marshals, he joined up with the bounty hunters. I hear he specializes in the posters that say dead or alive. It's always easier to bring in a dead man for a bounty than a live one."

Rose cringed. If he'd seen the poster Slade put out on Cam, he would know there was no such stipulation. Even so, would Frank take it upon himself and decide to deliver his man dead was easier than taking him all the way back to Nebraska alive?

She listened as Cam explained everything they'd learned so far, including the rustler they'd captured, but who was killed before he could tell them anything about the person hiring him.

"You say the sheriff took this Kent into town?" George said.

"That's right. We gave him a letter we found in the man's saddlebags, but nothing else. Rose was quick enough to remove his journal and some other papers, before she handed the saddlebags over to the sheriff." Cam reached into his shirt and produced the wanted poster Slade had put out on him.

George nodded. "I've seen this before. We checked it out with the office in Omaha and they said it wasn't anything they issued. After looking into it, they said it was some sort of personal vendetta. They tried to get the man who put it out, but they were told he left Omaha."

"That doesn't surprise me. It's possible he's out here somewhere. I'm afraid for some reason he thinks I own the Rocking M, and he's out to break me. It's a long story, but the old man wants my son. I'll fill you in on the way back to the ranch."

Cam went out to send the men back to the ranch while he, Josh and Rose remained behind until the train arrived and their cattle were loaded. Once they left, he returned to the stationmaster's office. "So how do we handle this?"

"My guess is between the rustling, the killing, and having a woman boss, you're running short handed. Your men haven't seen me. You can tell them I came out after they left, looking for work on one of the surrounding ranches. Since O'Brien has never met me, I doubt he'll suspect anything. It's possible he's involved in this. We got that wanted poster from one of the bounty hunters who works out of Denver. I wouldn't be surprised if there were more of them in on this. That reward is pretty attractive to men like the ones who join up with the bounty hunters."

* * * *

Cam was glad to return to the Rocking M. Even with three guns between the four of them, they were sitting ducks riding out in the open.

"Another new man?" Dave said once Cam sent George to the bunkhouse.

"Met up with him at the railhead. He saw us driving in the herd and said he was looking for work. Being shorthanded, I hired him. With two new hands, we can relieve Rose and Josh from having to ride with us."

"'Course, with a smaller herd there won't be as much work. If Darius were here, he'd say you were too soft hearted and fall for every sob story from every saddle tramp that crosses your path. Well, the damage is done. We'll find something for him to do."

"Was Dave serious?" Rose asked, once they were back at the main house.

Cam carefully closed the door before replying. He knew they were safe talking there since he'd seen O'Brien at the bunkhouse. "It's all part of the act. Dave knows as much as you and I do. It's not like we don't have work to do. After the rustlers hit the first time, Darius wanted to fence in the entire ranch. With the steers in so early, we can get a lot done by the time the snow flies. We've had the wire and posts for months just waiting for the time to get it done."

"It seems like a waste of time to me. If the rustlers are determined enough, they'll be able to cut the wire and take the cattle. I don't know if I agree with fencing off the open range, but if it was my father's idea, it must have some merit. Since Josh and I won't be riding with the men, will you allow him to come up to the house so we can go over the books from St. Louis I requested?"

Cam felt like he'd been blindsided. In the past couple of days, Rose had ceased being the woman who arrived at the Rocking M inappropriately dressed and had become the owner of the Rocking M. He no longer had any doubts about her being able to stick things out for the remainder of the required year.

"I've been meaning to talk to you about those books. I wish you would have told me you sent for them."

"Why? So you could tell me you didn't want your son to associate with the likes of me? I knew you were concerned about his education and so am I. I know a lot of people at the schools in St. Louis and getting the books that would help him was relatively easy."

Cam could have kicked himself for being so open about his feeling concerning Rose. She'd turned out to be someone he found he could respect. "I didn't mean I was upset about the books, it was just I wanted to pay you for them."

He wondered if he imagined her sigh of relief. "There's no need to pay me. It's the least I could do. I know my father talked about helping you with the cost of higher education for Josh, in his letters. I honestly like your son. He was the only person on the ranch to see the person I am rather than equate me with the life I've lived. You've done a good job in raising him. Not only is he intelligent, but his manners are not what I expected to find on a Montana cattle ranch. After what you told me last night, I can understand. I'm only sorry once this rustling business is over, you'll be returning to Nebraska."

"What are you talking about?"

"One doesn't have to be a genius to realize this isn't the kind of work you're trained to do. Added to that, it has to be hard to be away from your family."

Cam was surprised at how perceptive Rose was. He missed his family and working with his mind, but he knew he would also miss the Rocking M and working with his hands even more. "I miss my family, but this is my life now. Darius gave me a chance, and I've come to love the Rocking M almost as much as he did. I honestly can't see myself chained to a desk again. I like the freedom of riding the range more."

"Well, that's a relief. I was afraid I'd have to look for a new foreman. I know you didn't approve of me when I first arrived, but lately we've been working well together."

As she spoke, Cam found himself fixating on her full lips and wondering how they would feel beneath his lips if he kissed her. Where had that come from?

He knew damn good and well where it came from. For the first time since Martha's death, he was acting like a man. Martha wouldn't want him denying his feelings because of her. If the tables were turned, would he have wanted her to remain a widow?

Of course he wouldn't, but that was different. A woman needed a man.

And a man needed a woman…

"Did you hear me, Cam?"

"Ah… yes I did. I was thinking about something. Have you ever thought about settling down?"

"Not until I came here. I was saving to buy the Purple Moon from Celeste, but now I realize that's not what I want. I grew up there and never saw anything wrong with it, but since I've arrived here, I'm seeing another side of life. I wish I'd grown up with my father, but I realize he only did what he thought was right for me. He gave me a good education and readied me for whatever life threw at me, and I thank him for that. Why do you ask?"

"Just wondering. You've made yourself at home here. You talked about me going back to Omaha. I thought maybe you were going to go back to St. Louis. If you're going to stay you'll be needing a—"

"A husband?" Rose interrupted, anticipating what he was going to say. Why did men always think a woman couldn't survive if she didn't have a man in her life? "Are you applying for the job?" Oh good Lord, why did she say something like that?

"Well... I mean no. I was just wondering that's all. Your prospects out here are pretty limited."

"Really? I thought they were quite open. That is if a certain foreman would be available."

Her comment flustered Cam. "Are... are you trying to seduce me?"

Rose laughed. "I wouldn't do that. Only real ladies veil their true feelings with seduction. I'm more forthright than that. What I'm saying is I like you. I like you enough to want to get to know you better. Don't get me wrong. I'm not inviting you into my bed. I need all the friends I can get out here. I know friends, true friends, are few and far between. I'd be honored if I could call you my friend."

Cam hoped his relief wasn't noticeable. He could always use a friend, and who knew, it could grow into so much more. He'd allowed his mind to run wild earlier. Now he knew where he stood and it would work well for him. "That makes two of us," he replied. "You're right about friends, a body can never have too many of them."

The smile that crossed her lips told him she hoped they would become more than friends once this business with Cornelius was over and done with.

Chapter Eleven

Several days had passed since they'd taken the cattle to the railhead. Other than receiving a wire saying the steers had brought top dollar at market, things had remained relatively quiet.

To everyone's relief, there had been no further trouble from the rustlers. Even though Cam had become a frequent visitor to the house, they'd talked only about ranch matters. Their previous conversation had not been mentioned.

She knew they had both been surprised when they talked about settling down and marriage. She certainly wasn't ready for a life with one man and he was still living with the ghost of his first wife. Neither of them was suitable for a permanent relationship.

The woman she had been in the past wondered what it would be like to take him to her bed, but the new Rose McKinney understood she'd put her former life behind her. Until she did decide to marry, she wouldn't want another man in her bed.

With George keeping an eye on Frank, Rose found she was relaxed enough to unlock her front door. She certainly enjoyed catching the southern breeze. It aired out the house that had been closed up tight after Frank arrived.

Just yesterday Josh returned to school, so her afternoons were now quiet. She missed the hours she and Josh spent together discussing the contents of the books she'd purchased for him.

This afternoon she concentrated on the ranch books and continuing the journal her father had so faithfully kept.

"Where the hell is Addison Cameron?" a deep voice boomed from behind her.

She turned to see an older man who could only be Cornelius Slade standing in the doorway of the library. "I beg your pardon, sir, but I didn't hear you knock on my door."

"Your door! Like hell it is. I know Addison calls himself Cameron Blake now, but he also owns this ranch, at least that's what I've been told. You're nothing but his whore. I've been watching you ever since you got here. I've decided I can't break him by taking his cattle, so maybe if I take something more personal he'll come around. I think he might consider swapping my grandson for you."

His words came as such a shock, Rose had no time even to reach for something with which to defend herself before two men burst into the library and pinned her arms behind her back. She tried to scream, but one of the men shoved a gag in her mouth.

The only thing she could think to do to save herself was to put up a fight. If they were going to take her, she wasn't going to go easily. She squirmed and refused to walk on her own. She even made herself go limp and become a dead weight. As they dragged her through the house and out onto the porch her only prayer was one of the men would return and see what was happening to her.

As soon as she made it to the porch, she saw someone had saddled Renegade. Seeing him standing there made her want to laugh at her captors. That horse would allow anyone to saddle and lead him around like a puppy dog, but unless he got his mandatory sugar, he wouldn't allow anyone on his back.

She knew today would be no different. The minute these men put her on his back, he'd rear and buck relentlessly until the load in his saddle had been removed. With this in mind, she tried to remain limp in anticipation of the fall she would be taking.

Around her Slade and one of her captors mounted their horses while the third man hoisted her up onto Renegade's back. As she knew he would, her blessed horse began to buck, throwing her from his back to the dirt packed dooryard. The moment her head hit the ground, a welcoming blackness encompassed her entire being.

* * * *

Rain clouds were beginning to gather over the mountains, when Cam called a halt to the fencing for the day. They were making good progress. Even if the cowhands weren't adept at stringing wire when they first started, they had soon gotten the knack of it. George had been invaluable, since he'd worked on a farm back east for one of his assignments.

Working on the far edges of the ranch, Cam knew George was on the lookout for signs of the outlaws, but after the last raid it was as though they had disappeared from the face of the earth. He was beginning to think George would leave soon, saying he'd only been crying wolf.

"This is where we held off them rustlers," Adam bragged as they rode through the winter pasture where the last raid had taken place.

"Here's as good a place as any to water the horses," Cam said when he noticed George was interested in the location of the pasture.

"Right over here is where Dave and I hid behind that rock. I thought we were goners for sure. Then Cam came in with his gun blazin'. Dropped that rustler right out of his saddle, was the damnedest thing I ever saw. I thought we were going to find out who was behind it until someone in them there woods shot the man in the head."

Cam watched George while Adam relived the gunfight between them and the rustlers. Cam cringed at the telling of it as did Dave, but the younger man was filled with the excitement of the battle that ended almost as soon as it started. George was intrigued.

"Wasn't much of a fight," Frank declared. "Soon as Cam and I came in, them rustlers turned tail and ran like the cowards they are."

"That seems to be the way with rustlers," George said. "They're a pack of cowards who can't make an honest living."

Cam watched Frank's face for some expression that would tell him if the man was involved in all of this. Unfortunately, he decided O'Brien was one man with whom he would never want to play poker.

Once the horses had drunk their fill and were rested, they continued on toward the ranch. Cam rode in by one of the corrals that contained the breeding cattle and yearlings when he saw three men come out of the house, dragging Rose with them. He knew he was too far away to get to her before they could leave, and he didn't dare shoot, because a stray bullet could easily find its way into her body.

As he watched, two of the men mounted their horses while the third hoisted Rose onto Renegade's back. As could have been predicted, Renegade reared, throwing Rose to the ground. Shock sent the two mounted men out of the yard, while the third swung into his saddle and followed them.

Cam was the first one to reach Rose. By the time he got there, Renegade had calmed enough one of the hands could take him back to the corral and remove the saddle.

A spot of blood soaking the ground told him Rose had been badly injured in the fall. Picking her up, he headed into the house, closely followed by George and Dave.

"It looks like she put up a struggle," George said, picking up the papers scattered across the floor of the library. "Did you recognize any of them from that day in the winter pasture?"

Dave returned to the room, carrying a basin of water from the kitchen. "I did," he responded. "The one riding roan was at the winter pasture. He was one of the rustlers. I'd recognize that roan with the white blaze on his face anywhere."

"That's what I thought," Cam added, rinsing out a cloth in the water in order to wipe the blood from Rose's head. "The man on the white horse looked a lot like Cornelius Slade. That bastard came here and tried to kidnap Rose. I'm sorry she got hurt, but thank God that horse won't let anyone on his back without getting his lump of sugar."

"Cam?" Rose's whispered question brought everyone's attention to her.

"I'm right here. You're safe. I'll be sending someone for the doc as well as the sheriff."

"No, I don't trust him, and there's nothing the doctor can do for a bump on the head. It was your father-in-law. He thinks you own this spread. He said he hadn't broken you by taking the cattle, but maybe if he took your whore you'd trade Josh for me. If Renegade hadn't been as skitterish is he is, they would have taken me away. I can't thank that horse enough for saving my life. I'm certain he would have killed me when he found out you weren't going to give him Josh." She closed her eyes and then sat upright. "Josh. Oh my God, he's due home from school soon. If Slade finds him, you'll never get him back."

Cam's stomach churned. The men hadn't ridden off in the direction of town, so perhaps they hadn't run into Josh, but he had to know for sure his son was safe.

"I'll go and find Josh," Dave offered. "You stay here with Rose. If Slade is out there, he won't know me, but if he sees you, he could be foolish enough to shoot to kill."

"Pa, Pa, what's going on? Everyone says they think Rose is dead, and there were people here trying to take her away."

Everyone turned their attention to Josh as he entered the room.

Cam was immediately on his feet. "Thank goodness you're home. Did you see anyone riding hard between here and town?"

"Didn't see a soul. Who was I supposed to see?"

"I don't want you leaving the ranch for a few days," George said. "Your grandfather was here and tried to kidnap Rose. Until he's found, you and Cam are going to have to stay here at the house where we can guard all three of you."

"Look you can't do that," Cam protested. "I want to be in on this fight. It's me Slade is after and—"

"That's all the more reason for you and Josh to hole up in the house. Slade wants you, but he wants Josh more. He won't think a thing about sacrificing one to get the other. Consider yourselves under house arrest and that's an order. We all know why I'm here, and if you want me to do my duty, you'll abide by my orders. I've dealt with men like Slade before."

Cam knew George was right. Somehow he had to protect both Josh and Rose from the danger Slade posed.

"Whatever you say. Someone has to take care of Rose. I'm guessing I'm as good as anyone when it comes to that. Just don't kill him if you can help it. He was Martha's father, and he's Josh's grandfather. He's family. I don't know what happened to his mind, but like I told Josh, everyone handles grief in their own way."

"I don't care if he is my grandfather, Pa. He tried to hurt Rose. He ain't human."

"Isn't," Cam absently corrected his son. "You don't know him, and you can't fault him for his grief over the loss of his daughter."

Cam understood his son's feelings. As much as he wanted this to be finished, he knew he and Cornelius would never again be friends. The man was guilty of murder and rustling. It was entirely possible he would hang. Even in death, he wouldn't be reunited with his daughter because his misplaced hatred of Cam hadn't earned him a place in the same heaven as Martha. If anyone was a saint it was her and the little girl who hadn't even drawn a breath after leaving her mother's body.

* * * *

Rose's head ached but more than that she chafed under Cam's watchful eye. He sat in the chair next to the sofa where she lay not allowing her even to get to her feet. On the other side of the room, Josh did the homework that wouldn't be turned in because it would be several days before he would be allowed to return to school.

"We've got problems," Dave said as he came into the library.

"Of course we do," Cam scoffed. "What else can be wrong?"

"O'Brien is missing. No one has seen him since we rode in from building fence."

Rose's heart plummeted to the pit of her stomach. She wanted to be wrong about Frank. She actually liked him as a person, but this was the clincher. It was entirely possible the man had been working for Slade all along. It was more than she could take.

"It's what I feared. As soon as Cornelius made himself known, O'Brien took off. He has to be the one who's feeding our information to the rustlers. Now he's joined them. At least he doesn't know George is actually a marshal."

"I know the evidence is there," Rose agreed, "but..."

"There are no buts, Rose," Dave interrupted. "The man was loyal to us until Slade showed his face. Now he's missing. In my book that puts him in cahoots with the rustlers. How else would they have known where to find the herd after we moved them to the winter pasture?"

A commotion on the porch relieved Rose of the burden of trying to defend Frank. "I have to get in there and talk to Cam and Rose," she heard Frank shouting.

Cam got to his feet and went to see what was going on. When he returned it was with both Frank and George.

132

"Where have you been?" she said to Frank.

"I've been doing what you asked me to do. I've been out trailing the rustlers."

"Look O'Brien, we know you're not a U.S. Marshal," Cam said.

"That's right. I wasn't honest with Rose on the train and even less honest once I got here. I have to admit, I saw that wanted poster that's been put out on Cam. When I first saw you, I thought about contacting the man who had issued it. There's a lot of money being offered for you, but then we got acquainted. I asked a lot of questions and decided there was something wrong about the whole thing.

"Today when I saw those men riding out after Renegade threw Rose, I followed. Over the years I've learned how to trail outlaws without being detected. I know where they're hiding. It's only right the real U.S. Marshals be contacted. There's no papers out on these men, so I have no right to go after them. I used to wear a badge, but because of my temper I lost that privilege. Now I depend on wanted posters to find the men who are fair game for the bounty hunters."

"If you're not in on this, who is feeding them the information about what goes on at the Rocking M?" George asked.

"I don't know why you're asking questions, but I saw someone else at the hide out. I recognized Sheriff Pollard's horse as soon as I got there. He's in this up to his eyeballs."

"I tend to agree with you. As for why I have the right to ask questions, I came when I knew you were here. You have a reputation that's far from sterling in the marshal's office in Denver. I worried about why you came to Miss McKinney's aid posing as one of us."

"Look, I met Rose on the train. She didn't look like anything other than, well, you know what I mean. We had a good time, but I knew she wouldn't have given me the time of day if I told her I was a bounty hunter. Some women are funny that way. I told her I'd come if she needed me. When I got her wire, I figured she'd liked what she had on the train. Of course after I got here, I realized she'd become an entirely different woman, and she was one who was in trouble. Like I said, I recognized Cam right away, but once I got to know him, I realized it was something I didn't want to handle. I was hoping to get to the bottom of the rustling and then send for back up."

"You know," Dave said, "what he's saying sounds just crazy enough to be true."

"I swear it is the truth. Since you have the authority to stop these men, I'm sure the hands here will back you up."

"That should work," someone said from the doorway. Both George and Frank turned at the sound of what Rose assumed was a familiar voice. "We thought you might need some help on this one, George, especially since we received a wire from Frank asking for our help. We knew if he was sending the wire there had to be real trouble here. The boss said we should hightail it up here and help you out. It looks like we got here just in time for all the fun."

"It looks like we owe you an apology, O'Brien," Cam said, extending his hand.

"There's time for that later," Frank replied. "There's hard telling how long they'll still be at their hideout. If we move fast, we can catch them all in one fell swoop."

Everyone agreed and Dave went out to round up the hands to act as a posse. Rose worried Cam would demand to go with them, but didn't dare say anything.

"I'm going, too," Cam insisted, getting to his feet.

George got up and stood toe to toe with Cam. "Not this time. You and Rose are the only ones who can identify Slade. We can't take the chance you might get hurt or worse yet, even killed. What would happen to Josh then?"

Rose was relieved when Cam hung his head in defeat. "You're right, of course. It's just hard to sit back and let someone else fight my battles."

Rose looked around the room, suddenly aware of the fact Josh was no longer in the library. "Where is Josh?" she demanded.

"I haven't seen him since Frank got here," Dave said. "I'll check outside."

Within minutes, Dave hurried back into the house. "Somehow Josh slipped past the guards, probably out through the back. I saw him riding out when I stepped out onto the porch. I'm going to follow him. My horse is still saddled, and he's a lot faster than Josh's pony. I'll catch up with him."

"I'm going with you," Frank declared. "I know where the outlaws are. Hopefully, he went in a different direction. The last thing we need is for Slade to get his hands on the boy."

Tears filled Rose's eyes. She'd felt the brutality of Slade's touch when he tried to abduct her. She couldn't stand the thought of something like that happening to Josh. Cam sat next to her on the sofa and pulled her into his arms.

"Nothing's the way we thought it was," Cam whispered in her ear. "Now my son is out there looking for his grandfather. He has no idea how dangerous Cornelius can be."

"That's where you're wrong. He saw what he did to me, and he's heard you tell what happened the night his mother died. I think he's decided he has to be our avenging angel. Hopefully he rode in a different direction than the outlaws."

Chapter Twelve

Josh rode away from the ranch. He had no idea which way to go to find his grandfather and the men who were riding with him, but somehow he'd find him. He had taken his rifle and was ready to use it if necessary. He wanted nothing more than to put a bullet into his grandfather's dark heart.

From behind him, Josh heard hoof beats and turned to see who was following him. Recognizing Dave, he knew he had no chance to outrun the horse that was much larger than his pony.

"Just where in the hell did you think you were going?"

"Out to find my grandfather and put an end to him." He glanced at Frank as he rode up on the other side of him. "Why is he here? Pa says he's not to be trusted."

"There's a lot you don't know, Josh. Thank goodness you took off in a direction opposite the one Slade took. Now, you're going back to the ranch and stay with your pa and Rose while we go and flush them out."

"But I want—"

"I know what you want," Frank said. "The problem is we can't let you take the law into your own hands. You may think killing a man is an easy thing to do, but believe me it stays with you for the rest of your life. Slade isn't worth wrecking your life over. As for why I'm here, it's a long story. I'm sure your father will explain everything once we get you back to the house. After that, we're taking a posse out to capture Slade and his men, alive. Justice needs to be handed out in a courtroom rather than at the end of a gun."

* * * *

Cam paced nervously. What if Josh ran smack dab into Cornelius? Would he leave the hideout and take Josh with him? If he did, would he ever see his son again? The questions without answers plagued his mind and made him sick to his stomach.

Rather than dwelling on them, he went to the window and watched the men mounting up to go out in search of Slade and his men. In the distance, he saw three riders approaching. He breathed a sigh of relief when he recognized Dave and Frank with Josh riding between them.

"Now get your tail in the house and don't leave until we come back," he heard Dave scold Josh. "There will be guards at the front and back doors, so don't get any ideas about following us the minute your pa's back is turned. This is dangerous business and no one wants to see either you or Cam hurt."

The door opened and Josh sheepishly entered the library. "Just what did you think you were doing?" Cam demanded.

"Don't you start, too," Josh growled. "I've already gotten that speech from Dave. I went out to do what should have been done before this. If someone had put a bullet between his eyes, he wouldn't be trying to ruin our lives now."

"Don't sass me," Cam said, anger building within him.

"I didn't mean to, Pa. I just want this to be over and done with."

"Killing the man isn't the answer," Rose said as she hurried to give Josh a hug. "We have to remember your grandfather isn't in his right mind. I can't begin to understand how it would feel to lose a child and a grandchild at the same time. It has to have altered his thinking where your father is concerned. He does love you and wants you with him, but he went about it in the wrong way. If he'd realized your father had lost his wife and daughter things would have been different. He would have seen you grow up and been a part of your life. Instead, his warped reasoning has sent you into hiding, made your father change your name and kept you from the family who undoubtedly loves you unconditionally. I feel sorry for your father's family for not getting to know you."

Cam watched Rose embrace his son and realized he, like his son was crying. It had been years since he had allowed himself the luxury of tears for Martha, the child they had lost, and the family he had left behind to keep his son at his side.

* * * *

Darkness was falling and still there had been no word from the men who had ridden out earlier to where Slade and his outlaws were hiding.

Over an hour ago, Cookie had brought up food for supper, but Rose found she, like Cam and Josh, had no appetite.

"When do you think we'll hear something?" she asked.

"I doubt anything will happen much before morning," Cam responded. "If Cornelius thinks he got away, he'll let his guard down. I know I'd be planning to go in just before dawn. It gives a better element of surprise."

"I don't know if I'll be able to get any rest until I know that man is in custody." Rose sighed. "I understand he's sick, but his sickness has cost this ranch dearly. No matter what happens to him, it won't bring back my father or change the fact Dave was shot trying to defend our herd."

Just the thought of how badly Dave had been wounded brought images of men being wounded in the fight that was bound to erupt at dawn. "Maybe it's best if I check my medical supplies," she said, getting to her feet.

"Do you think you'll need them?" Josh questioned.

"Unfortunately, I do. Those men thought nothing of murdering my father, shooting Dave, and killing one of their own men. They won't go down easily. At least getting everything ready will help pass the time until we hear something."

"That sounds like a good idea," Cam agreed. "I'll have one of the men guarding the house bring up the supplies Cookie keeps in the cookhouse. Between what you have here and what we have there, it should be enough. Are you sure you have enough expertise to take care of these men?"

"Have you forgotten the doctor left me alone with Dave when he was wounded? I've some willow bark left from what Verna brought out, so I can take care of fevers."

The thought of wounded men being brought to her for treatment cause a knot in Rose's stomach. Even though she'd been trained to care for the sick, the waste of lives in the gun battles seemed ridiculous. Why men thought using a gun was the only way to settle arguments was beyond her understanding.

* * * *

Rose awoke with a start. She didn't remember falling asleep, but now the first light of morning was streaming in the window. Sometime through the night, someone had covered her with one of the quilts normally stored in the closet of her bedroom. From the chair where she had spent the night, she saw Josh sleeping on the sofa and Cam on the floor in front of the fireplace.

She made no attempt to rise. There was no use in waking Cam and Josh. They, like her, had probably had very little sleep in light of what was occurring with Slade and his gang of outlaws.

Considering dawn had probably been over an hour ago, she wondered what was going on with Dave and the others. Would there be loss of life? Would she have to tend to several wounded men or would no one need her skills? Whatever the answer to her questions, the price paid by everyone involved today was far too great.

"Are you awake, Rose?" Cam whispered.

Rose turned her attention to Cam and saw him sit up to face her. She smiled at the early morning stubble growing on his chin. Having never seen him first thing in the morning, she had only seen him clean-shaven. To be truthful, she rather liked the look of the beginnings of his beard.

"Yes, I'm awake. I didn't want to wake you or Josh."

"You don't have to worry about waking him. That boy could sleep through anything. At least it seems that way when I'm trying to get him up to go to school. I don't know about you, but I could use a cup of coffee and some breakfast. I'll send one of the men down to have something brought to us. This might be the only chance we'll have to get something to eat. If I'm not mistaken, we should be hearing from Dave and the others soon."

"I think you're right. I'm not looking forward to having them return. I'm so afraid one of more of them has been injured. We should be getting ready, just in case. Maybe we can have some of the men bring up bedding from the bunkhouse. If we have wounded men here we'll have to have places for them to recuperate. There are plenty of rooms upstairs as well as the downstairs bedroom. The problem is there won't be enough beds if there are several of them wounded."

She got to her feet and began to fold her quilt as well as the one Cam had used while he talked to the man stationed outside the front door. It wouldn't be long before the man returned not only with coffee, but also with the bedding she had requested.

After going to her bedroom to splash her face with water and change her clothes, she returned to the library. When she did, she saw Josh was up and taking care of the quilt that had covered him throughout the night.

"They just brought us up some breakfast," Cam announced when he came out of the kitchen. "I think we should eat it while it's hot."

Rose followed Josh as he led the way to the kitchen. Unlike last night when no one had wanted to eat, they were all hungry enough they made short work of the food.

While Josh cleared the table, Rose and Cam lingered over their coffee. It was a quiet moment like ones shared by husbands and wives all over the country.

She wondered what it would be like to have a real family. She would like a man like Cam in her life, but no matter what he said, once this was settled, she was certain he'd be leaving the Rocking M forever. He had family in Nebraska, and that's where Josh would have a better chance for an education.

Did she really want him out of her life?

Of course, she didn't, but what chance did she have? He was a good man and deserved a lot more in a wife than a reformed whore, and that's just what he'd be getting in her. She'd lived the life in which she was raised and now she regretted it, but she couldn't change the past.

"They're back!" The shout from one of the men guarding the front door silenced Rose's mental ramblings.

Cam was immediately on his feet and running toward the front door. Rose followed, unable to keep up with the strides of his long legs.

When they stepped out onto the porch, she stifled a scream when she saw two horses being led with bodies draped over their backs. One of the marshals leaned low over the neck of his horse indicating he had been shot, as did the man Rose recognized as Cornelius Slade.

The thought of using her nursing skills on Slade made her stomach roil and her mind spin with indecision. How could she treat the man who had accused Cam falsely and tried to kidnap her? It would be hard, but she knew she had to do it.

"We got them," Frank said as he dismounted and took the steps to the porch two at a time. "There are some of them that need doctoring, as well as a few of our men. Dave says you can take care of them if you let us bring them into your house."

Rose swallowed down the lump in her throat. As much as she wanted to say no and tell them to take the outlaws as well as Slade into town, she knew she had the skills and couldn't turn them away.

"Bring them in. I'll do the best I can. You'll have to send someone into town for the doctor so he can help me. Maybe they can ask Verna Johnson and Minnie Cranston to come out as well."

"Well, ain't you Miss High and Mighty," Sheriff Pollard taunted her.

She looked up to see him sitting on his horse, his hands tied in front of him. "I wouldn't be talking that way if I were you. Do you have any idea how much trouble you're in?" she demanded. "Were you the one who killed my father? Did you enjoy watching him die?"

"I didn't kill Darius. I only gave Slade the information he wanted. It was me who recognized Cam when I saw the poster out on him. He's the one who's wanted for murder. I contacted Slade, and he asked me to break Cam."

"Why did you let him believe I owned this ranch?" Cam said, as he reached up and pulled Pollard from his saddle. "Why didn't you just arrest me and have it over with?"

"Because I wanted to hurt Darius as much as Slade wanted to hurt you. I didn't pull the trigger on him, but I didn't shed no tears over his death either."

"The other marshal, as well as several of your men, are taking the ones that aren't wounded into town and locking them up in the jail, Cam," George said. "I'm staying here to keep an eye on the wounded ones. It was a good thing you and Josh were here. Slade was adamant he wanted to see you dead."

"I'm sure he was. Well, don't just stand there. Help me get the old man into the house. Rose and I talked about this last night, and we've got all the medical supplies on the ranch in the house. I've pulled out a bullet or two, and she knows nursing, but with so many shot, we'll need help from the doctor."

Rose listened to the conversation between the two men for only a moment, before going into the house. The first thing she had to do was assess the men's wounds and see, which ones needed her first. Of course, she didn't have to examine them to know the marshal and Slade were the worst of the lot.

"We've put a second bed in the downstairs bedroom," she said. "Take the marshal and Slade in there. I'll check the other men and be in immediately. Cam, bring in the majority of the medical supplies and some hot water. While I'm seeing to the other men, you can get them undressed."

Cam nodded and helped George get the marshal from his horse. Rose eyed Slade, knowing someone would have to help him as well. "Josh, you'll have to help Frank get your grandfather into the house."

Josh looked at her with distrust in his eyes. "I won't touch him."

Rose put both hands on his shoulders. "I don't have time to argue with you. Like it or not, this man is your grandfather, and he's badly wounded. I need to help him, and I can't do that with him still on his horse. Now, you will get him into the house. It matters not who or what he is. What you need to understand is he's in need of our help. Do I make myself clear?"

Josh hung his head as though shamed by her words. "Yes Ma'am, but I ain't going to care for him. Once he's in there, he's your responsibility."

"I shouldn't take the time to correct you, but I will. You should have said I'm not, but I don't expect you to care for anyone. I know this is hard for you, but you can't continue being disrespectful. It's over now. From here we have to go on and let the old hurts heal. Just do as I say and then get out to the kitchen and keep a kettle on the stove with hot water. I'm going to need plenty of it."

Josh gave her one last look before turning to help Frank with Slade. It galled her to have had to make Josh tend to the man who had caused him such pain, but she had no other option.

"This man has a shoulder wound," she said after checking the first outlaw. "He can wait. Take him upstairs and put him in the first bedroom." She looked at the back of the man's shirt. "It looks like the bullet went completely through. There's no bullet to dig out. I'll have someone bring up a basin of warm water. Make certain the wound is thoroughly washed. As soon as I take care of the more severely wounded men, I'll be up to bandage it." The outlaw looked at her as though wondering why she was doing this, but went upstairs with Adam without saying anything.

It was the same with the second outlaw as well as two of her hands. Only the outlaws protested. Her own men knew what she could do when it came to medical treatment and understood she had to take care of the men in danger of dying from their wounds.

With all the wounds assessed, Rose hurried to the downstairs bedroom. While the marshal had lost a lot of blood, Slade was the one most in need of her attentions.

"Wash off the marshal's wound," she told Cam. "His wound is bad, but Slade's is the worst. I'll tend to him and see if there's anything I can do and then get to the marshal."

"You'd treat that old bastard before the marshal here?" Cam said.

"I'll treat the man most in need of my skills first. The marshal will live. I don't know if I can say the same for Slade. If we're lucky, he's merely weak from the loss of blood and the bullet didn't hit any major organs. I don't think I can wait for the doctor to get here. I'm going to have to remove it and do it quickly. That's the only way I can assess the damage."

Rose helped Frank take off Slade's shirt and saw where the bullet had entered the old man's body. Luckily, it wasn't close to his heart, but it had entered at the top of his stomach. She had heard one of the doctors at the hospital in St. Louis talking about people who were gut shot not having much of a chance, but in this case all she could do was pray she had enough skill to save the man's life.

"Sterilize this knife," she told Cam. "I'm going to have to dig out this bullet."

Cam stared at her in disbelief. "Have you ever done something like this before?"

"No, but I've assisted with enough surgeries to know what I'm doing. Thank goodness he's already unconscious, but I'll need some whiskey to wash out the wound and to use just in case he wakes up. I know the men have some in the bunkhouse, bring me all you can find."

Cam shook his head but got to his feet to do what she told him. Once he returned with the knife, she made the first cut. With luck, the bullet wouldn't have taken a wayward path and would be close to where it had entered his body.

She was pleased when she found it lodged against the last rib. After taking it out, she sterilized the wound and prepared to begin stitching up the cut she had made. Once finished, she bound him with the strips of white cloth she'd torn for bandages.

"I've done what I can. Now we just have to watch for infection."

Cam looked at her with admiration in his eyes. "Damnedest thing I ever saw. I know you took care of Dave, but I also know it was Doc who did the surgery."

"I could have done it as well, but I knew the bullet was too close to his heart. I didn't have to worry about that with Slade. Now, let me see what I can do for the marshal."

The man had lost a great deal of blood and looked pale, but until she knew if the bullet was still in him, she wouldn't be able to treat him effectively.

"I got here as quickly as I could." She turned to see Dr. Myers enter the room.

"Thank goodness," Rose said, getting to her feet. "I took the bullet out of one man, but I don't know if I can do it again."

Doc looked beneath the bandage. "That's a damn good piece of surgery. Are you up to assisting me with this one?"

Rose nodded. "There are several more upstairs, but I assessed their wounds and they weren't as bad as these."

Doc bent to examine the marshal. "We're in luck. The bullet went clean through and I doubt it hit anything major. What we're dealing with here is the blood loss. I can take care of him, if you want to get started on the men upstairs. I'll join you as soon as I finish."

Rose sighed with relief as she left the room.

"You did a good job in there," Cam said. "As much as I wanted to see Cornelius dead, I'm glad you were able to save his life. Josh needs to know his grandfather."

"I'm afraid he won't have much time to get acquainted. He's guilty of murder, attempted murder, and cattle rustling. You know as well as I do any one of those are hanging charges. At least with him gone, we can get back to normal."

"Not unless he tells us where our cattle are. I know he has them stashed somewhere around here."

"If he regains consciousness, hopefully he will tell us."

"If, don't you mean when?"

Rose shook her head. She had seen the damage done by the bullet. It wasn't as bad as it could have been, but it was bad nonetheless.

"If you'll excuse me, I need to get upstairs and take care of the other wounded men."

As she turned away from Cam, she thought she was going to cry. The look of indecision in his eyes about his former father-in-law was heartbreaking. At one time he had loved Martha Slade Cameron with all his heart. Along with that love had come love for her parents. Martha's death had killed that and more than likely haunted him for the past ten years.

Josh was the one who would suffer the most because of this. Until a few days ago he hadn't even known he had grandparents who loved him. Now suddenly, he had a grandfather who not only wanted him in his life, but also condoned murder in order to gain custody of him. Then there was Cam's family. Rose was certain they wanted to know their grandson and nephew. Unfortunately, that wouldn't happen as long as Cam stayed in Montana. It was only a matter of time before he would want to return to Nebraska and lead a life much different from the one he had been living on the Rocking M for the past seven years.

She knew she would be able to rely on Dave to take over the position of foreman. That wasn't the problem. For her it was learning how to live without seeing Cam on a daily basis. As much as she had fought it, she knew she was falling in love not only with Cam, but also with Josh. His eager mind had intrigued her, and she considered him to be a good friend. She would miss both of them, but Rose knew she would never hold them back, if leaving was what they wanted.

Even though the surgery she'd performed on Slade exhausted her, she opened the door to the first bedroom and prepared to tend to the wounds of the men who were waiting for her.

Chapter Thirteen

Cam watched as Rose went up the stairs to care for the men who were not as badly wounded as Cornelius and the marshal. His feelings were mixed about everything that transpired in the past few months.

He'd lived for ten years as Cam Blake, but always in the past had been Addison Cameron. He'd faced that past when he first told Josh. Cam knew he cracked the shell he built around everything that happened in Omaha ten years earlier. For the first time, he had been able to put Martha, as well as the little girl who never even drew a breath, to rest. They would always be a memory from the past, but now he could put them where they belonged.

When had the woman who went up the stairs become more than just Darius's daughter, the owner of the Rocking M Ranch and his boss? When had he stopped thinking of her as a bad influence on his son and begun thinking of her as a woman he wanted to know better?

Had it been when she nursed Dave and helped him recover from the gunshot wound he had received at the hands of Cornelius and his gang of rustlers? Had it been when she rode with the men, or when she sent to St. Louis for the books to help Josh with his education?

It didn't matter when it happened, but that it happened. She had said she knew he would be going back to Nebraska and over the years it was something he longed to do. Now everything had changed. He couldn't think about leaving the Rocking M because it would mean leaving Rose.

"Is he going to die, Pa?" Josh said.

Cam turned to face his son. By his red-rimmed eyes, Cam knew the boy had been crying. Yesterday he had wanted to kill his grandfather, today the thought of the old man dying without Josh getting to know him brought Josh to tears.

"I don't know. He was badly wounded, but Rose did her best for him. Doc said she did a great job and I agree with him."

"I thought I wanted him dead," Josh said, his voice hardly more than a whisper. "But—but he's my grandpa, he's Ma's father."

"I know. As much as I've feared what he would do over the years, I never hated him, not like I thought. When I saw him this morning I realized he was nothing more than a broken old man. I was wrong to run away from him, but at the time I wasn't thinking properly. If I'd stayed in Omaha maybe we could have worked out our differences."

"Can I see him?" Josh asked.

"We'll have to wait until Doc says we can. I won't deny you getting to know the man for whatever time he has left. I remember when you were born, he was so proud. I think he handed out cigars to every man in town. He and his wife could never have any children after your mother was born. She wasn't much older than you when her mother died. From what Cornelius told me, his wife was a frail little thing and when she got sick she died within two days. It hit him hard. After raising you alone, I can see why he was so protective of your mother."

"Were you being protective when you said I couldn't spend time with Rose?"

Damn kid is too perceptive for his own good. "I guess I was. I know what kind of life she'd lived, and I was afraid she'd teach you things you don't need to know."

"Ah, Pa, I know about all of that. How could I help but know listening to all of the men on this ranch. Besides, Rose and I talked about what her life was like before she came here. She told me having grown up in the Purple Moon, and she didn't see anything wrong with it then. Now, she knows better. She's not ashamed of it, but she knows it's not the life she wants. I think she enjoys riding with the men and running this ranch."

Cam agreed with his son. Rose seemed to be as much in her element when she was on horseback as she was working on the ranch books. He'd seen her neat lines of figures that made Darius' hen scratching look like a child's scrawl.

"The old man is awake," Dr. Myers said, as he came out of the downstairs bedroom. "He's asking for you Cam."

"Can I go in, too?" Josh asked.

Dr. Myers looked at Cam before he answered.

"The boy deserves to at least meet his grandfather," Cam replied.

Josh smiled, sending a stab of jealousy through Cam's heart. The last thing he wanted was for Josh to bond with Cornelius, and yet, he knew he couldn't keep his son and Cornelius apart. He'd done that for the past ten years and now that the old man had very little time left to live, he couldn't continue.

Cam let Josh lead the way into the room. He glanced first at the marshal who seemed to be sleeping peacefully and then at Cornelius. "This is your grandson," Cam said, pushing Josh closer to the bed where his grandfather rested.

"He favors Martha," Cornelius commented, his voice weakened from not only his wound but also the loss of blood.

"That he does." Cam watched as Josh pulled a chair next to the bed and took Cornelius' hand in his.

"I've seen the picture Pa has on his dresser. She was a beautiful woman. I don't really remember her, but sometimes I think I see her when I'm dreaming."

"I wanted you with me, boy, but I can see your father has done a good job with you."

"Thank you," Cam said. "I've tried. I couldn't have given him a stable home for these past seven years if it hadn't been for Darius. He gave us a home here and helped with Josh's education."

Slade nodded. "The doctor tells me the woman patched me up. I thought she was just your whore."

Cam wished Josh hadn't heard the old man's description of Rose. "She's a trained nurse and there was no time for her to wait for the doctor to get here. If she had, you would have died. She saved the life of my best friend, Dave, when your rustlers shot him. If it hadn't been for her, he would have died of the infection that set into the wound after the doctor left."

"Why did you bring her here, Addison?"

Cam chafed at the sound of his given name. "She owns this ranch. It was her father your men killed in one of the early raids on our cattle. I'm only the foreman here."

"I was told you owned this place." Cornelius said no more as he began to cough, bringing up blood.

"Doc, you'd better get back in here," Cam called.

"Don't die, Grandpa," Josh begged. "Don't die until I get to know you."

Cam's heart ached for his son. If Martha and the baby hadn't died, his son would have had a close relationship with Cornelius. For the old man to die now just wasn't right.

"He just needs to rest, Cam. He overexerted himself is all. I've given him something for pain. You and Josh will be able to talk to him later."

Cam left the bedroom, but Josh stayed behind and held the old man's hand until he finally slipped into a deep sleep.

Alone in the library, Cam thought about what Cornelius said. Someone told him Cam owned the Rocking M. There could only be one person who had started a rumor like that.

When Cam first came to the Rocking M, Pollard had been one of the hands in Darius' employ. It had been Cam who told Darius he'd found Pollard drinking on the job, resulting in him being fired on the spot. There had never been good blood between the two of them.

From the Rocking M, Pollard had moved into town and taken a job as the deputy to the sheriff. When the old man died, he'd slid into the position and somehow duped the voters into electing him to the office months later.

"He squeezed my hand when I first went in there, Pa," Josh said, as he entered the library. "I think he really likes me."

"Of course he does, he loves you desperately, just as I do. I hope you'll have the time to get to know him. I want you to wait here until he wakes up."

"Where are you going?"

"I need to ride into town. Tell Rose where I went. I shouldn't be gone long."

Although Josh said nothing, Cam knew his son wanted to know what was going on, but until he could prove his suspicions, he didn't want to make any accusations.

* * * *

Rose stood and rubbed the aching muscles in the middle of her back. As much as it galled her, she'd bandaged the outlaws along with her own men. None of them was badly hurt, but they still needed medical care.

Once she was convinced they were resting peacefully, with Frank guarding the door to the room where the outlaws were sleeping, she slumped into the chair that sat in the hallway.

"You look beat," Frank said.

"I feel beat. Do you need someone to spell you out here?"

Frank shook his head. "I guess I owe you an apology. How long have you known I wasn't a marshal anymore?"

"Quite a while. Cam sent a wire to Denver to check you out. The marshals seem to think you're a dangerous man, are you?"

"Not in my mind. I've got a bad temper and got into a fight with my superior. Of course, he fired me on the spot. I didn't know much else other than being a lawman, so I became a bounty hunter. I worked with several other men who had been in either the Texas Rangers or the marshals."

"They said you were dangerous because you only went after men who were wanted dead or alive."

"They're right about that, but what they don't know is I took in more men alive than I did dead. I saw the paper out on Cam when I was back east. I recognized him immediately, but then I got to know him and realized he couldn't have been involved in the death of his wife. Trust me, I want these men to pay for what they've done not only to this ranch, but also to your father and Dave. I respect him and Cam. Before all hell broke loose, I had decided to send a wire to the marshals and ask for help. Thank goodness they got here when they did."

Rose was relieved. She'd come to like Frank and could not stand the thought he might have been working with either Slade or the rustlers in order to break her.

"I'll send someone up with some food and coffee for you once I see what's going on downstairs," she said, as she got to her feet. "You have to be starved."

"Now that you mention it, I do feel like my stomach is scraping against my backbone."

She smiled and then turned to go back downstairs. She found Verna and Minnie making themselves at home in the kitchen preparing food for the people in the household as well as broth for the patients in both the upstairs and downstairs bedrooms.

"Thank you so much for coming out to help. I don't think I could have handled the cooking and the patients at the same time. Our cook was one of the men who was injured. His helper is doing what he can to feed the men, but I can't expect an inexperienced man to cook for them and for everyone in the house as well."

Verna came away from the stove and put her arm around Rose's shoulders. "You look plumb tuckered out. Just sit down here and have something to eat. If I'm not mistaken you haven't had much to fill your belly for the past couple of days. Adam told us what had been going on out here when he rode with us from town."

Rose sat down at the table and allowed Verna to put a plate of stew in front of her. The aroma of the food made her mouth water. It had been a long time since she'd had a decent meal. What she had eaten hadn't been enough to keep a bird alive. She smiled to think of the words Celeste had spoken to her many times when she had been growing up. Now that all things were settling down, she would have to write her old friend and mentor to tell her she'd decided to stay in Montana as the owner of the Rocking M. The money she'd saved to buy the Purple Moon would be better spent on restocking the ranch her father had built from nothing.

"I told Frank O'Brien I'd send him up something to eat," she said, once she took the first taste of the food they had put in front of her.

"I'll take it up," Minnie offered.

Verna sat down across from Rose. "All you had to do was mention Frank's name to Minnie and she was off and runnin'. I swear that girl has a bad case of puppy love for that handsome devil."

"But isn't Minnie married?" Rose said, shocked that Minnie would chase after another man if she had a husband at home.

"She was. Her man, Paul, was killed during a bank robbery here in town. He worked at the bank and those dirty outlaws gunned him down like he was a dog. The posse caught up with them, no thanks to Amos Pollard. That man is as lazy as they come, but the men from town were mad and went out looking for them. Luckily they caught them just outside of town. Strange as it sounds, once they were in jail, they magically escaped. Now it all makes sense. If Amos was in cahoots with the rustlers, it's possible he was working with the bank robbers as well."

"So, what does Pollard have against the Rocking M that he would be in on the rustling that was eventually bound to ruin us?"

"Amos drifted into town about a year before Cam. Darius hired him. At the time, my Andrew said Darius made the biggest mistake of his life when he let Amos on the Rocking M. The next year, after Cam came, Cam caught him drinking on the job and Darius fired him. How he got to be our sheriff is anyone's guess. I know my Andrew didn't vote for him, but he must have had enough support from his drinking buddies to get him the office."

Rose nodded. The information Verna had just given her explained a lot. She knew there had to be a reason why Slade thought this place belonged to Cam and called her a whore. It had to have come from Pollard.

Chapter Fourteen

Cam rode into town, ignoring the questioning looks from the men who were gathered on the street, apparently wondering why their sheriff had been brought into town in shackles and now was residing in his own jail.

Rather than stopping to answer any questions, he tied his horse to the hitching rail in front of the jail and went inside.

"Cam, is something wrong out at the ranch?" George asked.

"No. I just wanted to come in and have a talk with one of your prisoners."

"Do I have to ask which one?"

"I doubt it."

"I didn't think so. Pollard has been calling you everything but white ever since we left the Rocking M. That man hates you with a passion."

Cam nodded. "He thinks he has reason. I don't agree. I was the one who found him drinking on the job and went to Darius. Of course, Pollard got fired on the spot, and he blamed me. After that, there was a big shake up on the Rocking M. Anyone who had seen Pollard drinking when he should have been working, found themselves out of a job. That was something Darius didn't tolerate. He always said what the men did in their off time was of no concern of his, but when they were working they had to be sober."

"I can understand that," George said. "Before you go back there, you have to leave your gun with me. I don't want to take any chances of some of the outlaws getting their hands on it and breaking out. I've already wired for a prison wagon as well as a judge to get here as soon as possible. 'Course, they won't get here for a few days. I've hired some deputies from town. I'm beginning to find out that the good sheriff isn't very well liked in this town."

"He lost the respect of most of the people when he let the bank robbers go last year. No one can prove it, but I doubt they could have broken out of jail without his help. Well, that's all past history. For now I just want to know where we can find Rose's cattle. Knowing Slade, he didn't profit from the rustling. I'm certain he has them stashed somewhere close by so he can give them to Josh, sort of like an inheritance."

Cam unbuckled his gun belt and put it on the desk that had, just hours earlier, belonged to Pollard. As much as he wanted to confront the men who were locked up in jail, he hesitated before opening the door leading to the cells.

Once he stepped through the doorway, he saw Pollard sitting dejectedly on one of the bunks. "I should have told the men to kill you when I had the chance," he spat.

"Then why didn't you?"

"Because Slade was paying me a lot of money to make certain you stayed alive. He didn't want me to kill you, just break you."

"Then why did you tell him I was the owner of the Rocking M?"

For the first time Pollard broke into a wide grin. "That bastard McKinney deserved everything he got, including being killed. Believe me, I didn't shed any tears at his funeral. If he hadn't been riding nighthawk and pulled his gun on my men he wouldn't have been killed. That wasn't in the bargain."

"Your men?" Cam questioned.

Pollard turned his back on him, indicating their conversation had ended. Cam knew he would get no more information from the former sheriff. Instead he would have to concentrate on the wounded rustlers in the upstairs bedroom of the ranch house.

* * * *

Rose finished the stew Verna insisted she eat before going back to the library. Once there, she saw Josh sitting in one of the chairs next to the fireplace cradling his head in his hands.

"Are you all right?" she asked, sitting in the matching chair on the other side of the hearth.

"I want to be," he said, without raising his head. "Why is it so hard? I should hate him for what he did to us as well as to your father, but I can't. Pa let me go in and see him and I held his hand. That was the same hand that held my mother's hand when she was a kid. I don't want him to die before I get to know him."

Rose cringed. She was the one who had cut the bullet out of Cornelius Slade and had seen the damage it had done. She prayed what she did would save his life. She'd lived her life knowing she had a father, but he was her father only on paper. She should have come to Montana as soon as she turned eighteen. That had been what Celeste suggested, but coming west had been the last thing Rose wanted to do at the time.

Even when she heard her father was dead and the Rocking M had been hers, she had been trying to decide how to get rid of it. That had been before she arrived and found out how much she enjoyed the fresh air and the people she'd met.

She knew she wasn't the woman for Cam. He neither wanted nor needed her in his life. Besides, once this was finished, she knew he would be returning to Nebraska and taking a bit of her heart with him. She hoped she would find a man who didn't care what she had once been — one the highest paid whores in St. Louis. Of course, if she didn't, she would survive.

"Rose." The sound of Dr. Myers' voice brought her out of her troubled thoughts. "Can you come in here?"

"What do you need?" She rose to her feet and went to the door of the downstairs bedroom.

"I need you to sit here with our patients while I get something to eat."

She glanced at Josh and saw him looking at her hopefully. "Would it be all right if Josh joins me? I think he needs to be with his grandfather for whatever time he has left."

"I don't think the end is anywhere near for Mr. Slade, but Josh is welcome to join you. I told you earlier, you did a good job with the surgery. There hasn't been any sign of infection, and he seems to be breathing much easier than he was when I first got here."

Rose turned to nod at Josh to find he was already on his feet. She knew he was more than ready to follow her into the room where not only his grandfather but also the marshal who had been wounded in the gun battle slept.

Rose busied herself by checking on the patient who needed her attention, while Josh seated himself next to the bed where Cornelius slept.

"Do you think the doctor is right?" he asked, when Rose turned her attention to the old man.

"His color looks a lot better. I think it's a distinct possibility he'll make a complete recovery. I doubt he ever thought he'd be involved in something like this. When your father told me about the life he led in Omaha, he said your grandfather was the head of the bank."

"Pa said it was his grief that changed him. It must have been hard for him to lose his only child, but I lost her too. She was my ma, and Pa says she loved me very much. I don't remember her other than by the picture of her that Pa has in our room. She was very beautiful."

"I'm sure she was." Rose allowed her mind to return to Cam. He was a handsome man and even though she hadn't seen the picture of his wife, she knew the woman had to be beautiful. Cam deserved nothing less. Surely, he would find a woman back in Nebraska who would love him and his son in the way they both deserved.

"Pa says I can go anywhere I want for school. I think he'd like me to go back to Nebraska to be close to his family, but I've been talking to my teacher. He went to school in Denver and says they have a good program for live-in students."

"Why Denver?"

"Because it's closer to the Rocking M, of course. I'd be able to come home for holidays and help out on the ranch. If I was in Nebraska, I wouldn't make it home during the school year."

"But you would be close to your father's family. I'm also sure your grandfather must have family in that area as well. You could get to know them."

"I haven't had any family other than the men on this ranch for most of my life. I don't really think I need them. I love everyone here and will miss them too much to be too far away."

She let the subject drop. Where Josh went to school was between Josh and his father. She had no say in it. The only thing she could do was offer financial support as well as open her library to Josh and help him to prepare for the higher education he deserved.

"Boy," the sound of Cornelius' weak voice startled Rose. "I didn't think you would still be here."

"I wanted to be here, Grandpa. I want to get to know you."

"How long has your father owned this ranch?"

The old man's question came as a surprise. "Pa told you earlier Rose is the owner of the Rocking M. Pa is just the foreman here."

Rose watched as the old man nodded his head. "I forgot."

"Why did you take the cattle?"

Cornelius closed his eyes, as though trying to decide what to tell his grandson. "I thought I could trade them back to him for you. I wanted you to take your rightful place at my side. I have so much more I can offer you than your father."

"I don't think you do. My father loves me and so did Darius. He was Rose's pa and he built this ranch. Your men killed him."

"I didn't know about that. I told them I wanted no violence, only the cattle. When I got here, I found the men I'd hired were not what I thought they were."

"Then why did you try to take Rose away with you?"

"She was like the cattle. The man I hired out here told me she was nothing more than a whore who your father brought out for his pleasure. I couldn't stand the thought of him being with a woman like that in front of you."

Rose turned away from Cornelius' bedside so Josh wouldn't see the tears forming in her eyes. All through her life she had been loved. She had been called a precious child and a paid companion. It hadn't been until she came west that she had been labeled a whore. Looking back on her life, she was exactly what Cornelius called her. She didn't ply her trade on the streets of St. Louis. Instead she had lived and worked in one of the most exclusive houses in the city. The men who came to her bed were men like Cornelius, wealthy businessmen who were looking for something outside their marriages. They certainly weren't the rough cowboys who patronized the girls who worked above the saloons in the areas of the city where proper ladies didn't dare to walk.

"I did it for you, Josh. I was going to give you the cattle so you could sell them and have money of your own."

"I have money of my own, Grandpa. Pa told me my mother had an inheritance and he invested it for my future."

"When he took the money I thought he meant to use it for his own profit. I didn't think he would put it away for you. I always considered him too shallow to think of anyone but himself. Why else would he have gotten your mother pregnant when it cost her life as well as her child? He killed my daughter and your mother, can't you see that?"

Rose could stand to listen no longer. "Cam loved your daughter. He told me losing her was the hardest thing he ever had to endure in his life. They had no reason to think she would die in childbirth."

Cornelius turned his head to look at her, anger burning in his eyes. "What do you know of my daughter? How could you understand what it is to lose a child?"

"I know her son is a fine young man and even you said he favors her. As for knowing about loss, I lost my father. It's true that I'd never met him, except through his letters, but I loved him nonetheless. Cam did what he thought was best for his son, just as my father did what was best for me.

"Maybe it wasn't right that he took Josh away from Nebraska but he was grieving just like you were. My father knew that at the age of sixteen he couldn't care for a baby on his own. He left me with people who loved me and made certain I had the best education money could buy. In times of crisis, maybe the decisions aren't always the best, but they are the ones with which we have to live."

When Cornelius made no reply, she checked and saw he had fallen asleep. She knew he needed his rest, but she couldn't help but wonder if he even heard anything she had said.

"Is he..." Josh said, unable to put voice to his worst fears.

"No, Josh, he's not dead. He's only sleeping. For now, that's the best medicine he can get, that and getting to know you. What he and his men did was wrong, but he thought he was doing it to save you. The way it sounds the cattle are safe and will eventually be returned to the Rocking M."

* * * *

Cam rode back to the ranch. If he'd stayed at the jail any longer, he would have begged George to unlock the cell so he could have choked the life out of Pollard. The man who had represented the only law in the area had been so deep in the rustling that had plagued the Rocking M there was no doubt he would hang for his crimes. Even if rustling wasn't a hanging offense, murder was, and as far as Cam was concerned, Pollard was behind Darius' murder and the wounding of Dave.

Thinking about the punishment facing Pollard, Cam turned his thoughts to Cornelius. The man was behind the rustling even if he hadn't participated in the crime. The problem was his hanging would be devastating for Josh. He'd seen the look on his son's face when he touched the old man's hand. How could he insist he be prosecuted with the men who actually took the cattle from the Rocking M and pulled the trigger that sent the bullet into Darius' body?

Dave waited for Cam when he rode into the dooryard. "Did you find out anything in town?" he asked.

"Not a damn thing, other than why Pollard got in on this. How about you? Was there anything at their hideout to tell where they're hiding our cattle?"

Dave shook his head. "All we found were a lot of empty tins from the food they ate, a pile of dirty clothes, and some cards. We poked around the area, but there wasn't a steer to be seen."

"Well, they have to be somewhere. I'm planning to talk to the rustlers upstairs. Now that Rose has them patched up, it's possible they can tell us something. It could be that they're like Nathaniel Kent and have only joined the gang recently, but it's worth a try."

Dave agreed and followed Cam to the house. It came as a surprise to find the library deserted, but once he looked in the downstairs bedroom, he saw both Rose and Josh sitting at Cornelius' bedside. As soon as Rose saw him, she got to her feet and came out to talk to him.

"How is he doing?" Cam asked.

"Better than I expected. Dr. Myers went up to check on the men I patched up and then was going to get something to eat. I would imagine you'll find him in the kitchen."

"I don't need to find him. After what happened with Dave I don't

160

know how much I trust him."

"He's a good doctor," she said in the man's defense. "He couldn't have predicted the infection that set in. Did you find out anything in town?"

Cam shook his head. Just thinking about the smug expression on Pollard's face when he talked about Darius' death made Cam want to vomit.

"What about the rustlers upstairs? Can they talk to me?"

"I don't know. They were both in a lot of pain, so I gave them some laudanum so they could sleep. It's worth a try though. We talked to Slade, and he says he hasn't sold the cattle he stole from us. We've told him a couple of times that you don't own this ranch, but if he remembers it when he wakes up is anyone's guess."

"How are our men?"

"About the same as the rustlers. Their wounds aren't life threatening, but they will be laid up for a while. It looks like I'll be riding with the men again until they can return to the saddle."

Cam wondered if he saw a hint of excitement in Rose's eyes. "Something tells me you don't think having to ride with the men is a hardship."

"It isn't. I rather enjoy it. Of all the things my father insisted Celeste teach me, I think I enjoyed the riding lessons the most. To be truthful, I never did learn to cook or keep a house like most women. Verna tried to teach me, but once she found out about my past, the lessons came to an end."

"Guess that stuff is all right if you're going to live in town and be a good little wife, but out here, you need to know a lot more. I have to admit, I rather like it when you ride with the men. To be truthful, they do too."

He thought about the way she looked in the tight britches with her breasts pushing against the plaid shirts she wore with them. He knew he wasn't the only one on the ranch who enjoyed the view when she climbed into the saddle to ride out with them.

"Am I interrupting anything?" Dr. Myers said when he entered the library.

"We were just talking about whether I can talk to the men upstairs or not," Cam replied.

"Don't see why not, but I doubt they're awake yet. They were sleeping soundly when I was up there earlier."

"I'll go with you," Rose said. "That way I can check on them."

Cam nodded and headed toward the stairs, Rose trailing behind him. At the top of the stairs, he was surprised to see Frank and Minnie in a passionate embrace.

"Ah... Cam, I... we didn't expect to see you up here."

Cam chuckled. "Apparently not. Rose wants to check on the rustlers, and I want to see if either of them can tell me anything."

Minnie smoothed down her hair as well as her wrinkled skirt before she brushed past them and ran down the stairs.

"It looks like you have an admirer," Rose said.

"I met Minnie when I first came to town. I've been in to see her several times since I got here. Now that all of this has ended, I've decided to give up the bounty hunter business and settle down. I'd just asked Minnie if she'd marry me, and she said yes."

"I'm happy for you, Frank," Rose said. "Minnie is a good woman. You know you can have a job out here if you want it."

"I understand that, but from what I figure, this town could use a good sheriff. I'm going to apply for the job. It's not like I don't have any experience in law enforcement. Minnie was the one to suggest it. She says considering Pollard's involvement with the rustlers, the town will be looking skeptically at the deputies. If they find those men are in on this, it leaves the position of sheriff unfilled."

Cam thought over what Frank just said. It made sense. He'd talked to Frank earlier and asked him about why he'd left marshals and realized it wasn't because he couldn't handle the job, it was because of his temper. Perhaps the position in town was exactly what he needed.

The upstairs bedroom was darkened, and the curtains drawn against the bright September sunlight. Even in the dim light, it was easy to make out the two men who lay not only on the bed that belonged in the room but also on the one been brought in last night in anticipation of the gunfight.

"You're the man Slade wants," the first rustler said, his eyes as large as saucers. "You look just like that picture he's got on that wanted poster."

"How long have you been riding with this bunch?" Cam demanded.

"Long enough that we'll probably hang with the rest of them, including that sheriff."

"Where are the cattle?"

The man laughed wickedly. "Now wouldn't you like to know?"

"If I tell you," the other man began, "will you speak for me so I don't hang? I haven't been riding with them all that long. Up until a week ago, I was workin' with the herd."

"I'd be willing to talk to the judge on your behalf if it means we get Miss McKinney's cattle back."

"Don't you mean your herd?" the first man said.

"No, I mean exactly what I said. This ranch as well as the cattle belonged to Darius McKinney. At least they did until Pollard's men killed him. Now they belong to his daughter, Rose."

"That whore? Pollard said she was a fancy whore from St. Louis, and you sent for her to warm your bed."

"It's true, I'm from St. Louis," Rose said, as she entered the room. "I am also the owner of this ranch. The cattle you rustled belong to me, and the man you killed was my father."

The look on the faces of the rustlers were ones of shock. "But... but we were told this man..." the first man began pointing at Cam.

"Then you were told wrong," Cam interrupted. "I have the ability to talk to the judge and ask him to go lighter on you if you tell us what we want to know. Where are the cattle that belong to the Rocking M?"

The men exchanged glances before the second man answered. "Can you keep us from the hangman's rope?"

"Only if you cooperate with us," Cam replied.

Chapter Fifteen

Rose considered the information the rustler provided as she changed her clothes. Cam left the house as soon as the rustlers talked to get the men ready to ride to where the cattle had been stashed. He'd promised to get Renegade saddled and wait for her.

"Just where do you think you're going?" Frank demanded, as she left her room.

"Cam told you what the rustlers told us. We're going out to retrieve my cattle."

"I don't think you should go out there."

"Why not?" She was getting more and more irritated with Frank and his questions.

"From what Cam told me, one of those men had been guarding the herd until last week. If they had someone guarding your steers a week ago, what makes you think there won't be someone guarding them now? There could be gunplay, and I bet you're less than handy with a handgun to say nothing of a rifle. It would be too dangerous for you to do something like this."

"Look, Frank, I can understand what you're saying, but these are my cattle and this is my ranch. I'm not going turn tail and run back to St. Louis, so I think it's high time I stood up for what's mine. I have to do this. Whether you like it or not isn't the issue here. I need you to guard these men. With luck, we'll be back by nightfall."

She turned away from him and hurried back down stairs. As she got to the foot of the stairs, she heard Cam and Josh arguing.

"Why can't I ride with you to bring back the herd, Pa?"

"I told you, it was because I don't want you in the middle of this thing. It's too dangerous."

"But Rose is going, why can't I?"

"They're Rose's cattle, it's her right. Besides she's my boss, and I know better than to cross her."

"Your father is right," Rose said as she entered the room. "I need you to stay here. If anything happens to us, someone has to know where we went and why. You stay here with your grandfather, and we'll be back before you know it."

To her relief, Josh stopped his protesting. She and Cam were able to leave the house without any further argument.

"What the hell was that all about?" Cam demanded as they made their way to the corral. "What kind of trouble are you expecting?"

"The same kind you are," she replied. "Frank reminded me if there were guards with the herd last week, there will be guards there now. We could be riding into an ambush. I'm no good with a gun, but you and the others are. Be sure we have enough fire power before we go riding there."

"Then you should stay behind."

"Don't be silly. You said it in the house. I'm the owner of the ranch as well as the cattle. As such, it's my right to be there, and as my employee, you have no reason to argue with me."

"Maybe not, but I should take you over my knee and give you the spanking you were probably denied as a child."

"Just try it and you might find you bit off more than you can chew. We can talk about all this when we get back. This is something we have to do before any guards get wind of the fact we raided the hideout. We don't want them running off the herd before we get them back."

By the time they got to the corral, Dave was waiting for them. "What's up? Did you find out anything from the rustlers at the house?"

"We sure did," Cam said. "Get everyone together. I know where the herd is. We're going out to get them, and there could be gunplay. Make sure everyone is armed and ready to ride in five minutes."

Rose grabbed her tack and began to saddle Renegade. She knew they were riding into trouble, but she didn't care. The raid on the outlaw camp had netted them the people responsible for her father's death. The only thing left was for her to get back the stock for which he gave his life.

* * * *

To reach the canyon where the cattle were hidden took an hour of hard riding. Once close, Cam motioned for the men to wait, while he took Dave with him to scout out the men guarding the cattle.

Once he was satisfied there would be little problem in getting the steers back, he returned to where Rose waited with the men. "This is going to be easier than I thought," Cam said once he dismounted.

"What are we up against?" Adam said.

"There are three guards, one in the front and two in the rear. It doesn't look like they know about our raid on the hideout. They're not heavily armed. I say half of us go around the back and the rest of us take the front."

"What about me?" Rose said.

"Much as I hate to do this, I think you'd make the perfect decoy for the guy in the front. I want you to ride in and tell him the boss sent you out here to give the boys a reward for the job they're doing."

Rose smiled broadly. "Why Mr. Blake, are you saying you want me to ply the trade I learned in St. Louis?"

He didn't like the way she spoke. It was like she was taunting him. "I want you to play pretend. Do you understand?"

"Perfectly. It should work, just as long as I have plenty of men behind me. In case you've forgotten, that part of my life is over."

He nodded and watched as she unbuttoned her shirt far enough down so the man guarding the front of the herd would get a good look at the mounds of her perfect breasts. Once she finished with that, she took off her hat and unpinned her hair to let it fall loosely around her shoulders in reddish brown waves.

To Cam's surprise, his response to her was one he hadn't had since he married Martha. This woman was special. He'd visited whores before, when the ache in his groin was more than he could stand. Even though he'd relieved his needs, he never felt the way he did now. Cam wished he could be with the men guarding Rose to make certain the man she would be seducing kept his hands to himself. Instead, he needed to stay with the men who were taking out the two guards at the rear of the herd.

* * * *

Rose had never played the seductress in her life. What she did at the Purple Moon was entertain the paying customers. She didn't have to sell herself, because they knew exactly what they wanted and she'd been trained to give it. This would be all new to her.

Confident the men behind her were close enough to help her out if she got in trouble, she rode up to the guard.

"Stop where you are," the man shouted. "Who are you?"

Her heart beat out a frantic rhythm, as she raised her hands and rode closer to the man. "I'm not armed," she called out. "Your boss sent me here to take care of you boys. You're first."

"What boss?" the man asked without lowering his gun.

"Why honey," she drawled, "I was just servicing Amos and Cornelius and were so pleased with me, they told me where to find you boys. They told me you'd been doing such a good job you deserved to be rewarded. I agreed with them. I'm sure we can find a place to take care of business away from these smelly cattle."

The man motioned her to dismount and approach him. Once she was close enough, he pulled her into his arms and covered her mouth with his. The stink of his fetid breath made her sick to her stomach. While he was preoccupied with kissing her roughly and groping her breast, she watched as two of her men came up behind him.

Once they were in place, she brought her knee up into the man's groin. Before he could howl in pain, Dave brought his gun down on the back of the man's head.

"Tie him up," she ordered after wiping the man's saliva from her mouth with the sleeve of her shirt. "We can pick him up on the way back. Let's go and see if we can help Cam and the others. Adam, I'd like you and two men you pick to stay here and guard the herd. You'll know when we start driving them from behind."

Adam nodded and selected the two men he wanted with him. As Rose remounted Renegade, she saw the unconscious outlaw being tied and gagged and slung over his horse in order to take him back to the ranch.

* * * *

Cam rode around the rim of the canyon to where he and Dave saw the two rustlers guarding the back of the herd. He wished he hadn't sent Rose in as a decoy. What if something went wrong? What if the man raped her before he could be stopped? If he'd hurt her or worse yet shot her? Of course, he hadn't heard any shots fired, so he could at least put that fear behind him.

Below them, the two men sat at a campfire with their backs to the area where Cam and his men waited to ambush them. As silently as possible, they crept close enough to easily overtake the men who were oblivious to their presence.

Cam nodded to the man on his left. Together, they brought their gun butts down on the back of each man's head.

"Ours is secured," Rose called as she rode in to join him. "Looks like yours are too. Once you get them on their horses, we're ready to move this herd. I've sent someone back to tell Adam we're going home."

Cam stared at Rose. She hadn't taken time to button up her shirt and her face was flushed with the excitement of a job well done. Added to her hair hanging around her shoulders the look made her more appealing than she had been earlier.

He didn't care that their men surrounded them. He suddenly wanted her in his arms to assure himself she was indeed untouched.

Pulling her close to him, he felt her body melt against his own. When he bent to kiss her, she put up no resistance. He'd forgotten how much he enjoyed kissing a beautiful woman. The feelings filling his body were ones he hadn't felt since he lost Martha.

Only the snickers of their men prompted him to break the embrace. "I... I don't know what came over me," he apologized.

"I do. We've both been fighting this for weeks," she whispered so softly only he could hear.

He knew she was right. He wanted her, but she was far beyond his reach. He had a son to consider and family in Nebraska he needed to see. He couldn't fall in love with his boss and have everyone think it was only so that he could have more of an interest in the Rocking M than just being the foreman.

While the other men rode to the head of the herd, Rose stayed behind with Cam. He wondered if their kiss had unnerved her as much as it had him.

After giving the men enough time to get back to the head of the herd, he urged the last of the cattle forward. Even the dust couldn't take away the warmth of the kiss he had just shared with Rose. He could only pray the long ride back to the ranch would help the ache that tugged at his heart.

He was glad they'd decided Dave should ride back to the ranch and let Josh and Frank know they had the cattle back before people started to get concerned about them. It would be several hours before they could get the slow moving herd back to the safety of the ranch.

Chapter Sixteen

Rose was surprised at how quickly the circuit judge arrived for the trial of the rustlers. The first man to be tried was Amos Pollard. The trial lasted only two hours before Amos started to rant and rave about how Darius deserved to be killed because he had fired him several years earlier. After that outburst, the jury, made up of the townspeople, took only twenty minutes to find him guilty of murder, attempted murder, and rustling and sentence him to hang.

When the verdict came, Rose felt her stomach begin to knot. The next trial would be for Cornelius. Once it was over, Cam would be one step closer to leaving Montana and walking out of her life forever.

Josh sat beside her clenching and unclenching his fists in frustration. Although weak, Cornelius was dressed impeccably and sat with the dignity of any wealthy man she'd ever known.

When the judge banged his gavel for the trial to begin, Rose watched as Cam get to his feet.

"Before this trial starts, your honor, I would like to say something."

"Since you and Miss McKinney are the injured parties here, I have no idea what you want to say, but I will allow you to say it."

"Thank you, your honor. To begin with, Mr. Slade is the father of my late wife. When she died, we both did things we weren't proud of. They were done out of grief. He wanted my son taken away from me and I wanted to keep him with me. In his mind my wife's death during childbirth was my fault.

"It took almost ten years for anyone to contact him regarding the wanted poster he had put out on me. When he did get an answer it was from Amos Pollard. Amos told him I was the owner of the Rocking M. It was Cornelius' contention that if he rustled the cattle, I would allow him to have my son in return for the herd. He had no idea Amos was getting revenge on both Darius and myself. Cornelius is an old man and his reason has been clouded by grief. Even though he was behind this, he did not profit from the theft of the cattle and they have been returned to the Rocking M. He was also not aware of the murder of Darius McKinney. I am certain he has not been in his right mind since the death of his daughter and granddaughter. I'm asking that he pay a fine to Miss McKinney but not be made to spend the remainder of his life in jail or be hanged."

There was a hush in the courtroom, and Rose felt Josh reach for her hand and hold it tightly.

"Do you agree with this, Miss McKinney?" the judge said.

Josh let go of her hand before she got to her feet and walked to the front of the courtroom. "Yes your honor, I do. Mr. Slade did not have all the facts about ownership of the Rocking M. He thought he was doing something that would help him gain custody of his grandson. I spent my entire life estranged from my father. In all good conscience, I can't deprive Josh of his grandfather."

The judge sat quietly for a moment, as though contemplating what he was going to do with the statements she and Cam had made.

"This is, indeed, the most unique case I've ever had," he finally said.

"Let me ask you, Mr. Slade, have you spoken either with Mr. Blake or Miss McKinney about what they just told the court."

Laboriously, Cornelius got to his feet. Rose could see the pain his injury caused in his eyes as he stood. "No sir, I haven't. I only wanted my grandson. It has been ten years since my daughter died and my former son-in-law took the boy from me. I didn't know what was going on here until I came out at Mr. Pollard's request. When I got here, he told me my son-in-law had brought in a fancy woman from St. Louis and was flaunting his relationship with her in front of my grandson. Since the loss of his cattle hadn't gotten me my grandson, I figured maybe he would swap him for his woman. I didn't know until later she was the owner of the ranch and he was merely her foreman. I am sorry for any pain I have caused either of them. The only good thing to come out of this has been that I have gotten to know my grandson. I misjudged his father. He has done a good job with the boy. He's a fine young man who has made me very proud."

The judge indicated Cornelius should sit down. "Miss McKinney, since the crimes this man is accused of were against you and your property, do you have a suggestion of how I should sentence him?"

Rose ran her tongue over her lips. "Like I said, I can't deprive Josh of his grandfather. I will take full responsibility for him and give him a place to live on the Rocking M until he recuperates from his wounds. When he is well, if he wants to return to Nebraska, I won't stop him. He can check in with the law enforcement authorities there. I'm certain Cam will see to it that he does what he is supposed to once they are back in Nebraska."

The judge took a moment to consider his decision. While he thought about what he was going to do, the courtroom buzzed like a hen house full of chickens.

Rose went back to where Josh was sitting with Cam by her side. "I can't believe the two of you said those things," Josh said, once they were all seated together.

"The man is your grandfather," Cam assured his son. "I was wrong to take you away from him ten years ago, especially since I knew how much he loved you. He's not really an evil man. Rose and I talked about this and we want you to know him."

Rose knew how Cam agonized about what he would say today. Last night they had talked until almost midnight, trying to decide what they should do about Cornelius. Rose knew what it was like not to know her father, she wanted a reconciliation between Cam, Josh, and Cornelius.

"I have thought long and hard about this," the judge said, after banging his gavel several times for order. "I am inclined to take what Mr. Blake and Miss McKinney told us to heart. I have talked to the marshals who have been in charge of Mr. Slade. They have told me when it comes to Mr. Blake and his son, his mind is not clear. You are a generous woman, Miss McKinney. I will release Mr. Slade into your custody. When and if, he should decide to return to Nebraska, you will both appear before me prior to his leaving."

Josh clasped Rose's hand in gratitude. She was surprised when Cam put his arm around her shoulder and leaned close to whisper in her ear.

"Thank you, Rose. This means a lot to Josh."

Did it mean a lot to Cam, too?

* * * *

Cam reluctantly left Rose's side to bring Cornelius back to where they were sitting. The lost look in his former father-in-law's eyes told him the man didn't completely understand what had just happened.

"Why did she do this for me?" Cornelius said.

"Because she's a good woman. She thinks highly of Josh and wants him to get to know you. When I first told him about the wanted poster you put out on me, he asked me why you did it. I told him it was your form of grief, just as my running away and changing my name was mine. No matter what, we're family, and it's time we got to know each other again."

"Are you really going back to Omaha?"

"I honestly don't know. I want to see my mother and my brother, but I had a wire from them yesterday saying they are coming out here. I've made a new life for myself and I can't imagine leaving it behind."

"Would you be content to stay here as a ranch foreman when you are so much better suited to working in a bank the way you did when you and Martha were married?"

"I'm not the same man I was then. There I was Addison Cameron. Here, I'm Cameron Blake and I assure you our names have been legally changed. I realize now I enjoy working on the ranch and doing things with my hands."

* * * *

As much as Rose wanted to return to the Rocking M, she knew she had to stay for the trial of the rustlers. The two men who had given Cam the information of where they could find the herd had already made a deal with the judge allowing them to serve shorter sentences. The others were facing long jail terms, and those who had been involved in her father's murder faced the hangman's noose.

By the end of the day, five of the men were set to hang with Amos Pollard the next day at noon, and the rest would be going to prison for long terms. For Rose, the sentences were just, but they didn't bring back her father or change the fact everyone on the Rocking M suffered because of their actions.

"Are you ready to go home?" Cam asked, once the trial ended.

"I most certainly am. I'm sure Cookie has supper ready."

"I'm not a man without means, dear lady," Cornelius said. "Please allow me to take you and Addison, along with Joshua, out to dinner."

Rose exchanged a glance with Cam.

"I think that would be nice, Mr. Slade," Rose replied. "I know you have always thought of Cam as Addison, but he told you today he has legally changed his name. Here he is known as Cam, and I would appreciate it if you would remember that."

As they left the courthouse, Rose felt as though she was with her family. If only it would be the same way forever, but she knew it was far too much to ask. Instead she would take what she could get while she could get it.

At the café, she ignored the curious looks sent in their direction. It was the first time she had actually come to town since arriving at the Rocking M. There had been far too much work to do at the ranch. She knew the people in town had heard all the terrible rumors Amos Pollard spread about her. She wondered if the modest attire she'd worn to the trial, as well as the generous offer she had made to Cornelius, surprised them.

Cam and Josh each ordered a well-done steak. She opted for chicken and dumplings, but Cornelius studied the menu as though he had no idea what to order for himself.

"I remember how much you always liked Martha's roast beef," Cam said. "I been told the roast beef they serve here is very good."

"Have you ever had it?" Cornelius said.

"Well, no. I prefer a good steak. Besides, until today, the roast beef always brought back memories of Martha. Now I realize I have to put her to rest. It's time for all of us to move on."

Throughout the meal, Rose watched Cornelius intently. At the ranch she had thought his disorientation had been due to his wound, but now she saw things that bothered her. Cam had been right. The man was not in his right mind. More than likely, the shock of losing his daughter and granddaughter hastened the onset of the mental ramblings of a much older man. She was glad she'd agreed he shouldn't be sent to prison or, worse yet, hanged for his planning of the rustling on the Rocking M.

To her surprise, at one point during the meal, he reached across the table to take Josh's hand in his. "You are my only heir, Joshua. I have left everything I own to you. As soon as I can, I will contact my lawyer and have your name changed to Joshua Blake. I never want you to have to worry about where the money will come from for your education."

"What about your bank?" Cam said.

"I sold that several years ago. When I was tracking you, I couldn't be there on a regular basis to carry on business. I know now I was wrong about you, but that is in the past. I hope with the time I have left, we can once again become family."

Rose smiled at the exchange. The man sounded as normal as any older man facing the end of his life. The slip into normalcy of the situation soon was gone, as he began to talk about how Martha should be having supper with them tonight.

With the end of the meal, Cornelius made a big display of reaching for his wallet, only to find it was empty. Rather than embarrass the older man, Rose reached for the check.

"Tonight you will be my guests," Rose said, as she reached into her bag for enough money to cover the cost of their meal.

"It isn't right for a woman to pay for dinner," Cornelius protested "I am certain my credit is good enough in this establishment that they will put our meal on my bill."

"Please," Rose pleaded. "Since I've gotten my cattle back, I can certainly afford it."

After paying the bill, they went out to the carriage they'd brought into town in anticipation of having Cornelius with them on the return trip to the ranch. Rose was content to sit in the second seat of the carriage with Cam while Cornelius shared the front seat with Josh, who proudly drove out of town and toward the ranch.

She smiled when Cam put his arm around her shoulder. "Did you notice the way Cornelius was acting?" he whispered.

"I've seen men like that in St. Louis. It's an affliction of many older men. They lose touch with the present and live in the past. It's not surprising considering his grief over the loss of his daughter. I'm certain it hastened his confusion. Thank goodness we asked for leniency from the judge."

"I watched him at supper as well as at the trial," Cam replied, his voice still low enough only Rose could hear what he was saying. "He's not well. I'm glad you agreed with me about letting him get to know Josh during the time he has left in life."

"I wondered about his health when I was caring for him after the shooting. The trip from Omaha to Montana has taken its toll. I'm certain he doesn't have much longer to live. At least he will be getting to know his grandson."

They rode in silence for several minutes. As they did, she remembered Cam saying something about his brother and mother coming to Montana.

"When will your family be arriving?"

"They should be here by the first of next week. I asked around and was told they could get rooms at the boarding house."

"They'll do no such thing. The ranch house has more than enough space. You know how many bedrooms there are upstairs. I have no idea why my father built such a large home for himself, but you'll have to agree with me there's no need for your family to stay in town when they can stay with us."

"You're amazing. I'm certain they'll only be here for a short visit. I was actually surprised when my brother said he was leaving his store in his son's hands to bring my mother out here. If they had waited until Christmas, I had planned to take Josh to Nebraska so he could meet his family."

Rose felt her heart start to break. Was this the way he intended to tell her she should start looking for a new foreman? If he had been planning to go to Nebraska at Christmas, would he be looking for a position where he could use the education he'd received as a young man? There was no reason for her to expect him to stay on now that no one was looking for him because of the wanted poster that Cornelius had put out.

Chapter Seventeen

Rose enjoyed having a full house. Although Cam's brother, Brock, was older, they looked so much alike it was uncanny. She especially liked Cam's mother. At first, she didn't want to put Rose out by staying at the ranch, but finally agreed provided she could do the cooking for all the guests at the house.

Rather than riding with the men, as she had planned, Rose spent her days with Nancy learning the art of cooking.

"You're a good student, my dear," Nancy observed.

"These are things I should have learned as a child, but..." she really didn't want to talk about growing up at the Purple Moon and learning the facts of life along with the studies her father insisted she undertake, instead of what was needed to make a home.

"You don't have to say anything more," Nancy said, patting Rose's arm reassuringly. "Addison—I mean Cam, told me all about your past."

"But we agreed he wouldn't tell you," Rose protested.

"Cam and I don't keep secrets from each other. I'm his mother. I knew he was keeping something from me, that's why he finally told me. Even though I don't agree with the kind of lifestyle you lived, I can see you were raised with love. Just the way you have taken Cornelius into your home after what he did to you proves you have a good heart."

"It's strange, when I first came here all I could think of was how quickly I could sell this ranch and go back to St. Louis. I missed the women who had been my surrogate mothers more than I did the lifestyle. I don't know when I began to change my mind, but I do know I don't want to go back there. I've come to love this ranch. I may change my mind after the first winter here, but I doubt it."

"I'm glad. I think you've been a very positive influence in my grandson's life."

Her statement took Rose by surprise. "When I first came, Cam forbid Josh to even come up to the house."

"That was because he hadn't had time to get to know you. You have to admit your background had to be intimidating to him. He knows you now, and I know he admires you as much as we do."

When Rose made no response, Nancy stopped what she was doing and came to her side. "What's wrong?"

She wondered if she had any right to talk about her worst fears. Throwing caution to the wind, she put voice to the thing that terrified her the most. "Once Josh's formal schooling is finished here, I'm afraid Cam will be moving back to Omaha. With his education, he won't have any problem getting a good job."

"Oh, is that what's worrying you?"

Rose nodded, unable to stop the tears beginning to run down her cheeks.

"We've talked about this for years. When my son changed his name, it nearly broke my heart, but I understood why he did it. I knew, from his letters, there was more to it than changing his name. He told us he had found a new life here, and it was one he enjoyed. I doubt he'll ever be content to be stuck behind a desk now he's had the freedom to ride the range and do something with his hands. You've fallen in love with him, haven't you?"

"Am I that easy to read?"

"Not to a man, but women know these things. It's been a long time since my son had a woman who loved him. Josh isn't the only one who has benefited from being here with you. Almost as soon as you arrived, I could see a difference in the letters Cam was sending home. He's been writing once a week ever since he arrived at the Rocking M and changed his name. It broke my heart to realize how depressed he really was. Since you've arrived, I could tell he was smiling more. At first, he was concerned about your influence on Josh, but then the tone of his letters changed completely."

Rose prayed what Nancy just told her was true and not something he told his mother to put her mind at ease.

"Well, now, dinner is ready. Why don't you go and get Cam and Josh? I'm sure they're in the library with Brock. I'll go in and get Cornelius."

Rose found Cam, Josh, and Brock in the library and told them to come out to the kitchen to eat. Before they could get to their feet, Nancy's scream turned their attention to the downstairs bedroom.

Rose was the first one to reach Cornelius' bedside. "I couldn't wake him, and he feels so cold," Nancy said, her voice flat and emotionless.

Instinctively, Rose put her fingers against the pulse point in the old man's neck. When she felt nothing, she carefully pulled the sheet over his face. "It looks as though he died in his sleep," she said.

Behind her she heard Josh stifle a sob. "It's all right to cry, Josh," Cam said. "I wish you could have known him when he was in his right mind. He was a shrewd businessman. I'm certain you would have liked him a lot better then."

Rose shed her own tears. They were the ones she should have shed for her father, but she had only known him on paper. For her, he had never been a flesh and blood man until she arrived at the ranch he had built and left in her care. Cornelius had been real. He was a man who had lost his mind because of his grief and at the end of his life couldn't tell past from present.

"Do you think we should make arrangements to take him back to Omaha with us for burial?" Brock asked.

"No," Josh replied, his voice heavy with tears. "He should be buried here, by us."

Rose wished Cam would take his son's words to heart, but his family was in Nebraska. It would be too much for her to ask to have them stay in Montana just to be close to her.

"I agree with Josh," Cam said. "With the weather so unseasonably warm, taking him back to Nebraska would be out of the question. With Martha gone, there's no one there for him. No matter where his remains are buried, he isn't there. What was Cornelius Slade is with his wife and daughter now. It's possible he's been dead since the day he buried Martha."

"He can be buried in the cemetery behind the house, alongside my father," Rose said. "I'll send someone into town to get Frank. He'll want to know what's happened."

Rose left the family to be alone with Cornelius. Once outside, she saw Adam and hurried to tell him what had happened, and that she wanted him to go into town and get Frank and the undertaker to come to the ranch.

Once she returned to the house, she found everyone waiting for her in the kitchen. The one who seemed to be the most upset about the old man's death was Josh. Rose understood his grief. She also understood the reasoning behind Cam's calm demeanor. For the past ten years he had lived in fear of the man who had once been his father-in-law. There hadn't been enough time for the two of them to mend the rift that separated them for so many years.

* * * *

The funeral was held the next morning. Frank O'Brien and George Wilson joined the mourners. Between Frank and George they'd found Amos' deputy was in on the rustling and, after Amos made his trip to the gallows, his deputy followed him.

After Frank told his side of why he had been fired, George did some investigation and found the story to be true. Once Frank's story was confirmed, George did everything in his power to convince the town fathers to hire Frank to replace Pollard.

"I didn't think I'd still be here when Cornelius died," George said once they returned to the house to eat the meal Nancy prepared.

"I knew he wasn't well," Rose replied. "After the trial he seemed to fade quickly. I think the only thing keeping him alive was finding his grandson."

"Speaking of that," Frank said. "The kid from the telegraph office stopped me when I was leaving town. He said Cam sent a wire to Omaha last night, and an answer arrived today. I told him I'd bring it out with me."

Rose watched as Cam opened the wire. Once he scanned it, he broke into a wide grin.

"Well, I'll be damned. I honestly didn't believe Cornelius about the inheritance for Josh. I went into town yesterday and sent a wire to his lawyer to tell him about Cornelius' death. This says he will be catching the next train out here with the paperwork for Josh to receive the money set aside for him. It looks like you're going to be a very wealthy young man, son."

Josh made no response. Rose knew exactly how he felt. Money meant security, but it didn't bring back the man who left it to him.

Chapter Eighteen

Cam was shocked when the lawyer arrived with the paperwork for Josh's inheritance. He knew Cornelius had money, but over the past ten years it had been entirely possible he'd spent most of it trying to get Josh as his own. The amount of money left to Josh was enough so he wouldn't have to work for the remainder of his life if he decided he wanted to do that.

"I don't really want the money, Pa," Josh said once the lawyer read the contents of Cornelius' will.

"You have no obligation to take the money," the lawyer said. "What I want you to consider is grandfather wanted you to have the money. At this point in your life, I know you don't think you want it, but if you agree, I will continue to invest it for you. The day may come when you might need the money for your education or even for a place of your own. When that happens, it will be waiting for you. With the proper investment you may even earn more money with it."

"The man makes a lot of sense," Rose said. "When I was growing up, my father sent money for my care and education. Celeste refused to take any of it for my care and spent only what was necessary on my education. When I came of age, I had a sizable bank account."

"Can you invest it for me, Rose?"

Josh's question came as a surprise to Cam. The lawyer was a reputable man, so why would his son want Rose to invest his money for him?

"This man has done a good job with your money so far. I looked over the papers he brought with him and your investments are making money for you. I think he will continue to do the best he can for you. Living in Omaha he has the ability to find better investments than I can find here. That's the reason I left my money in St. Louis. I knew the lawyer who has been looking out for my best interests over the years would continue to do so."

Josh remained quiet as though considering what Rose had just told him. "I guess you're right, Rose. I just didn't think it was best to have my investments so far away from home."

Cam thought long and hard about his son calling the Rocking M home. Over the past few days he'd considered returning to Omaha to be closer to his family now he realized his mother and brother were his family, but Josh considered the people at the Rocking M family as well. He had grown up living and working with the hands as well as Darius for the last seven years. It was apparent now Rose had become an important part of his life as well. Could he take his son away from the only stable home he'd known since his mother died?

* * * *

Rose was pleased when Josh asked her to invest his money for him, but she knew the lawyer would do a much better job for him. What she wondered was what Cam thought of the question. Hearing Josh call the Rocking M home warmed her heart, but did Cam feel the same way? After meeting Nancy and Brock, she doubted it. Cam missed his family and with good reason. She knew she would miss Nancy once she and Brock went back to Omaha with the lawyer at the end of the week.

She was glad Josh had listened to her and signed the paperwork to allow Cornelius' lawyer to continue overseeing the money he had been left.

By the end of the week, everyone left the ranch to return to Nebraska. With the house empty for the first time in weeks, Rose felt terribly lonely. Rather than stay in the house alone, she put on her britches and headed out to the cookhouse.

"Are you going to ride with us today, Rose?" Cam asked when she joined the men for breakfast.

"I was considering it. We're still running short handed. With everyone gone from the house, I decided it would be a good time for me to get back to work."

"I'd like that," Cam replied.

Rose smiled, pleased he wasn't protesting her right to be riding with the men. As she thought of something more to say, Josh came into the cookhouse.

"Haven't you left for school yet?" Cam inquired.

"I'm all ready, Pa, but I found something in the book Rose loaned me last night. I took it up to the house to give it to her, but she wasn't there. I thought she might be here having breakfast."

What Josh said piqued Rose's interest. "What did you find?"

Josh opened the book and produced an envelope with her name on it. As soon as she took it from him, she recognized the handwriting of her father. Just seeing her name written in his familiar hand made a lump form in her throat. Over the years she had read and reread her father's letters. Now, months after his death, this new letter had the same effect on her that it had when she was a child.

"Thank you Josh. I guess my father wrote me one last letter."

Rose waited until Josh left before she found an empty seat and sat down to read the letter her father had left for her to find. She remembered the book Josh had borrowed the night before. It had been a volume of Dickens' A Tale of Two Cities. Had things not been so hectic since her arrival, she would have sat down and read it for herself and found her father's last letter.

My dear Rose,

If you are reading this letter, I am already dead. I had prayed someday you would come to me on your own, but I can understand your reluctance to come to this untamed country.

By the terms of my will, the Rocking M will belong to you only if you stick it out for a year. It may sound harsh, but I am praying you love it here as much as I do.

Before you make your decision, there is something I want you to know. I loved your mother with all my heart. As soon as she turned sixteen, I was going to ask her father for her hand in marriage.

Unfortunately, an older man took advantage of her and left her carrying his child. That child was you. Her parents were so embarrassed they sent her away.

It took me several months to find her, but when I did it was too late. When Celeste asked if I was your father, I lied and said I was. Once I held you it was like looking into Josie's beautiful face.

I wanted to take you with me, but Celeste knew I was too young to care for a newborn. She promised me she would raise you like her own. When she asked what I was going to do, I told her I was going west, and I wanted a ranch of my own. She said she wanted to help me out.

She promised me when I found a place I wanted to buy, she would advance me the money to buy it. Her condition was I was to build my ranch and leave it to you on my death. She wanted more for you than a life in the Purple Moon.

She was the one who suggested the courses you should take and the training she was going to arrange for you. I paid her back completely and made certain you never wanted for anything.

Now I am certain you want to know who really fathered you. It pains me to say you are not my daughter, but instead you are my sister. My own father raped your mother. Since I learned the truth, I have not spoken to him.

I have no idea if he still lives in Missouri or if he burns in hell for what he did to your mother. The only good thing to come from it was you. I am so proud of you and have never thought of you in any way but as my daughter. If your mother had lived, we would have married, and this would never have been revealed.

As it is, I feel you have the right to know the truth. In my heart, I am your father, but in reality we are brother and sister. Never forget I have loved you since the first moment I held you in my arms and your little hand curled around my finger.

I pray you will love the Rocking M as much as I have and you will make it prosper. The one thing I ask is that you never forget the love Celeste gave you throughout your life.

Rose's tears blurred the words on the page, but not so much that she missed the change in her father's signature. Instead of Your Loving Father, it read, Your Loving Brother. His change in status hit her hard.

What kind of a man raped a child? Knowing of the rape, how much courage had it taken Darius to go in search of Josie and lay claim to her child?

When she'd been a little girl, she had often questioned her father's love. Now she realized how deep that love had run. Often she'd heard to father a child had taken only a few moments of the physical act, but to be a father took a special man. Darius McKinney had been that man to her.

"Are you all right?" Cam asked, putting his hand on her arm comfortingly.

Rose shook her head and handed him the letter.

"Can this be right?" he questioned after scanning the contests of her letter.

"I'm afraid so. Everything I've believed about my life has been a lie. As my father, I loved him. As my brother, I now realize what an exceptional man he was."

"Of anyone on this ranch, I understand what you mean by living a lie," Cam said. "What are you going to do now?"

She knew it was a foolish question, but at the same time, she realized he had to say something. "I honestly don't know. It's been over twenty-five years. Could there be any of them left? Do they care?"

"You'll never know if you don't ask. Since the letter was in a book, it's entirely possible the information you need is in the library as well."

"I suppose you're right. I'll go up to the house and start looking right away. Of course, that means you'll have to do without me today."

"Whoa, not so fast. You've waited twenty-five years for this information, if it's in the house, it will still be there after you get something to eat."

Rose took a moment to comprehend what Cam just said. The letter had taken all thoughts of food from her mind. As though Cam's words brought back her earlier hunger, her stomach began growling. Obediently, she sat down in time for Cookie to put a plate of hot food in front of her.

"You go ahead and eat," Cam said. "I've got something to take care of."

As Cam left her side, Rose felt abandoned, but at the same time relieved. Like a good meal, the information she'd just received would need time to digest. If she discovered the name of her true father or her maternal grandparents, would they be happy to hear from her or would they not remember the woman who gave birth to her or the man who claimed her as his daughter?

Her mind spun with so many questions, she ate automatically, hardly tasting the food on her plate. Thoughts of who would be the most help to her rushed through her mind. She could send a wire to Celeste, but dismissed the idea. Instead, she decided to ask for help from the U.S. Marshal's office in St. Louis. With George still in town helping Frank establish an effective sheriff's office and restore order to the chaos Amos had left behind, she decided she should start there.

"I'm going to come up to the house to help you," Cam said, as he slid onto the bench beside her.

"Shouldn't you be out with the men today? I thought you had to get the branding finished so you could drive the remainder of the herd to the railhead next week."

"Dave can handle the branding. We're almost done, so it will probably be finished by noon. I think there's some bad weather moving in, so they won't be out there too long. It's more important for me to stay here and help you today. You know what they say, two sets of eyes are better than one."

She looked at him, pleased he wanted to help, but confused about his motive. "That's funny. I've never heard that saying before."

"Could be because I just made it up. I have a feeling what you're looking for could turn into a needle in a haystack. Besides, it will give me some time to spend alone with you."

Cam's words came as a surprise. Ever since her attempted kidnapping, she had longed to be alone with him. To hear Cam put voice to her thoughts made her wonder if she could hope for a future for the two of them.

"I'd like that," Rose said, hoping she didn't sound overly anxious.

After taking her plate back to the cook, Rose and Cam left and walked across the yard to the main house. Entering through the front door, she experienced a completely different feeling than she'd ever had before reading the letter she now clutched in her hand.

From the letters she'd received all her life, she knew every inch of the house and equated it with her father. Now everything was different. The house was the same but now she knew the man who built it was her half brother. Just as the letter confirming her parentage had been hidden, she knew the answers she sought would be in similar hiding places.

Outside a cold wind blew from the north. Being from St. Louis, she wasn't used to falling temperatures in October, but Cam assured her it was normal here. It was one reason the men were anxious to finish the branding. Driving the steers to market would be much easier without having to contend with snow.

"It's cold in here," Cam observed when they entered the library. "It's no wonder; the fire is just about out. I'll add a couple of pieces of wood, and it will warm up in no time."

Rose appreciated his take-charge attitude. Looking around the room, she was defeated. A large roll-top desk dominated one wall while another contained a floor to ceiling bookcase filled with dozens of volumes. Any one of them could hide the names of her family.

By eleven, Rose had searched the entire contents of the desk, while Cam had been through every book on the top two shelves that lined the wall.

"I think I've found it," Cam shouted, bringing Rose to full attention. "Why didn't I think of it before?"

"What did you find?"

"It's a family Bible, but it was hidden behind some of these books."

Rose watched as Cam came toward her carrying the black leather bound book in his hands. In St. Louis, Celeste made certain Rose went to church and Sunday school on a regular basis. In St. Louis, it was the cook and her husband who took her to services and tucked her in at night after she said her prayers. Of course, once she was grown, she'd opted not to accompany them.

Just touching the book brought back the happy memories of the time she spent with Alice and Pete. She'd abandoned the practice of going to church because it no longer had fit into her lifestyle, but the argument made little sense now. Just holding the book in her hands brought more peace than she'd felt in a long time. Somewhere within its pages, she knew she would find the answers she sought.

She laid the book on the desk and opened it to the place between the Old and New Testaments. Just as she thought, the page to which she opened contained a family tree. Under the names of Richard and Ardella McKinney, were listed four children, the oldest being Darius. Looking down the list of names, she was disappointed not to see her name listed.

"At least I have the names of my other brothers and sisters," she said, absently turning the page. As she did, she found a single piece of paper folded in half and tucked between the pages.

Opening it, she saw another family tree. Under the heading of Father was the name Richard McKinney and under Mother was Josie Sullivan. Beneath them she saw her own name listed along with her date of birth. Lower on the paper were the names of her mother's parents, brother, and sisters, along with the name of the town closest to the family farm. To her surprise, they lived only a few miles from St. Louis. Her mother's family as well as her father, had been within driving distance, and they never even knew she existed.

At the very bottom of the page was a message for Rose in Darius' handwriting.

My dear Rose
Within these pages are the names of our family. I was sixteen when I learned the truth and left home. I give you this information now in the hopes you will have the courage I lacked and decide to contact them. Now you have found this, all the secrets are out in the open. I wish you luck in finding the family denied you for so long.—Darius.

He'd signed the note with his given name, which saddened her. No matter what she found out today, she knew he would always be her father. Whether father or brother, she loved him with all her heart. Of all the gifts he had given her over the years, this was the most important of them all.

* * * *

Cam knew Rose needed to check on the information she'd found in the Bible. Because of the wind that howled outside, he insisted they take the closed carriage into town. Even with the heavy buffalo robes around them, it would be a cold ride. It always amazed him how early the cold weather set in this far north.

"I think we should go down to the cookhouse and get some dinner before we go into town," Rose suggested. "Business like this is best conducted on a full stomach. Besides, if we leave later we can stop at the school and pick up Josh. I don't like the idea of him riding home in the cold."

Cam agreed. It saddened him that in the excitement of finding the information on Rose's family, he had forgotten his son. With the change in weather it was entirely possible they could see the first snow of the season before they arrived back home.

When they stepped into the warmth of the cookhouse, Cam was relieved to see the crew there eating the noon meal.

"We finished up as fast as we could," Dave said when they sat down across from him. "With this weather setting in I wanted to get the men back here as soon as possible."

"That was a good idea," Cam agreed. "It's good to have the branding done. Let's hope we won't get much snow out of this storm and we can drive the cattle to the railhead on Monday like we planned. I'm leaving you in charge for the rest of the day. Rose and I have business in town. We'll be picking up Josh from school and be back in time for supper." He was glad Dave didn't press him for the reason he and Rose were going into town in the face of the coming storm.

After they ate, Cam drove toward town, thinking how different things were without Amos Pollard in charge of the sheriff's office. Beside him, Rose fingered the letter Josh found in the book as well as the single page family tree from the Bible. He could tell she didn't want to talk about what they'd found.

"What brings the two of you to town on a day like today?" George greeted them when they entered the office.

"I found some papers and was wondering if you could check on these names through the U.S. Marshal's office in St. Louis." Rose said, holding out the letter and family tree toward George.

From behind them, Frank entered the office accompanied by a gust of cold air. "Is this a private parry or can anyone join in?" he asked.

George handed Frank the papers. "See what you make of this. Rose wants to see if she can locate her family. I can contact the marshal's office in St. Louis, but if they aren't wanted for anything, I might not find out much. Do you have any contacts back there that could help?"

"It's possible. I can send a couple of letters off and see what I can find out for you." He reread the letter that had been the catalyst for Rose's search for her family. "If this isn't the damnedest thing I've ever read. Between the two of us we'll find your family for you. Would you be willing to write a couple of letters to put in with my request? That way your family would know it wasn't a hoax."

Cam watched Rose as she contemplated doing what Frank was requesting. Once she agreed, he left her alone to compose what would probably be the hardest letters she had ever written in her life. He wanted to pick up the mail for the ranch and go over to the school to meet Josh before they started for home.

* * * *

Rose thought about the letters she would compose to the family who knew nothing of her existence. It took only a moment for her to compose the first of the letters to send to Frank's contacts in St. Louis.

Dear McKinney Family,

My name is Rose McKinney and all my life I have considered myself the daughter of Darius McKinney and Josie Sullivan. My mother died giving me life, and my father left me with a woman in St, Louis to be raised. As I was growing up, he supported me from the money he earned from the ranch he built in Montana, the Rocking M.

Recently, I received news my father had been murdered, and his ranch had been left to me. Since my arrival in Montana, I helped to find the men responsible for his death as well as the rustling of his cattle, and I learned he was not my father. In a letter he left for me, he detailed the circumstances of my conception and that his father, Richard McKinney, was my father.

I am now looking for the family I have been denied my entire life. If I have any McKinney family left, I would appreciate hearing from you.

After adding her address at the Rocking M, she signed her name before copying the letter for the Sullivan family. After twenty-five years, she had no high hopes of ever hearing back from either family, but she had to try.

Chapter Nineteen

Although there had been a light dusting of snow on the day Rose and Cam went into town to talk to Frank and George, the first heavy snow of the season held off long enough for the men to get the cattle to the railhead. By getting them there so late in the season, she knew they wouldn't command top dollar, but at least she wouldn't have to feed them over the winter.

In the excitement of the drive, along with the snow that fell with a vengeance, Rose almost forgot the inquiries George and Frank had made on her behalf.

In the month that had passed, Cam made it clear he had no desire to go back to Omaha, even though his family was there. Once his decision was made, Rose found they were spending more and more time together. Although he had never been improper, Rose could feel a strange sensation growing within her. All her life she had considered men playthings, but Cam was different. If she didn't know better, she would think she'd fallen in love with her foreman.

During all the troubled times surrounding the capture of the rustlers, she thought about it, but knew he would, more than likely, return to Nebraska once things quieted down. Then love had been only an unattainable dream. Now she realized it had turned into reality, but if Cam felt the same way he showed no signs of it.

As was their practice in the afternoon, Rose and Cam were going over the ranch books when Josh came home from school. With him being in town every day, Rose suggested he be assigned the task of picking up the ranch mail. It gave him a new responsibility to replace riding with the men on a daily basis.

"How was your day at school?" Cam asked, after Josh handed Rose the stack of letters.

She only half listened to what Josh said as she thumbed through the envelopes that contained bills as well as chatty letters from Celeste and the girls at the Purple Moon. It came as a surprise when she came across a letter from Ralph McKinney as well as one from Sarah Sullivan-Bennett. She recognized the first name as belonging to her half brother and the second as her mother's sister, her aunt.

Her hands trembled as she tore open the first envelope and gazed on the handwriting that could have belonged to Darius. Since Cam had known about the letters she sent to Missouri, she didn't hesitate to read the first reply aloud.

Dear Rose,

I read your letter with great interest. Yes, I did know the reason Darius left home. He was a year older than me and my best friend. Before he left, he told me what our father did to Josie that made her leave home. That was the last I ever heard from him until receiving your letter. I always assumed he had found her, and they went west together. The news of her passing saddens me.

I have often wondered about the child she was carrying when she left home. I am pleased to know after all these years the sibling I have been preparing for is a sister.

I, too, left home at an early age. Our father was an abusive man, and I could no longer take his physical beatings. I secured employment at the local livery stable, and when the opportunity arose, I was able to purchase it. I now run it with the help of my sons.

Our father died five years after Darius and I left home, so our youngest brother, Emmett, took over the farm and still runs it. Our sister, Margie, married a man and headed west. Amazingly, she lives near Billings, although I do not know how close that is to your location.

My mother never believed our father was guilty of raping your mother and died of a broken heart a year to the day after his passing.

Emmett and I have talked of this and decided to make a trip out to Montana to meet you and see Margie after Christmas. We understand the weather will not be in our favor, but it is the only time either of us can leave our homes.

We look forward to your reply and hope you will allow us to make the journey to Montana to be reunited with you at last.

Your Brothers—Ralph and Emmett

Tears rolled down Rose's cheeks when she finished reading the letter. Before making comment on its content, she reached into her pocket to get her handkerchief. After wiping her eyes and blowing her nose, she looked up at Cam and Josh.

"They want to meet me," she half whispered. "They really want me as their sister."

Cam came over and joined her on the sofa. After putting his arm around her shoulders, he pulled her into a warm embrace. "I never had any doubts about that. Why don't we see what the other letter says?"

After reading the first letter, Rose felt a bit more confident about the second. It helped to have Cam's arm around her shoulder for support.

Dear Rose,

I am so excited to know you are alive and well. It saddened me to learn of Josie's passing. I was older than your mother, but knew of her love for Darius as well as his love for her. I also knew when your father raped her and left her carrying his child.

My father flew into a rage and sent her away. On the night she left, I begged her to stay in town with my husband and me, but she refused. She wanted to be nowhere near our father, and I couldn't blame her.

Even though her leaving was at his request, my father grieved her loss to us. It took several days for him to come to his senses and when he did, he was shocked to realize she hadn't come to stay with me. Until the day he died, he begged God to forgive him for what he had done to his youngest daughter.

My brother, Hal, now runs the farm, and we have talked to both Ralph and Emmett about the letters you sent. Since they are planning to come to meet you after Christmas, we would like to come as well. We anxiously await your next letter.

Aunt Sarah

The thought of both sides of her family wanting to meet and accept her was almost overwhelming. She mentally calculated the number of people who would be coming and realized she would need all five of the bedrooms of the house to accommodate them. Of course, it wouldn't be impossible, especially if the men and women were willing to share rooms.

"With your entire family coming, maybe this is the time for me to ask you the question that has been on my mind," Cam said. Without giving Rose a chance to say anything, he took her hand in his.

"I was going to wait until spring to give you time to get to know me better, but with your family coming after Christmas, would you do me the honor of becoming my wife while they're here?"

"W... wife?" Rose stammered.

"And my ma," Josh added. "Pa and me talked it over, and we both want you, if you want us."

"Pa and I," Rose automatically corrected him. "And I would be honored, but only on one condition."

Both Cam and Josh looked at her in amazement. "Condition?" they said in unison. "What condition?"

"Don't look so scared. I want to be married before my family arrives. I want some time alone to adapt to my roles as wife and mother before I meet them."

Cam pulled her into his arms and kissed her lovingly. "We can talk to the parson on Sunday when we go into church. With luck, he'll marry us after the service."

Rose knew it wouldn't happen so quickly. What she wanted was for the parson to come out to the ranch and perform the ceremony in the library with the hands and Frank, as well as Verna and Minnie in attendance.

Since the secret of her parents had been hidden in the library, Rose thought it a fitting setting for their wedding. Ever since she had touched the old Bible, she had renewed her relationship with God, but she still knew she would be more comfortable in this room than the church when she joined her life with those of Cam and Josh.

* * * *

Three weeks later, Verna and Minnie fussed fixing Rose's hair and helping her into the dress she and Minnie worked so hard to make. Although the wedding night held no mysterious secrets, Rose was as nervous as any new bride.

She'd received word Celeste was arriving on the morning train from St. Louis, and Frank had assured her he would meet the train so Celeste could be at the ranch in time for the wedding.

As soon as Minnie and Verna heard of Rose and Cam's plans, they came out and insisted on helping Rose fashion the perfect wedding dress. When Rose told them she had brought a length of blue satin with her from St. Louis, they were even more anxious to help her with it.

"Whose idea was it to use all these tiny buttons?" Minnie complained, as she worked buttoning up the back of the dress.

"As I recall," Verna teased, "this is the same pattern you picked out for your wedding dress when you and Frank were married."

All three women enjoyed a good laugh at Minnie's expense. She and Frank had been married over a month ago and although the dress was from the same pattern, it was of a soft brown cotton with a print of yellow and orange flowers that accented Minnie's coloring perfectly. She wore it again today because she was Rose's matron of honor.

"Where's my baby?" Celeste's voice drifted up the stairs. "I hope I'm not too late to play the part of mother of the bride. I intend to cry at your wedding, Child."

"I'm up here, Celeste," Rose called. She almost dreaded seeing her surrogate mother, friend, and mentor.

As soon as Celeste breezed into the room, Rose breathed a sigh of relief. Rather than the flamboyant dresses that showed more of her ample breasts than was necessary, she looked perfect in her blue serge traveling suit with its crisp white blouse.

"That nice young man who picked me up said I have plenty of time to freshen up, but I was worried just the same."

Rose hurried to embrace Celeste. "I have the room down the hall ready for you. It won't take long to heat some water and…"

"And nothing child. This is your wedding day, and you won't be doing any work. I took an earlier train and arrived at the railhead yesterday. The stationmaster generously took me back to his house, and his wife arranged for me to take a bath.

"All I need is to freshen up and change my clothes. I can hardly wait for you to see the dress I brought with me for today. I asked my dressmaker, you remember Kristine, don't you? Of course you do. Well, I told her the dress had to be special because I was sure you would be making a dress from that blue satin she gave you before you left."

Rose smiled at the predictability of Celeste. As usual, she talked non-stop giving no one a chance to say a single word and immediately took over the entire situation.

* * * *

Cam waited nervously in the library. Josh stood beside him acting as best man, while Dave played hymns on his guitar. The only guests who didn't work at the Rocking M were Frank, Minnie, Verna, and Celeste. Cam would have liked George to attend, but he'd left a week earlier to return to Denver for his next assignment with the marshals.

Minnie was the first to enter the library. From the look on Frank's face, he knew the man was proud of his new wife. Once she stood opposite Cal and Josh, Rose entered the room with Celeste at her side. When Rose first said Celeste was coming to the wedding Cam worried. He remembered, all too well, the dress Rose wore when she first arrived at the Rocking M. It was a relief to see Celeste wearing a dress of the latest fashion, complete with a high neckline and matching hat.

Rose looked beautiful as the blue of her dress matched the color of her eyes perfectly and the style accented her slim waistline. She, too, wore a hat made from the same material as the dress.

"Who gives this woman to this man in marriage?" Parson Webster asked.

Celeste took a step forward. "Since her father is no longer with us and I had the pleasure of raising her, I do."

Cam was shocked to see tears pooling in the older woman's eyes, as she kissed Rose lightly on the cheek and placed Rose's hand in his. "You've made your father proud," Celeste whispered. "I know you and your young man will have a good life together."

When Cam at last said the words that made Rose his for the rest of their lives, he was happier than he had ever been. His marriage to Martha had been when he was an inexperienced youth and she a trembling virginal bride. Today he knew exactly what to expect in the marriage bed and so did Rose. Rather than frightened youngsters, they were mature adults and their union was based on their love for each other rather than lust for the unknown.

Chapter Twenty

After their marriage in November, Cam and Josh moved to the main house. Rose loved playing wife and mother, especially when a late December blizzard kept them snowbound for the better part of a week.

Because of the weather, the visit from her family was postponed until February, giving Rose more time to adjust to her new lifestyle. Since neither Ralph nor Emmett was bringing a wife, it had been agreed they would share a bedroom. Sarah and Margie were also traveling without their husbands, so they too would share a bedroom, leaving only Hal with a room to himself.

By the first of February, Rose realized she would be having a baby by the end of August or the first of September. She almost wished she'd said nothing about it to Cam, because he had become so protective it was a wonder he allowed her to dress herself.

On the morning their guests were to arrive, the men set up the extra beds and brought in enough wood to supply the fireplaces in each bedroom.

As much as Rose wanted to go to the station, Cam would hear nothing of it. He contended that even though the day was bright and sunny, it was far too cold for her to make the trip. He enlisted Frank to bring his carriage from town to help transport their guests and Dave would be bringing the buckboard to accommodate the bags.

As cold as it was, Cookie helped her make a pot of rich soup. Last night, he had come up to the house to help her set the dough for the bread she made under his watchful eye this morning. The aroma now wafted from her kitchen made her proud. When she first arrived here, just seven months ago, she had no idea how to cook a meal. Now she was not only making bread and soup, but she was also getting ready to entertain a houseful of guests.

* * * *

As soon as the train arrived at the railhead and the passengers got off, Cam recognized Ralph and Emmett McKinney. They so closely resembled Darius; there was no denying they were brothers. The other man and woman who got off the train were undoubtedly Sarah and Hal. The last woman to step onto the platform bore a strong resemblance to Ralph and Emmett, so she had to be Margie.

"I'm Cam Blake," he said, stepping forward to greet the passengers who would be making the trip out to the Rocking M.

"So you're our new brother-in-law," the older of the two men said, shaking his hand. "I was a little disappointed the two of you couldn't wait so I could give the bride away, but I know how you young people are."

Cam was a bit put out by Ralph's attitude, but tried not to show it. How dare he imply Rose was with child before they married?

"Getting married when we did was Rose's idea. I suggested waiting until you arrived, but she wanted a quiet affair so she'd have time to adjust to being a wife and mother before meeting her family."

"Mother?" both women said in unison. "Are you telling us Rose was in a family way when the two of you married?"

"That's the not what I'm telling you. What I'm talking about is I have a thirteen-year-old son, Josh. I've been a widower for ten years, so Rose sort of walked into a ready-made family."

Both women smiled, as though relieved to think Rose hadn't been pregnant on her wedding day. He wondered what they would think if they knew she was already expecting their first child.

* * * *

Rose heard the jingle of harnesses and hurried to the front door. She held her breath as the five people who represented her family got out of the carriages and stepped onto the porch.

The first woman to enter the house had tears in her eyes as she embraced Rose. "You are, indeed, Josie's daughter. You look so much

201

like her it's uncanny. I'm your aunt Sarah and this you your Uncle Hal."

Rose allowed the man, who seemed more reserved than her aunt, to embrace her.

"And you're our sister," the other woman said, taking her turn at hugging and kissing Rose.

"You kept asking what Darius looked like honey," Cam said, coming to her rescue. "Well, all you have to do is look at Ralph and Emmett and you'll know."

The two men who greeted her were very handsome. As a child she remembered Celeste telling her how handsome her father had been and now she had proof.

While the men went into the library with Cam, the women insisted on joining Rose in the kitchen.

"We asked Cam if you were in a family way when you got married," Sarah began. "Haven't you told him about the baby?"

Rose felt a blush creep into her cheeks. "Does it already show?" she said, her hands going immediately to her still flat belly.

"Only in your eyes." Margie assured her.

"We talked about a family when we first got married. I just didn't think it would happen so quickly. Of course, Cam is thrilled, but I was hoping for some time alone when Josh goes away to school next fall."

"School?" Sarah questioned.

"He has a fine mind. Both Cam and I are well educated and we want Josh to have every opportunity."

The two women looked at her skeptically. "With a fine education, what is your husband doing working on a ranch?"

Rose completely understood the question. She'd asked herself the same thing when he decided to stay rather than go back to Nebraska where he could make more money than she could pay her foreman.

"That's the beauty of a good education," she replied. "It allows one to check out all the avenues open to you. My—Darius made certain I received training in many areas. It's amazing that since I've come here I've used many of the skills I learned in St. Louis."

She was relieved to see Cam come into the kitchen. "My wife is far too modest. Without her skills in nursing, my best friend to say nothing of a U.S. Marshal would have died from their wounds. Add that to her ability to straighten out the ranch books and you'd realize she's invaluable. As for me, it's a very long story and one better told over dinner. The men sent me out here to tell you they're starving and the smell of that soup is driving them crazy."

Rose said a silent prayer of thanks that Cam didn't mention the other skills she possessed. Those were best kept a secret between the two of them and wouldn't be shared with her newfound family.

* * * *

What had started as a tense reunion ended on a much lighter note. Sarah and Hal had finally put to rest all their questions concerning their sister and the child driven her from their family home. For the McKinney's, the whispered rumor of a half-sister had finally been substantiated. Rose knew they wished Darius was still alive, but a reunion with the oldest McKinney brother was not to be.

By the time they left for the railhead, each promised to keep in touch with Rose through letters and perhaps another visit in the future.

With her house quiet for the first time in over a week, Rose went into the library, chose a book from the shelf, banked the fire, and sat down in one of the overstuffed chairs.

She had read barely two pages when sleep overtook her and a dream invaded her subconscious. In the dream, a man who looked like a younger version of Ralph stood side by side with a girl whose resemblance to Sarah was uncanny looked down on her.

"Had things been different," Darius began, "I would have been your true father. It mattered not that you were my half sister. I loved your mother as I loved you. We are together now and our families know our story. Thank you for being a daughter to make us proud."

"I know you fear giving birth," Josie said. "There is no need for fear. Your child has been conceived in love. When I carried you, things were so different. I was not strong enough to survive. You and Cam will have a healthy daughter. When she is born, do not be hurt if he asks to name her Martha for his first wife."

Epilogue

Five years later

Rose sat on the porch with Cam and watched their children at play. Five-year-old Martha pumped herself higher and higher on the rope swing, while three-year-old Darius played with the carved horses Dave loved to give him and six month old Addison slept in his cradle, oblivious to anything but his afternoon nap.

"Our children are growing up," Cam observed.

"Indeed they are," Rose agreed. "Speaking of children, where is Josh today? I haven't seen him since we left church."

"The last I saw of him, he was leaving with Frank and Minnie. Minnie's niece is visiting for the summer form Sheridan and from what I saw she's an attractive young lady."

"He'd better not be interested in her. If he wants to become a doctor, he has a lot more schooling ahead of him. I just don't think…"

Cam began to laugh before she could finish. "As his mother, you won't think any girl is good enough for him. I seem to remember my mother insisting Martha wasn't good enough for me. It really came as a surprise when she told me not to let you go when she first came to visit."

"That surprises me as well. Martha was more your equal than me. I was brought up in a cathouse for goodness sake."

"Somehow I don't think it was your background that Ma liked. I agree with her, we are well suited by not only our education but also our personalities."

Rose smiled. Whatever lives they'd lived in the past were behind them. Their future lay not only with their three younger children, but also with Josh and the Rocking M. The ranch Darius McKinney had founded almost thirty years earlier would be there for Rose and Cam's children and grandchildren as a grand legacy.

About the Author

Mild Mannered wife, mother and grandmother by day, Shari Dare spends her nights writing and writing and writing. Having been inspired by an English assignment in her sophomore year of high school, she had never quite finished the assignment. New stories pop into her head every day with never enough time to write them all.

A Wisconsin native, she grew up a country girl, but enjoys her "city" home. She and her husband of over 50 years, Bob, live in a mid-sized town close to the Illinois border. Deeming Bob "A Saint" for putting up with her she has never regretted marrying her high school sweetheart just two days after graduation in 1964.

http://www.derr-wille.com

Other Books by the author with Melange

Family Secrets
Hattie's Preacher, Book 1 of the Outlaw Series
Outlaw's Son, Book 2 of the Outlaw Series
Outlaw's Daughter, Book 3 of the Outlaw Series
Outlaw's Secrets, Book 4 of the Outlaw Series
A Father's Love